YOUR NAME IS PETER DAN-
ZIGER?
　Yes.

YOU ARE HERE OF YOU WN
VOLITION?
　Yes.

IN ORDER TO C EAR YOUR
NAME OF VARIOUS ACCUSA-
TIONS AND TO FURNISH VOL-
UNTARY INFORMATION TO
THIS INFORMAL INQUIRY?
　Just to clear my name of various
　accusations.

YOU UNDERSTAND MY QUES-
TIONS WILL TAKE ANY DIREC-
TION MY INTELLIGENCE AND
INSTINCTS LEAD ME?
　You've got it on the record, Major.
　Let's go.

*You will never guess what
you are about to learn in—*

THE DANZIGER
TRANSCRIPT

"Adventure, romance, chilling, merci-
less suspense!"　—*Chicago Sun-Times*

"In the tradition of *Th I*
Tapes . . . f

D1397402

THE
DANZIGER
TRANSCRIPT

A NOVEL

Carl Fick

A DELL BOOK

This one is for B. L.

Published by
DELL PUBLISHING CO., INC.
1 Dag Hammarskjold Plaza
New York, New York 10017

Reprinted by arrangement with
G. P. Putnam's Sons
Printed in the United States of America
First Dell printing—June 1974

Monday

V HOW MANY TIMES YOU WENT TO
BATHROOM IN 1937. WHAT WAS
NAME?

is necessary?

name was Stella. As in starlight.

NAME?

son.

LONG HAD YOU KNOWN HER?

e grammar school.

TINUOUSLY?

and on. Why does Stella enter into this?

ILL EMERGE. WHAT DO YOU MEAN
F AND ON?

lived nearby. Grammar school, high school,
nally when I went home from college,
f course, later in New York.

N IN NEW YORK?

r the war. I came back and bumped into

DENTALLY?

T WAS SHE DOING THEN?

ng a little. She looked something like
Oberon, and that's all the goosing one of
bitious Muskegon kids needs.

WERE MARRIED WHEN?

e day before Thanksgiving, 1946.

YOU BROKE UP THE NEXT DAY?

y do you bother me with all this if you al-
have the answers?

T HAPPENED?

pretty personal.

YOUR NAME IS PETER F. DANZIGER?

Yes.

YOU ARE HERE OF YOUR OWN VOLI-
TION?

Yes.

IN ORDER TO CLEAR YOUR NAME OF
VARIOUS ACCUSATIONS AND TO FUR-
NISH VOLUNTARY INFORMATION TO
THIS INFORMAL INQUIRY?

Just to clear my name of various accusations.

THE TWO OBJECTIVES ARE SYNONY-
MOUS.

Let's find out.

YOU UNDERSTAND MY QUESTIONING
WILL TAKE ANY DIRECTION MY INTEL-
LIGENCE AND INSTINCTS LEAD ME?

You've got it on the record, Major. Let's go.

VERY WELL, WE'LL COMMENCE. NAME?

Peter Danziger. We just did this.

MIDDLE INITIAL?

F.

F FOR WHAT?

F for Fahnstock.

AGE?

Forty-four.

PLACE OF BIRTH?

Muskegon, Michigan. You already know this.

THEN YOU CAN HAVE NO OBJECTION TO REPEATING IT ACCURATELY FOR THE TRANSCRIPT. CURRENT ADDRESS?

Shoreham Hotel. Washington, D.C.

FOR HOW LONG?

Since three P.M. yesterday afternoon.

BEFORE THAT?

I lived for two weeks with a man named Gil Ketchum on West Eighty-ninth Street. Manhattan.

HIS ADDRESS?

On the corner of West End. Tenth floor.

BEFORE THAT?

Before that I was in Miami. Florida. Living with a guy named Jack Walsh.

ADDRESS?

I don't remember. It was Northwest somewhere. On the Miami River. For two and a half months. Before that—

THAT WILL SUFFICE. OCCUPATION?

None.

WHAT DO YOU DO FOR A LIVING?

Nothing in particular, as you know.

HOW DID YOU EARN YOUR LAST DOLLAR?

Writing a speech.

FOR WHOM?

For a nameless executive fron
tion which subcontracts to the go

I SUPPOSE YOU KNOW I CAN

Go ahead. I won't help you bit

YOU TEND TO DRAMATI
ZIGER. BEFORE THAT?

I free-lanced some publicity.

FOR WHOM?

I forget.

BEFORE THAT?

I wrote two-thirds of a book
mated on Jack Walsh's party boa

MATED?

Not broads. I sold bait and
gled reels, and spelled Jack at
that—

ARE YOU MARRIED?

Before that I worked for W
for many years.

YES. ARE YOU MARRIED?

Don't you want to know why I

PLEASE. ARE YOU MARRIEI

No.

WIDOWED OR DIVORCED?

Yes.

WHICH? YOU COULD MAKE

I don't want to. Divorced.

TELL ME THE CIRCUMSTA

Of which? The marriage or th

BOTH.

Why? This is ancient history.

BEFORE I'M FINISHED I

SO IS THIS INTERVIEW. AT ANY RATE,
IT'S ON A POLICE BLOTTER. WHAT HAP-
PENED?

Maybe you'd better ring for the thumbscrews,
Major. This has nothing to do with you.

EVERYTHING ABOUT YOU HAS SOME-
THING TO DO WITH ME. WHO DO YOU
THINK YOU'RE PROTECTING? THE
GIRL? YOURSELF?

The residue of a twenty-year-dead marriage
couldn't protect a bluebottle fly.

WELL, THEN?

Let's just say we decided it had been a mistake.
We agreed to disagree. Et cetera.

DID YOU TRY TO KILL HER?

I guess she thought so.

DON'T MAKE ME DRAG IT OUT OF YOU,
MR. DANZIGER. WHAT HAPPENED?

There was a little screaming. The superintend-
ent arrived with two state cops. Broken heads and
broken hearts.

WILL YOU TELL ME WHY?

No.

AND THAT EPISODE DESTROYED THE
MARRIAGE?

Oh, yes, that destroyed the marriage all right.

WHERE WAS THE DIVORCE GRANTED?

Juarez.

YOU KNOW, OF COURSE, THAT SHE
WAS OPENLY ACTIVE IN SUPPORTING
TWO COMMUNIST ORGANIZATIONS IN
GREENWICH VILLAGE FROM MID-1942
THROUGH 1945?

So was Franklin D. Roosevelt. At any rate, Stella wasn't a Communist, she was an enthusiast.

THEY CAN BE EQUALLY DANGEROUS.

Do you keep a file on enthusiasts, for God's sake? When I met her again she was rooting for Tennessee Williams.

WERE YOU FAMILIAR WITH HER POLITICAL ADVENTURES?

Anyone who knew Stella was familiar with every little thing she did.

DID YOU TRY TO DISSUADE HER?

In my era, she had already switched to Tennessee Williams. I tried to dissuade her from that.

YOU MENTIONED COLLEGE. WHERE DID YOU GO?

Ann Arbor. University of Michigan.

DID YOU GRADUATE?

No. I left after three years.

WHY?

War coming. Boredom. Money. That was the year my mother remarried and things in general seemed to be coming apart. Are you just curious, or is all this in aid of something?

IN AID OF TRUTH. WHAT DID YOU STUDY AT MICHIGAN?

English major. What about you? Ancient history?

ANY OUTSIDE ACTIVITIES?

Aren't we a little far afield?

I REPEAT: ANY OUTSIDE—

I swam. Messed around with the drama club. Wrote sports for the newspaper one year.

DIDN'T YOU BOX?

Yes. Two years.

YOU MIGHT HAVE MENTIONED IT.

Dreadfully sorry. How did you know? Spot the old broken nose and deduce?

I DON'T HAVE TO DEDUCE. WHAT ABOUT POLITICAL ACTIVITIES?

I've been waiting for that. Yes. Once I had a diaper rash too.

SOMETHING ABOUT ARRANGING A SPEECH BY ROBERT MINOR, WITH AN ACCOMPANYING CAMPUS RIOT?

I didn't arrange the riot. I didn't have to.

BUT YOU ARRANGED THE SPEAKER?

Yes.

WHO WAS YOUR CONTACT?

For God's sake! I took the devious underground route and wrote a letter to the *Daily Worker*.

WHY?

Were you alive then, Major?

VERY MUCH SO.

The hell with it. Read some books and consult your memory and then come back to me some frosty afternoon.

NO EXPLANATION OFFERED?

Now? To you? Absolutely none.

VERY WELL. IS YOUR MOTHER ALIVE?

Yes. Was she a Communist too?

HER NAME?

Mrs. Walter Hasbrouk.

ADDRESS?

Riverdale Drive, Columbus, Ohio.

DO YOU SEE HER?

Rarely. Hasbrouk and I don't dig each other.

DO YOU CORRESPOND?

Mostly cards. An occasional long letter.

WHAT IS HASBROUK'S OCCUPATION?

He's something with an accounting company. Like in charge of digits.

WELL-TO-DO?

I guess so.

WHAT DO YOU THINK OF THIS COUNTRY?

You mean here? Around Washington?

I MEAN THE USA.

For God's sake, Major! What do I think of the Apostle Paul? What do I think of the stately oak? What do I think of frontal lobotomies? May I stand up? The air is getting a little heavy down here.

PLEASE YOURSELF.

Have I told you anything you didn't know?

NOT YET. WE'LL TAKE A BREAK FOR A CIGARETTE NOW.

What if I didn't smoke?

NO MATTER. I DO. THE MEN'S ROOM IS DOWN THE HALL.

ALL RIGHT? COMFORTABLE?

Sure.

VERY WELL. LET'S SEE. YOU WENT TO MUSKEGON NORTH JUNIOR HIGH SCHOOL. YOUR HIGH SCHOOL WAS MUSKEGON CENTRAL.

Yes.

NO PREPARATORY SCHOOL?

No.

WHEN DID YOUR FATHER DIE?

1935.

OF WHAT?

Of bird shot. He was killed in a duck blind.

HE WAS A LIEUTENANT IN THE FIRST WAR?

Yes. Field artillery.

HE WAS ALSO NAMED PETER DANZIGER?

Yes.

NO MIDDLE INITIAL?

Peter C. C for Carl.

OF GERMAN DERIVATION?

Yes. Today you'd say East German; three generations removed. Danziger—Danzig. Get it?

AND YOUR MOTHER?

Her name was Ruth Fahnstock. She was born in East St. Louis. Her father owned a clothing store. She was Jewish. Maybe she still is.

WHAT IS YOUR OWN RELIGIOUS AFFILIATION?

None.

YOUR ARMY DOG TAGS CONTAINED THE ABBREVIATION J.

Sure. What else? You mix a Lutheran and a Jew together and you get a Jew. Maybe even if you mix a cocker spaniel and a Jew. In Muskegon I felt J and in the Army I felt J, and as a matter of fact, the longer I talk to you the more J I feel. It's not all bad, Maje.

YOU SEEM HEATED.

Funny, huh? You asked me a question and I answered None.

YOU HAVE A SISTER?

Yes.

OLDER, YOUNGER?

Younger. By five years. Maybe seven by now. She married a nice guy who works in an advertising agency in Boston. Lives in Weymouth, Massachusetts. She's half-Jewish too.

THIS ISN'T AN INQUISITION, YOU KNOW. I'M MERELY DIGGING INFORMATION.

Sure you are.

WHAT WAS YOUR ARMY SERIAL NUMBER?

Are you serious?

DO YOU REMEMBER?

As a matter of fact, I do. One-two-one-seven-five-seven-eight-three.

AND YOUR SERIAL NUMBER AFTER YOU WERE COMMISSIONED?

Do you mind telling me what you're trying to get at?

DO YOU REMEMBER?

Zero-seven-ten-three-seven-zero.

WHEN WERE YOU COMMISSIONED?

September, 1943, as though you didn't know. Are you trying to make sure I'm me? I admit it!

WHERE?

Good Jesus, Major. Coral Gables, Florida.

TELL ME ABOUT CORAL GABLES.

Sure. That's reasonable. It's only twenty-five years ago.

PROCEED.

It's hot, okay? In August the palms dry out and

turn brown. The sun hurts your eyes if you don't wear flyboy glasses. The lawns look like welcome mats when they're watered, but they're not. Children, dogs, nigras and servicemen not wanted. You get skin sores from your perspiration. You march to class and back. You sing. By God, how you sing! 'I've Got Sixpence" and "For Me and My Gal." Sing, Danziger!
CONTINUE.

All day you construct plane of the meridian problems and you're always surprised when they turn out. At night you either do star identification on your back on the grass with a bottle of Jax beer, or you fly a night celestial mission in a 1928 Boeing Commodore hung together with mirrors and fine wires. The flights aren't bad. They pack fresh milk and baloney sandwiches. From the air at night Miami Beach looks like a piece of costume jewelry. Miami, Havana, Nassau and home.
YES?

Major, really, what is this all proving?
IT'S NOT PROVING. IT'S DIVULGING.

Divulging what?
YOU, MR. DANZIGER. CONTINUE.

Divulge away, Danziger!
WE'RE WASTING TIME. IF YOU REALLY WANT TO BE CLEARED, MR. DANZIGER, WE DO IT MY WAY. CONTINUE.

Okay. If you've got a decent chauffeur he'll feather an engine and let down into Havana for a magneto check. Then you diddle around with girls and buy scotch and rum and nylons. Sometimes a tired old engine resigns all by itself and you taxi home from Bimini on one. Once I trolled for sailfish off the pontoon. There are girls in the bar of the Seven Seas restaurant in Miami, and eleven kinds of fried fish. When you graduate, a smiling type from Pan American Airways hands you your wings on the stage of the Coral Gables movie house. Your uniform smells as though the price tags are still on it. You figure you'll be dead in thirty days and you vow to stay away from planter's punch that night and just enjoy, but you don't.

(Pause for tape change.)

SORRY. CONTINUE, PLEASE. YOU WERE JUST NOT ENJOYING.

Yeah. So if you're lucky you have a date with a photographer's assistant from downtown Miami named Spencer. That's her first name. Her husband was killed in Africa. Spence talks about him as though he were around the corner getting a six-pack, and off and on all night she seems to pause and listen for him. Then she goes crazy and croons all over your clean newly commissioned body. Coral Gables. What else do you want to know?

WHAT FLIGHT WERE YOU IN?

Flight One.

WHO WERE SOME OF THE OTHER MEN? AND DO YOU SEE THEM?

Campbell. Deak. Drost. Ewing. It was alphabetical. I don't see them.

NAME SOME MORE.

Joe Alvarez. Never see. Tully Cartwright. He

belongs to the University Club. Occasionally see. Eddie Brennan. No. Hank Drago. Nice guy. See him occasionally. Somebody Cruikshank. Never. I bump into Mike Chiapa every three or four years here and abroad. Dolph Bergen. Quite often for bridge. That's all I can remember. What's the object of this exercise?

DO YOU REMEMBER A MAN NAMED CROGER?

Croger? (Pause) No.

ARE YOU SURE? SIX FOOT ONE. BLACK HAIR. BROWN EYES. PITTED FACE. EMIL CROGER.

No. Sounds like that police blotter again. What did he do?

YOU DIDN'T KNOW HIM?

Repeat. No.

I'M AFRAID I DON'T BELIEVE YOU.

You don't? Tough shit. Who the hell is Croger?

ONE OF THIRTY-SIX MEN IN FLIGHT ONE WITH YOU FOR TEN MONTHS. AND YOU DON'T REMEMBER HIM?

Negative.

WE'LL COME BACK TO THIS. WHERE IS YOUR EX-WIFE TODAY, DANZIGER?

You got me. Did she run away with Croger?

DO YOU COMMUNICATE WITH HER?

Not since she got married. Before that I sent checks for a couple of years.

WHO DID SHE MARRY?

I never met him. His name is Ballantine.

WHERE DO THEY LIVE?

Last I heard, the West Coast. He's show biz.

WHERE WERE YOU ON JULY 14, 1944?

1944? I know this will sound like a flimsy excuse to you, but I left my total recall in my other suit.

THIS HEARING IS AT YOUR REQUEST. NEVER MIND. I'LL TELL YOU. YOU CHECKED INTO THE PARK LANE HOTEL IN LONDON.

It's possible.

SO DID EMIL CROGER.

Croger again. Major, believe me, you're demented.

WITHIN AN HOUR OF EACH OTHER.

I don't know what you're trying to get at, but I do remember. July fourteenth was Bastille Day. I checked into the Park Lane with Junior Brant from my squadron. He had a tiny French girl he named Penney. She brought little tricolors and we waved them off the roof at five o'clock in the morning. We had just come off a mission to Brux. That's in Czechoslovakia, Major. They used to shoot at you. What the hell is all this about? My sins are supposed to be more recent. Or are they retroactive too? Who's Croger?

I'LL CONNECT IT UP FOR YOU. YES OR NO, WERE YOU IN SAIGON THIS PAST JANUARY, FEBRUARY AND MARCH?

The great leap forward. Yes. As you know.

YES OR NO, WERE YOU IN HAVANA ON NEW YEAR'S DAY, 1959?

Yes.

SO WAS CROGER. YES OR NO, WERE YOU SPENDING A CERTAIN AMOUNT OF

TIME IN BOTH PLACES WITH A MAN WHO CALLED HIMSELF LOUIS ESTIMET?

Yes.

SO WAS CROGER. YOU SEE, MR. DANZIG-ER—

Did Croger work for a news outfit? I know three newspapermen and two broadcasters who were in both places when I was.

YOU TELL ME WHO HE WORKED FOR.

Sure. Old Croger and I lit the match. Estimet held the fuse. We were all on the University of Michigan boxing team.

THIS ISN'T EVEN REMOTELY FUNNY, MR. DANZIGER.

Let me see Croger's picture.

I THINK NOT.

Guilty until proven innocent.

I ONLY ACCEPT INCREDIBLE COINCI-DENCES.

Major, it gives me a small but sharp pleasure to realize I could pick you up and stuff you through that cement wall before a guard could get in here.

I'M GLAD TO HAVE THAT ON TAPE. YOUR OLD VIOLENCE SYNDROME.

What am I supposed to have done? Besides breach security and beat up a security captain? Isn't that why we're here? Or do these things keep growing, like fungus?

YOU'LL PROBABLY SEE A FORMAL IN-DICTMENT IN DUE COURSE.

You never heard of due course. You're insane. Where do we go from here?

TELL ME ABOUT CROGER.

Listen carefully. The only possible way this dialogue can progress is for you to assume literally that I do not know this man. I mean it. Otherwise, we're stuck.

IT ISN'T A DIALOGUE. AND WE'RE STUCK JUST IN TIME FOR LUNCH, MR. DANZIGER.

LET'S GET BACK TO THE WAR.

Wait. This is for the record?

YES.

Is the machine on?

YES.

Okay, I want to make a statement. Now.

PROCEED.

Quote. I, Peter Danziger, state that I am in the black book because someone decided they needed a whipping boy. Not for marital excesses, not for speeding tickets a quarter century ago in Michigan, not for forgetting some forgettable character in cadet training, but for writing about various hushed-up messes over the past few years. I understand my bureau well enough to know that it doesn't deep-six people for audacious journalism. Quite the contrary. They were delighted that I got to Cambodia, and even happier with the Buddhist story. When one of Bunker's Boy Fridays complained from Washington, Vince Schaefer personally told him tough shit. I got a raise instead of a wrist slap when I went back to Cuba. My bureau simply doesn't leave its people out on the end of a limb while big government saws it off. Until now.

So there has to be something else. What, Major? I want to know—now—what pressure you exerted to get Schaefer to drop me. What skeletons in what closets? Don't tell me it was for punching that captain? That's the biological hazard of having too big a mouth. Something else had to happen, and I want to know what it was. Something so stinking that at this moment in history I can't get a job writing obits. The only answers I get are embarrassed murmurs about security.

I'VE OFTEN PONDERED PRECISELY THE DISTINCTION BETWEEN CRUSADING RE-PORTING AND YELLOW JOURNALISM. IT MUST BE A TERRIBLY NARROW LINE TO FOLLOW, MR. DANZIGER.

I'm not on charges for yellow journalism, and I couldn't care less about your ponderings. What's the answer?

WHY DON'T YOU ASK MR. SCHAEFER?

You know as well as I that somebody put a gag on his mouth.

UNFORTUNATE. LET ME REASSURE YOU THIS IS NOT A WITCH-HUNT. WE'RE AF-TER REAL GAME. . . . NOW, THINK BACK, MR. DANZIGER. SHORTLY AFTER PARIS WAS LIBERATED IN AUGUST OF '44, A B-17 CREW WAS REQUESTED FROM THE FORTY-FIFTH COMBAT WING TO FERRY SOME FLIGHT SURGEONS FROM THE EIGHTH AIR FORCE TO THE VILLA COUBLAY IN PARIS TO SET UP EMER-GENCY HOSPITALIZATION FOR THE WOUNDED COMING IN FROM THE

THIRD ARMY IN THE VICINITY OF METZ. DO YOU RECALL?

Major, are you deaf? Didn't you hear what I just said?

OH, YES. YOUR REMARKS ARE ON THE RECORD. BUT THEY HAVE NO RELEVANCE TO THE SITUATION YOU ARE IN AT THIS MOMENT.

What situation am I in?

IT WILL EMERGE. TO CONTINUE. YOU AND YOUR FRIENDS, MAJOR JOHN CRANE, CAPTAIN FRANCIS VACCARI AND AN ENLISTED ENGINEER NAMED BURRAX CONTRIVED TO FLY THIS ASSIGNMENT. IS THAT CORRECT? YOU ALSO CARRIED AN UNSPECIFIED OBSERVER? WAS IT EMIL CROGER?

I never heard of Emil Croger. Do you know who you remind me of? The White Queen. One of us is barking mad. So twenty-odd years ago we flew a bunch of medics to the Villa Coublay. Carry on.

WHAT WERE YOUR ORDERS?

I don't recall. Fly them over, leave them off and return, I suppose.

PRECISELY. DID YOU?

Certainly not. Do you think we were idiots?

WHAT DID YOU DO?

Reported a broken oil pump, ordered one sent from Honington, England, by slow freight, and took off for the Champs-Élysées like scalded cats.

WHY?

(Expression of anger) For the same reason any-one goes to Paris. To contact the *Geheime Staats Polizei,* of course.

HOW YOU BECOMING RATTLED, MR. DANZIGER?

I bloody well am, pal. You have an other-world quality I haven't observed since my unfortunate late aunt fluttered off to the funny factory in Lansing, Michigan. She used to have a thing about moths.

HOW LONG DID YOU STAY IN PARIS?

About a week. Give me a demerit.

WAS THAT THE OCCASION OF YOUR FIRST MEETING WITH ESTIMET?

(Long silence) Major, seriously, this is hopeless.

I AGREE.

(Long silence) Let's see if we can't make some sense. You've got a lot of bits and pieces in your mind and in your files, like parts of a puzzle. You think that if you pick them up, one by one, and fit them together properly they're going to make a sensible picture. But they won't. None of the pieces you've tried can ever fit together. If your intention is to confuse me with sorties from all directions, you're to be congratulated, because you do. But you haven't added a single bit to your puzzle. And you won't.

CONTINUE.

If you discovered now that this man Croger, for example, had driven the cab that brought me here from the airport, I imagine you'd find it a significant piece—maybe even a conclusive one.

But it wouldn't be. It wouldn't be anything at all. No matter how you go at it you're not going to get a sensible picture, you see, because your premise, whatever it is, is wrong.

EVERYTHING YOU SAY IS PLAUSIBLE, MR. DANZIGER. BUT YOU HAVEN'T SHOWN ME ANYTHING YET OF THESE NON-FITTING PIECES, PSYCHOLOGICAL-LY OR FACTUALLY. I MUST CONGRATU-LATE YOU, HOWEVER, ON A CONVINCING TRY.

You remind me of a psychiatrist I went to once. Are you a psychiatrist?

AMONG OTHER THINGS.

We'll go back to my diaper rash after a while, won't we?

(Silence)

IF NO ONE SPEAKS WE MAY BE FINISHED, MR. DANZIGER.

My bet is you're practicing up listening for private practice. Okay, listen. I'll tell you about Louis Estimet. Nothing to hide. It's just your manner that puts me off. Remember that. (Pause) It goes back, but not as far as you think. I first set eyes on Louis at a press reception at Claridge's in London. Not during the war, but in 1956. Maybe 1957. I was on my way back from Bonn for reassignment and stopped over for a few days. Jim Severance, the head of our London Bureau, took me to a foreign press reception the Board of Trade was throwing to celebrate the opening of the British Industries Fair. There must have been three hundred people milling about with cocktail glasses and squares of anchovy toast. One of them was a short, bouncy, balding man with a dark complexion and gold-rimmed glasses. He introduced himself to me as Major Louis Estimet. He had a slight Mittel-Europa accent, but at Claridge's, who doesn't? Someone had told him I'd been in Bonn for a year or so, and he wanted to know if I knew Burt Ingebritzen, who at that time was senior member of Bonn's Export Control Commission. As it happens, I did. I'd been to Ingebritzen's home for a few weekends. He had a squash court and we were fairly evenly matched. I told Estimet that I knew Burt, and he asked if I would give him a note of introduction.

WHAT WAS ESTIMET SUPPOSED TO BE?

His card said he was managing director of some company with a fairly grand-sounding title. I don't remember. Trans-Europe Trading, Limited, or the like.

WHAT DID HE WANT WITH INGEBRITZEN?

As I recall, he'd been trying to go through channels in Bonn to purchase a rather large number of machine parts or something, but his order got stuck in the hierarchy. He thought Ingebritzen could expedite for him, particularly since the Ingebritzen family firm was one of the sources.

IT SOUNDS UNLIKELY. DID YOU GIVE HIM THE NOTE?

Sure. Our bureau knew of him. I had and have no doubt he's a reputable guy. He came over to the hotel the next afternoon and we had a drink and I scribbled an introduction for him.

YOU DIDN'T THINK HIS STORY SMELLED?

No. Why did it smell?

ONE: A PRIVATE COMPANY DID NOT PROCESS THROUGH BONN TO PURCHASE INDUSTRIAL GOODS. TWO: AN INQUIRY IN WEST GERMANY ABOUT A SIZABLE PURCHASE OF MACHINE PARTS IN 1956, FAR FROM GETTING LOST IN THE FILES, WOULD PRODUCE TWENTY-FIVE GERMAN SALESMEN ON YOUR DOORSTEP WITHIN TWELVE HOURS.

You had to have a federal export permit.

WHICH WAS APPROXIMATELY AS DIFFICULT TO OBTAIN AS A STEIN OF LAGER. VERY INTERESTING. DID THE NOTE DO HIM ANY GOOD?

Yes. I didn't know it until a couple of years later, though, when I bumped into him in Miami Beach.

MIAMI BEACH? REALLY? WHEN WAS THAT?

Oh—late fall, '58. November, I imagine.

WHAT WERE THE CIRCUMSTANCES?

I was sitting on the terrace of a hotel called the Beau Séjour watching the bikinis and whatnot around the pool. We were drinking and talking—

WHO IS WE?

A young lady named nameless.

INCIDENTALLY, WHAT WERE YOU DOING THERE?

I'd been in the bush in Cuba with the Fidelistas

researching a series. I came down with a bug, so the office flew me back and gave me a week on the beach to finish the writing and drown the bug.

CONTINUE.

Late in the afternoon, someone yelled, "My dear fellow!" It was Estimet, deeply tanned and very pretty in a white silk shirt and red linen Bermudas. As a matter of fact, he looked like a successful psychiatrist. He had called the bureau and found out I was in the vicinity. I was his long-lost son. Apparently Ingebritzen had pushed the right button and Louis had made buckets of money on the deal.

DID YOU SEE MUCH OF HIM AT THAT TIME?

We had dinner a few times. Played tennis once. He chartered a boat one morning early and we went deep-sea trolling. My last night there Miss Nameless got him a date and we all went dancing down the Strip.

WHERE DID HE GO FROM THERE?

I don't know. I left at dawn the next morning for New York. Six weeks later, of course, he was in Havana. So was I. So was Errol Flynn. So was Castro. So were lots of people.

WHAT WAS HE DOING THERE?

What he's always doing, I guess. Business.

I KNOW A LITTLE ABOUT THAT BUSI-NESS. WHAT DID HE TELL YOU?

Exactly nothing.

DID YOU SEE HIM AGAIN IN HAVANA?

Sort of, on the run.

IT'S ODD THE ATTRACTION YOU SEEM
TO HOLD FOR LOUIS ESTIMET.

Isn't it, though. Just think. I've seen him for all
of eleven hours since 1956.

DOES THAT INCLUDE SAIGON?

Make it fourteen hours. But forget that for a
moment. You left an accusation floating around
somewhere. I think you started it in Paris. Question: What possible relationship could there be
between Louis Estimet and my stolen week in
Paris in 1944? And who the hell is Croger? You
started out in a hurry, but I never caught the
destination.

I'M NOT BEING INTERROGATED. YOU
ARE.

I'm not being interrogated. I volunteered to
clear my name of some nonsense. Now the nonsense is getting deeper. In fact I'm up to my ass
in it at this moment. And in you, Major Pike.

LET'S TRY TO KEEP THIS IMPERSONAL,
MR. DANZIGER.

It's difficult. You admit that you're fishing?

NOT AT ALL. ALL THE LITTLE PIECES
YOU ARE FILLING IN HELP CREATE A
COMPLEX PICTURE ABOUT A NASTY
BUSINESS THAT HAS GONE ON TOO
LONG, AND I MIGHT ADD, TO WHICH
YOU HAVE FAR TOO MANY STRANDS FOR
SHEER COINCIDENCE.

I see the handwriting on the wall, Maje. What
would have happened if I hadn't volunteered to
clear my name?

YOU WOULD HAVE BEEN SITTING

THERE, ACROSS THIS DESK, AT EXACTLY THIS MOMENT, ANYWAY.

Shows you not to volunteer, doesn't it? I saved you an airline fare.

WE'RE WASTING TIME, MR. DANZIGER.

Time is what I've got. What do you want to talk about, Doc? I just decided I like "Doc" better than "Maje."

YOUR DEFENSE MECHANISMS ARE SHOWING, MR. DANZIGER. TELL ME ABOUT THE FIRST TIME YOU MET LOUIS ESTIMET IN SAIGON. OR DID YOU SEE HIM IN BETWEEN?

Who is Croger, god damn it?

IN DUE COURSE. CONTINUE.

I told you, Doc. Those words "due course" do not fall trippingly from your tongue.

HAVE WE REACHED AN IMPASSE FOR THE DAY? I SENSE SOME IRRITATION.

(Laughter) How did you get so sensitive, Doc? No kidding, how did you get so bloody sensitive?

WE WILL CONVENE AGAIN AT TEN THIRTY TOMORROW. A CAR IS WAITING TO TAKE YOU TO THE SHOREHAM HOTEL.

Shoreham Hotel

Darling:

Back at the hotel after a long wasted day, with scotch and ice in one hand and my small brain in the other. I feel as though someone is trying to take me apart. I wish you were here to share a hot shower and like that.

I don't know quite how to describe what's happening. Saigon may even be secondary. We've been probing around helter-skelter with the University of Michigan, marriage and divorce (poor Stella), with odd little pot-shots at everything that's happened since. No pattern—unless I'm stupider than I think. I almost get the feeling he's not after facts, but out to fill in some complicated mental picture of me personally.

The interrogator is a major named Pike. Bradford Pike. He sounds like a highway in Massachusetts, but he looks like Robespierre. I don't know how I know this but I do. Short, wiry, a little ascetic-looking. Very tweedy, but definitely West Point. Body more robust than you'd think from his face. Has read all but seven of the one hundred best books. Plays volleyball on the Agency Varsity. Married a girl named Pam who took her master's at Bryn Mawr on "The Role of Field Hockey in the Sumerian Civilization." They screw on alternate Saturdays, grounds permitting. He is thirty-five, thirty-eight. From New England—not Harvard but Swamp Yankee. I thought he was a lawyer, but he's a psychiatrist. Maybe he's both. We clash. In all ways. I'll get to know him well.

Their intelligence is superb . . . he has bits and pieces even I didn't remember. I may need a little G-2 myself before long.

Now that I'm actually in it, it no longer seems voluntary.

After you left me at Kennedy, I had a sleepy flight down fortified by all the brandies in all the coffees during all the hours of the night. Wasn't thinking about interrogations then, but about you. After this, shall we continue on down to Mexico City where I can still have that job with old Pat and we can get married. Quiet! Of course I can write film. Fade in: faded blonde . . .

Esterhazy darling, after soap and water. I'm a little spooked. They do it too well. The building masquerades as Commerce Dept. office. Immense. Met at the door by a full cadre of young noncoms in gray suits. Corporal-type turned me over to sergeant-type turned me over to lieutenant-type. My destination approx. one and a half miles from entrance. Kept passing hurried important-looking people in corridors. Wondered why the hurry? To get ham on rye, to pee, to deliver message for hot line?

The interro. started badly. I was too impressed by the panoply of power. Kept expecting a four-star to walk in and pin me to the wall in a burst of logic. You keep wondering: How can all this power, all these people be wrong?

Also learned that the tape recorder is a highly subtle inquisition device. Around and around, your fate whispering away. Almost hypnotic. Ever since that brutal Verranzo case in '64, I've felt that if someone asked me on a lie detector if I liked lamb chops for lunch the needle would quiver, the machine smash, and Danziger ho for the hot seat!

Darling, there's a trunk—an old footlocker really—under the bed at the Landing. Lieutenant P. F. Danziger stenciled on it with an APO number. Full of letters, records, etc. Appreciate if you'd call Gil soonest, get him the key, and ask him to find copy of 1943 Air Corps Yearbook called *Celestials*. Have him send it immed. If we can afford it, I think you'd better advance him some kind of retainer too. I have a hunch I'll be needing him. Show him this letter. Who knows? They brought me to the hotel with no hassle tonight, but I smelt a little man in tow, and two will get you five there's a body outside in the hall and another downstairs in the lobby reading the Washington *Post* and waiting for a tall, aging, angry-looking man with a broken nose to make a dash for it. And so I'd like to. And you know why.

All of it,
PETER

DARLING TRIED PHONE BUT DNA STOP SUSPECT MAIL INSECURED STOP ANONYMOUS TYPE ZEROED IN ON HOTEL MAILBOX AFTER I POSTED LETTER STOP ASK GIL TO VERIFY TAMPERING STOP WILL PHONE COLLECT FROM BOOTH TOMORROW 7 PM UP THE MIDDLE AGES EXCLAMATION POINT.

PETER

TO: A. J. KATIN
FROM: BRADFORD PIKE

(FORMAL REPORT TO FOLLOW)

As you will observe from the first day's transcript, the interrogation technique we devised is not yet fully effective—primarily because of subject's extreme defensiveness and hostility. He has not yet "opened up," although he is beginning. However, this holding back may be an initial indication of guilt and fear. I am abiding by the broad concept: confuse and conquer.

Appreciate any information available on Class of 1943 H, September, from AAC (Pan American) at Coral Gables, Florida, including class book, photos, records.

I am not concerned by the innocent tone of the foregoing private communications, inasmuch as subject obviously knows we are on watch, and quite probably the communications were designed for our eyes.

B.P.

In those days Duck Lake ran into Lake Michigan through a deep natural inlet of pure white sand. The water was ice-blue clean. Deep-swimming, the current whished you along in a kind of cool dream light.

Duck Lake itself was filled with perch and bass and sunfish. There are probably a thousand cottages and sewage problems surrounding it by now.

They used to say there were pickerel in the reeds on the east end, but I never hooked one.

Father used to say, "Prevail, god damn it!" when I got bored or tired rowing. He thought trolling was one of the noblest pursuits of man, provided someone else was on the oars. Even this unreason I still find admirable.

He was a big man, bigger than me, and he had a gift for the unexpected. His whole life and his death were unexpected. He had the kind of crag face and light-blue eyes that turned on you like the dazzling glare of honesty, and it gave you pause. It made you choke your youthful lies back in your throat and take a completely different gambit, a little nearer the truth. It wasn't that he'd check up on you; it was that you simply couldn't lie to a face and eyes like that. You didn't even want to.

A psychiatrist I went to once suggested that my awe for this man was the nub of my problems. It may or may not have been true, but if it were, the nub compensated for the other problems. I've always had this thing about penalties and compensations and no one has talked me out of it yet.

He liked, primarily, kids, language, football and outdoors. I've never really known whether he liked my mother or not. He threw all of western Michigan out of whack when, instead of accepting a publicized athletic scholarship to Michigan Aggie after high school, he somehow got himself into Harvard and stayed until he graduated. He had been pretty good in baseball and really good in football, with a couple of statewide honors, but he wanted Harvard and he got it and paid for it himself somehow. In his way he reflected Harvard all his life, deliberately or not. When he was truly angry he called his adversary a consummate ass, a phrase I have never otherwise heard or seen outside a period book. He used it on me twice, and I was rather pleased, being older then. Once was when I didn't know what peristalsis meant, the other when I told him I was in love with Stella.

He had always wanted to teach. He taught high school for a few years in Lansing, went to war, married mother and then was offered a position teaching English and History at The Lake Day School, a rather posh establishment outside Muskegon for manufacturers from Grand Rapids and Benton Harbor who wanted their foals out of their houses, as he used to say. He had been recommended by his ex-roomate from Harvard, Arjay Lindstrom, and stayed there all his life, with slight incremental raises and no promotions. Arjay later became headmaster and had as much trouble with Father as any preceding headmaster.

Once, when I was about eight, my admiration for him passed all rational bounds. He and Arjay and a few others decided to put a float into the Muskegon Founders' Day Parade, a big event. I was drafted to round up fourteen or fifteen dogs from the neighborhood. I got them together with enthusiasm, mutts and thoroughbreds, and when I saw the usage I was enkindled with imagination and fire. Their float was a fenced-in flatbed truck filled with howling dogs. In the center was a gigantic and fearsome homemade machine with a crank-handle. Arjay cranked the handle while Father with an honest glare at the world in general seized nearby beagles by the tails and dropped them into the feeder on top. There were horrible screams from an amplified phonograph up front, and then from a hole in the bottom of the machine emerged long strings of frankfurters. With an evil smile Father tossed them one by one to the crowds on either side. That's my old man, I told everybody.

Although he was a Midwesterner born, by habitat and inclination, he used to enrage his cronies by going into a dissertation on Eastern brains (his) versus Midwestern brawn (theirs). Unfortunates, he would tell us later. Good lads, but unfortunates.

We were sitting on the running board of his magnificent old robin's-egg-blue Buick touring car in the parking lot outside the football stadium at East Lansing, eating egg salad sandwiches. I drank root beer, he had a flask of his home-brewed medicinal. It was near the end. He told me why Michigan State would obviously overwhelm Michigan and then began to talk about himself to me, for the first and last time: "No one guarantees you are the captain of your soul. You are if you are. There's not one goddamn word in the Bill of Rights about that tender area. It's most important once in a while in life to be able to tell someone to go piss up a rope. Your mother tells me I do it too often, that it's become a game with me, but it hasn't. I just maintain a low boiling point. A low indignation point. It's hurt me, I suppose, in academic circles. But not with the kids. That's why I stay at the Day School. Arjay is an ass in many ways, but he's a free-thinker, and as long as I worry about it, which I do, he leaves the classroom to me. He thinks teaching is a private affair between the teacher and the student, and none of this nonsense about ordained methodology. I read somewhere once that the definition of an ideal education was Mark Hopkins on a log. I'm no Mark Hopkins but I can teach those bright misshapen little horrors to love their language."

And he was in love with language all his life. For years around the dinner table he carried on about best lines.

Best opening line of a novel was from Sabatini, a writer he detested as a merchandiser. From *Scaramouche:* "He was born with the gift of laughter and a sense that the world was mad."

His favorite title was: *Heartbreak House.*

The most evocative line of poetry he had ever read was from a child's verse: "Over the hills and far away."

He read from *Wasteland* to me, and it was only years later that I realized what he had been reading from some funny little magazine.

The only times he got involved in politics were once for Franklin Roosevelt and once against Father Coughlin, who made an appearance in Muskegon. Both activities worked subtly against him with the Day School Board. He genuinely believed that La Follette or someone like him would start the groundswell of a Midwestern progressive movement that (helped by Eastern brains) would spread out from the center and by its sheer righteousness occupy the conscience of the country and in time the world.

Once on a camping trip up near Cadillac he scorched the breakfast eggs and in one beautiful flowing motion heaved the black iron skillet over a pine tree into the river. It was a stupid thing to do, but I admired it immensely. I was about twelve. I still like the idea that Father wouldn't take any shit from a frying pan. I wonder whether he would have thrown Major Pike into the river.

I've reconstructed this in my mind a thousand times. The mallard came in that day from right to left. The wind had to be from the northwest, the way the blind sat. He was on the right side of the blind and stood up too fast in front of Arjay's barrel just as Arjay let go. Maybe eighteen inches away. In Jensen's funeral parlor I wanted desperately to see him, and desperately to not. To see what conceivably could have killed this man who couldn't be dead. They never let me, of course. I've always been relieved and resentful.

It killed Arjay too. He died seven or eight months later. They called it a coronary, but it was sheer unbelieving horror. They had been oddball friends since Harvard. The difference was, as Father used to say: "That goddamn Arjay knows how to *adapt*." In his vocabulary that was a kind of curse.

After he died, I cried every night for a hundred years. Prevail.

At eleven on Fridays a piano down the hall began to bang "Oh, beautiful for spacious skies" in march tempo and all the thirteen-year-olds stood up and filed out for assembly, stirred and excited and each feeling taller than a Michigan pine. Stella as in starlight was direct brown eyes and a pouty lower lip, from the beginning an intrusive little female without scruple or embarrassment. In assembly stared until I looked away, and me the champion out-starer.

In her father's barn the fresh-cut hay was fragrant and moss green and on the ground level you could hear Holsteins shifting and trampling, and occasionally the proud old bull let out a deep rolling sigh in his stall. It was raining that Saturday and her sister, Norma, and the two Latema boys and somebody's cousin Alice and I were diving off a high beam daringly into deep hay. I lay in the pocket I had made on my last leap and looked up at the high-vaulted barn roof with its rain leaks here and there, hay dust sticking to my perspirey arms and the smell of the place strong and marvelous in my nostrils, and then Stella was kissing me, rolling on me, wrestling with me while the other kids were running around down below at their own suddenly petty games. Sensations flashed and odd creepy exciting feelings sprang alive and the sweet mystery of life became less mysterious and even sweeter. We played every Saturday for what seemed the rest of our lives.

It was impossible to spend much time with Stella without being hypnotized by her intensity. That was the fall Father was killed on a gunning trip. He who was so much alive. In her own direct way Stella pulled me out of my absolute anguish into a kind of languorous blue twilight. My mother at that time could only flutter. It had been a patriarchal household, and, poor dear, she'd never had a chance.

Stella as in starlight. We would drift away to other people and suddenly come back secretly and whisper in each other's ears the idiocies other people could perpetrate. It was a private thing. She went with Tom Latema to the graduation parties and dances and I took someone I can't remember, but we always met later. I was reading a lot then and once I said to her, "Incestuous sister, my love," and she slapped me hard.

She signed on for secretarial school and I went off to Ann Arbor. When I invited her up for a football game and house party she was insecure about her wardrobe and her manners. Uncomfortably un-Stella. In a fraternity parking lot that night I told her to stop worrying, she was the best lay on the campus. She smiled viciously in the yellow of the streetlight and began to chant: "My Hymie is a colleger, my Hymie is a colleger" . . . I hit her rather hard—we were both full of manhattans—and then kissed her and took her to a hotel and we stayed in bed pleasing each other until it was time for her bus Sunday night. I had always been in love with her when I was with her.

Fortunately, we each let go easily.

One night in 1946, in New York, someone lowered a face mask in an Equity Library production of *The Great God Brown* and there stood Stella. We went home to Tenth Street together and laughed and cried and talked about high school and the barn and familiar old memories and idiosyncrasies and a week later got married the day before Thanksgiving in the morning. In the night she started calling me Donny, who was current; yesterday afternoon at three thirty and again at three forty-five. It turned out there were lots of Donnys. After a while the police came.

I saw her just once more, in Los Angeles, the night before Kennedy was nominated. On impulse I looked her up in the Beverly Hills directory and invited her for a drink at the Wilshire. I ducked an assorted group of perspiring press, all of us still groggy from the nominating inanities, and caught a cab to richer country.

We met in the lobby.

Our eyes locked and we both stood stupidly, wondering what to say. Her husband was a lean handsome man.

"You look better than ever, Stella."

"Thank you. Thank you, Peter. How has your life been?"

"Oh. On and off. You know."

Her husband moved past us into the security of the bar, no doubt diminished by the unexpected brilliance of the dialogue.

She looked flustered: "Mine too, I guess. I'm dying for a margarita."

We went in and sat down and chatted and I spent the rest of the evening wondering how my life had been, and how she stayed so damned good looking.

Tuesday

ARE YOU COMFORTABLE? WOULD YOU LIKE MORE COFFEE?

No, thank you.

ALL RIGHT. I WANT TO GO BACK AND TOUCH ON A FEW SHADOW AREAS BEFORE WE MOVE INTO MORE CURRENT ISSUES.

I thought you just might.

THIS HAS TO DO WITH THE PERIOD 1953-1954.

Yes.

I KNOW YOUR DISRESPECT IS INTENDED, BUT I ASSURE YOU IT IS UNWARRANTED. UNLESS YOU HAVE SOMETHING TO HIDE.

Nothing but me.

EXCELLENT. THEN WE CAN PROCEED. HAVE YOU REFRESHED YOUR MEMORY ABOUT CROGER?

Negative.

I HAVE, ON THE OTHER HAND, REFRESHED MINE. THERE IS NO QUESTION

THAT YOU KNEW HIM. ONE OF MY PEO-
PLE SUGGESTED YOU MAY HAVE HAD
LUNCH WITH HIM SIX DAYS A WEEK FOR
TEN MONTHS.

So it follows I remember him? Maybe he was a
musician. Did you ever eat with a musician?

IT DOES, INDEED, FOLLOW. WHY DON'T
YOU START TO DIG YOURSELF OUT?

I'll dig out as soon as I'm dug in. So far I've
heard nothing but funny hints.

YOU WILL HEAR SOME FACTS, MR. DAN-
ZIGER.

When?

SHORTLY.

My gratitude is exceeded only by my disbelief.

SHALL WE CONTINUE OUR LOOK AT '53-
'54?

Might as well.

YOU WERE IN EUROPE IN THE SUMMER
OF '53?

Yes.

ON ASSIGNMENT?

No. On vactaion.

FOR HOW LONG?

About two weeks in London, goofing around.
Then I went to Portugal.

WITH WHOM?

With a young lady—then—who has absolutely
nothing to do with this inquiry. Knew nothing,
cared less, and is probably laughing somewhere at
all of us disembodied characters.

YOU REFER, OF COURSE, TO THE WOM-

AN NAMED CYBELE McCULLOUGH WHOM
YOU HAD KNOWN MUCH EARLIER?

(Silence) You do have your surprises, Doc.
Now where in God's name did you get hold of
that? You're not reducing me to ashes, but you're
sure as hell reducing me to tears. Not about
Cybele. About me. Was I born in a dossier or did
it just grow? Who gave me the answers to the
arithmetic test in fourth grade? I can't remember, but Doc has it on page seven hundred and
seventy-three dash four. When did this start? Pre-
or post-umbilical? And do you keep one running
on yourself? I knew a guy who lives alone on a
farm in Vermont who goes to town twice a month
for supplies and talks to himself the rest of the
time. What have you got on him, Doc? Dangerous?
A sex maniac? Lonesome? You people frighten
me.

WHO IS CYBELE McCULLOUGH?

A girl. Correction. She was a girl. I don't know
anything that might have happened to her since
except the ravages of time. Do you people make
any allowance for the ravages of time?

UNDER WHAT CIRCUMSTANCES DID
YOU MEET HER?

Under the circumstances of drinking.

MR. DANZIGER, WHAT CAN BE THE AD-
VANTAGE TO YOU OF THIS OPEN HOS-
TILITY? CAN'T WE GET ON WITH IT?

That was a factual statement, as it happens,
Doc. Tell me what more you want.

IF YOU COULD THINK OF THIS AS OPEN

COMMUNICATIONS, FOR EXAMPLE—

It would be a pretty heady exercise. Which garden path would you like to lead me down?

SO LONG AS YOU DISTRUST ME—

Like a piranha. Cybele McCullough was a girl I was fond of. I don't know when she had the measles nor which of her uncles belonged to the Black and Tans—nor do I care.

NOR DO I. YOU KEEP PRETENDING THIS IS WORSE THAN IT IS. WHERE DID SHE COME FROM?

North Ireland, originally. Outside Belfast.

YOU'RE TURNING THIS INTO A ROOT CANAL EXERCISE, YOU KNOW.

That's because the whole thing seems a little dental, Doc.

YOU OWE US SOME EXPLANATIONS; AT YOUR OWN REQUEST.

Correct.

SO CAN WE PROCEED ON SOME KIND OF FACTUAL BASIS?

Factual basis? Why not? But don't ask me any current questions about Cybele McCullough. I thought she was Mary Magdalene about 1945. End of story.

AND PERHAPS AGAIN IN 1953?

And perhaps again. Correct.

AND SINCE?

Not since. Nothing since.

HOW AND WHERE DID YOU MEET HER?

The problem with unpeeling people, Doc, is that you have to look at unpeeled people. How does this ancient thing help you in any tiny way?

TO REPEAT: HOW AND WHERE DID YOU MEET HER?

At a tea-dance in the lounge of the Piccadilly Hotel on a summer afternoon in 1943.

THAT WAS SORT OF AN—AN ASSIGNATION PLACE, AS I RECALL.

Sort of, I suppose.

CONTINUE.

I wish I could. What if—now—having made the commitment to subject myself voluntarily to open-end interrogation, I decided to switch over?

TO WHAT?

To your subpoena. Or whatever you spooks call it.

WHY? WHEN WE'RE GETTING ALONG SO FAMOUSLY, MR. DANZIGER.

So what if I did?

CHANGE, YOU MEAN?

Yes.

YOU CAN'T, YOU SEE. AS YOU PUT IT SO FORCEFULLY, YOU HAVE ALREADY MADE THE COMMITMENT. YOU CAN STOP TALKING OF COURSE—

Very neat.

NOT REALLY. IT'S NOT THAT REWARDING AND, AS YOU SAY, MY ROLE IS DENTAL.

You know what you're running up against? The information gap. Maybe I should call it the Inquisition Gap. It probably drives you crazy. Example: I'm sure there's some cigar salesman in

Queens who by coincidence has ridden the E train with me more times than my girl. But you don't have a dossier on him. Consider *that* as food for thought! Wouldn't *that* foul up your inquiry? X-teen thousand more mutations of chance. Doc, you'd go out of your skull! How many times by chance have you got in the same cab? What a plot, hey, Doc? Throw the son of a bitch in jail— at least for lousing up your predetermined chart of probability. I could give you at this moment the names of about eleven people I've seen and talked to at all the places you're psyched up about, at all the right times. I could, but I won't because, like Stella and Estimet and Cybele, they're irrelevant. Just like your files and your point of view. Those people are parts of my life. They have nothing to do with anything else. This inquiry isn't about me. It's about you.

I'M A LITTLE BORED WITH HEARING YOU WHINE, MR. DANZIGER. YOU'RE RIGHT OF COURSE: THIS HEARING ISN'T ABOUT YOU. YOUR EXISTENCE DOESN'T MEAN A ROTTEN BEAN. OTHER EXISTENCES DO. MEN WHO MAY HAVE HAD THEIR PERSONAL ACTUARY TABLES SEVERELY CHANGED BECAUSE OF ACTIONS YOU TOOK OR DIDN'T TAKE. DON'T SHOUT AT ME ABOUT INFRINGEMENTS ON YOUR CIVIL RIGHTS OR INTRUSIONS ON YOUR FREEDOM OF SPEECH, BECAUSE THAT'S NOT MY DEPARTMENT. I'M CONCERNED

ABOUT ACTIONS. PROVABLE DANGER-
OUS ACTIONS. AND, SIR, I'VE GOT
THREE HUNDRED PAGES OF SINGLE-
SPACED EXPOSITION HERE THAT SO
FAR ADD UP TO DEEP INVOLVEMENT. I
DIDN'T ASK YOU TO COME HERE. PER-
SONALLY, I'D HAVE PREFERRED TO
HAVE YOU DRAGGED IN, BUT APPAR-
ENTLY THERE'S SOME UNWRITTEN
LAW ABOUT DOING THAT TO PEOPLE
WITH BY-LINES. BUT YOU DID VOLUN-
TEER TO COME HERE AND CLEAR YOUR
NAME—AND GOT HEADLINES AND
FRONT-PAGE STORIES INTO THE BAR-
GAIN. I UNDERSTAND YOUR COL-
LEAGUES ARE MAKING BETS IN THE
PRESS ROOM. VERY WELL. THAT'S YOUR
TACTIC. BUT I LIVE IN A COLDER
CLEANER WORLD. SO NOW SHOW THE
COURAGE OF YOUR PUBLICITY. TALK,
MR. DANZIGER.

By God, I finally pressed the right button.
SHALL WE CONTINUE?

You bet your ass. But you're going to hear a lot
more what you call whining before you're finished. As a matter of fact, I wondered for a minute whether you were going to zero in on my
patriotism or my manhood. Fifty-fifty, I decided.
Then you just took a sloppy half-whack each
way. Bad strategy, Doc.
AND NOW SHALL WE GET ON WITH IT?

(Pause)

You know, I just realized I have a tremendous advantage over you. I know where I am. And you're sitting balanced on a sticky wicket. Uncomfortably, I hope. And I've got twenty years of fatuous memories about the pods they clamp around okay brains like yours at that little gray factory up the Hudson. You talk about your responsibility, Doc. Fine. I've got mine, too. And it ain't to the military. It's to all us votin' chickens that just get shoved around if we ain't mindful, I'm mindful, Doc.

A PERSONAL QUESTION, IF I MAY DIGRESS. DID YOU REALLY THINK YOU COULD PUT ME THROUGH THAT WALL YESTERDAY, MR. DANZIGER?

Still do, Doc.

(Pause)

I BELIEVE I'VE HAD ENOUGH OF YOU UNTIL AFTER LUNCH.

So early? I assume I'm free to go back to my hotel? Is it bugged already?

OH, INDEED. SHALL WE BREAK?

You break first, Doc.

HOW WAS YOUR LUNCH?

The Shoreham blue-plate special should never be confused with lunch.

A PITY . . . WE ACCOMPLISHED SO LITTLE THIS MORNING THAT PERHAPS WE CAN MAKE UP FOR LOST TIME NOW. I WANT TO TRY TO CONNECT UP ONE MORE LOOSE ELEMENT BEFORE WE TRY,

AS YOU SAID YESTERDAY, TO FIT ALL
THE PIECES INTO ONE PICTURE.

I sincerely hope you know what you're doing.
The evidence, so far, is shaky.

WE'LL SEE . . . THERE IS ANOTHER MAN
WHO FITS INTO ALL THIS.

Into all what?

INTO THE SAME PICTURE WITH CRO-
GER, LOUIS ESTIMET AND CYBELLE Mc-
CULLOUGH.

You left out Stella.

SO I DID. BUT NOT YOU, MR. DANZIGER.

Who is this new unfortunate?

NOT NEW. YOU KNEW HIM WELL. IN
COLLEGE.

I went to college with six thousand guys. A long
time ago, Doc.

NO PROBLEM. YOU'LL RECALL HIM IN-
STANTLY. TELL ME ABOUT THE MAN AT
MICHIGAN YOU CALLED CHARLEY HSI.

(Pause)

I should have smelt that one coming. I must
be losing my instincts.

OR COVERING THEM WELL, MR. DAN-
ZIGER. TALK ABOUT CHARLEY HSI.
WHAT WAS THE ORIGINAL CONTEXT OF
YOUR FRIENDSHIP?

Contract bridge. He was the best bridge player
at Michigan; also one of the nicer guys.

DESCRIBE HIM. THEN, I MEAN.

Maybe five-feet-five. Moonfaced, but not fat. His
eyes disappeared when he smiled, which was often. Spoke without an accent. Had his clothes

tailored in New York and owned and operated a brain about the size of an IBM computer.

EXCELLENT. AND WHAT DOES HE LOOK LIKE NOW—OR AT LEAST WHEN YOU SAW HIM SO OFTEN THIS PAST WINTER AND SPRING IN CAMBODIA AND LAOS?

Identically the same except that his eyes disappeared faster.

MEANING HE SMILED MORE OFTEN?

Meaning he aged a little.

WHAT WAS HIS HOME OF RECORD WHEN YOU FIRST MET HIM AS COLLEGE STUDENTS?

Shanghai. His father owned a bank.

AND NOW?

Peking. That's where his family is.

DID YOU MEET HIM AT MICHIGAN THROUGH THE LEFT-WING ACTIVITIES WE DISCUSSED YESTERDAY?

God, no.

HOW DID YOU MEET HIM?

At a bridge table in the Student Union. All the Chinese stayed a million miles from politics. Out loud, at least.

DID YOU SUSPECT THEN THAT HE MIGHT BE A MILITANT?

A militant what? He was a banker's son, for God's sake, with a wardrobe from J. Press. He was a militant capitalist if he was anything.

WHY DID YOU SEE HIM REPEATEDLY IN THE FAR EAST, FULL WELL KNOWING HE WAS AS FAR FROM BEING ON OUR SIDE AS MAO HIMSELF?

Still a helluva bridge player, Doc.

YOU WERE IGNORANT OF THE FACT THAT HE MAINTAINED A HIGH BUT UNDISCLOSED STATUS IN HIS GOVERNMENT?

I'm not a cretin, Doc. I needled him about it. What's his sin? To stick with his country?

AT LAST REPORT, THE GOVERNMENT OF THE REPUBLIC OF CHINA WAS STILL IN TAIWAN.

At last report, the people of China were still in China.

FOR A POLITICAL REPORTER, MR. DANZIGER, DON'T YOU THINK YOUR STANCE IS A LITTLE NAIVE?

I haven't heard of any recent act of Congress telling me I'm at war, Doc. You're the naive one. There are hotel lobbies in Pessary, Ohio, that smell better than the old China Lobby. . . . Introducing Doc Pike—the last surviving member after those two greedy old horrors in Taiwan pass on to their little gelt-lined pagoda in the sky.

IT'S SINGULARLY UNREWARDING TRYING TO EXTRACT INFORMATION FROM YOU, MR. DANZIGER.

Maybe it wouldn't be if you'd stop trying to prewrite the script.

THE SCRIPT IS ALL WRITTEN—AND YOU WROTE IT, MR. DANZIGER.

What does it say I did with Charley Hsi?

GAVE AND RECEIVED INFORMATION, OBVIOUSLY.

Every time I open my mouth, here or in a bar

or on a telephone, I give and receive information, Doc. It's called talking and listening. It's how I make my living. You'd be surprised at how common it is, and how legal.

LEGAL, MR. DANZIGER, IF THAT TALKING AND LISTENING JEOPARDIZES THE STANCE OF YOUR COUNTRY?

By whose decision? Look. This is easy, Doc. Just trot out the old statute that says it's a crime to talk to Charley Hsi.

IN WARTIME, MR. DANZIGER—

We're not at war.

DID YOU HEAR THE CASUALTY REPORTS ON LAST NIGHT'S NEWS?

Tragic. But just an adventure, Doc. You can't have it both ways. There's a book about how to define war too. Have you read it? You couldn't make a formal wartime statute stick in this skirmish if you had Clarence Darrow as linebacker.

THERE ARE, AS A MATTER OF FACT, A SURPRISING NUMBER OF THINGS WE CAN MAKE STICK.

Pfui. Also, explain that line you dropped about jeopardy. Jeopardizing what stance? Our stance stinks. There's hardly anyone in the world who doesn't understand this almost automatically, through osmosis, excepting you people and your candy Saigon generals with the Ramon Navarro mustaches.

THERE'S NO QUESTION BUT THAT YOUR ACTIONS AND WORDS JEOPARDIZED IMMENSE PLANS AND MANY MEN,

MR. DANZIGER. BELIEVE ME, I COULD GO TO COURT WITH THAT TOMORROW.

Just for the hell of it, Doc—are you talking about treason?

PERHAPS TO ME: TREASON. PERHAPS NOT UNDER THE LAW.

Well, let's arrange that you don't pick the jury ... I'll bet you'd love it if I were in the military.

I CAN'T THINK OF MANY THINGS THAT WOULD PLEASE ME MORE, OR THAT WOULD SERVE THIS SMALL CORNER OF OUR GOVERNMENT.

Makes a fella glad he's not a soldier, Doc. . . . What am I supposed to have told Charley? The plan for the new armor-piercing shell? The strategy of the spring offensive across the Somme? Or just who was sleeping with who?

IT'S NOT MERELY WHAT YOU MAY HAVE TOLD THIS DANGEROUS MAN. IT'S WHAT HE TOLD YOU THAT YOU DID NOT COMMUNICATE TO OUR PEOPLE.

Our people meaning your people?

YES.

(Expression of anger) God damn it, I have nothing to do with your people. I communicate with my people. Meaning the people who pay me to use my brains and my ingenuity and tell what I find. And the people who plank out a nickel or dime to read those immortal words. If this is your case, I don't need a lawyer. Just a judge. You're screwed, Doc.

(Silence)

SO—WHERE ARE WE HERE? WE'VE ESTAB-
LISHED YOUR CONNECTIONS, BY YOUR
OWN ADMISSION, WITH LOUIS ESTIMET,
CHARLEY HSI, AND THE WOMAN
KNOWN AS CYBELE McCULLOUGH.

She's not known as Cybele McCullough. That's
her name.

THE WOMAN NAMED CYBELE McCUL-
LOUGH. NOW FOR MR. CROGER, AND WE
CAN QUICKLY GET INTO THE MEAT OF
THE THING . . . DO YOU STILL PROPOSE
TO ME THAT YOU DO NOT KNOW THE
MAN?

I sure do. Never heard of him.

TAKE IT FROM THIS POINT OF VIEW.
YOU CAN'T REALLY WIN WITH THIS
CONTINUING DENIAL BECAUSE WE CAN
PROVE IT. IF I SHOWED YOU, FOR EX-
AMPLE, A PHOTOGRAPH WITH YOU AND
CROGER BOTH IN IT, ABOUT SIX FEET
FROM EACH OTHER, WOULD YOU SAVE
US ALL THE TIME AND TROUBLE OF DO-
ING SO BY SIMPLY ADMITTING THAT
THE FIGURES ARE INDEED OF YOU AND
EMIL CROGER?

God damn it, nobody listens. Doc, if you
showed me a Kodachrome of me and Croger making love to the Dolly Sisters on the same hassock
it wouldn't put you one inch further.

THERE ARE TIMES WHEN THE PRICE OF
STUBBORNNESS, IN A DECLINING MAR-
KET, DROPS OUT.

So be it. What time is it?

WE HAVE AMPLE MORE TIME.

That's one of the cockiest statements I ever heard.

WOULD YOU LIKE A BREAK? THIS DAY IS AN ALMOST COMPLETE WASTE. YOU DEFEND YOURSELF LIKE A DEMON AGAINST WINDMILLS. IS IT PANIC, MR. DANZIGER?

I think I'll go back to the hotel now, Doc.

YOU AGREED TO FOLLOW OUR RULES FOR THE INQUIRY, MR. DANZIGER. IN WRITING. AND I'D LIKE ANOTHER HALF HOUR.

This is democracy? Let's pee.

YOUR TERMINOLOGY IS MOST SUCCINCT. MY CONGRATULATIONS TO YOUR PUBLISHER.

My ex-publisher. Thanks.

ALL RIGHT?

No. Are you interfering with my mail?

IT'S AN AXIOM THAT NO ONE CAN INTERFERE WITH THE MAIL, MR. DANZIGER.

I had a sudden hunch where you expect to get that picture you mentioned. Obviously, you don't have it here. People are probably looking for it. But you've told them I'll get old Danziger to deliver it to us. And the only way you could know that is by reading a letter I wrote and mailed last night.

IS ALL THIS YOUR TORTUOUS WAY OF

ADMITTING THE EXISTENCE OF CRO-
GER?

You really don't listen, do you? There is no
Croger. Not in my life. As I'll demonstrate when
I get the pictures—if, indeed, I do.

WE'LL SEE. SIT DOWN, PLEASE . . . (Pause)
. . . JUST LOOSE ENDS FOR A MOMENT
NOW, I THINK. I SEE YOU MENTIONED
THAT YOU LAST SAW YOUR FRIEND CY-
BELE McCULLOUGH IN 1953?

Yes.

SHE DIDN'T COME TO THIS COUNTRY
THE FOLLOWING YEAR, IN 1954?

No. Yes. About a year later.

WHY DID YOU FORGET?

It was forgettable.

WHAT WAS THE OCCASION OF HER
VISIT?

She was working on something. A ballet thing,
I believe. God knows why. She used to pick
things up and drop them.

EXACTLY WHAT DO YOU MEAN?

What I said. She bored easily. What possible
difference could it make to you?

THAT WILL EMERGE. DID SHE CALL YOU
OR WRITE YOU?

Yes.

WHICH?

Both.

SAYING WHAT?

What would you expect? Saying, "Peter darling
I'm going to be in New York."

DID SHE MENTION THE SPECIFICS OF HER DUTIES HERE?

No, she just mentioned that she had some, which I doubted.

DID YOU ACCOMPANY HER ON ANY OF HER BUSINESS ERRANDS?

God, no.

DID SHE INTRODUCE YOU TO ANY PEOPLE?

I think a bartender.

DID YOU INTRODUCE HER TO CHARLEY HSI?

(Silence)

You're one of those conspiracy nuts, did you know that, Doc? Shadows behind shadows. Where did you get your degree? The University of Graustark?

YOU HAVE NO RECOLLECTION OF CYBELE MEETING CHARLEY HSI?

No. Doc, you're on a dead end.

HOW ABOUT LOUIS ESTIMET?

That's logical, isn't it, Doc? I didn't meet Louis until three or four years later.

OR SEVEN YEARS EARLIER, MR. DANZIGER.

When you go into practice, Doc, just a tip from an old buyer. Don't let your patients suddenly feel that they're losing their senses, which is what you seem to do instinctively, old boy.

YOU LOCK YOUR MIND, MR. DANZIGER, WITH AN INTERESTING DEVICE. IT'S NOT UNCOMMON, HOWEVER.

I'm not really losing my senses either, however.
SO WE CONTINUE. . . . I'D LIKE TO GO
BACK TO THE BEGINNING OF YOUR AS-
SOCIATION WITH CYBELE McCUL-
LOUGH. WHAT KIND OF PERSON WAS
SHE?

Doc, we keep doing this.
BELIEVE ME, IT IS NECESSARY. FOR ME
AND FOR YOU.

(Silence)

Okay, Cybele was slightly mad.

(Silence)

She was tall, slight. She looked as though she
might disappear at any moment. Her eyes were
immense and dark. She was one of those Irish-
men with the white skin and dark-green eyes and
black hair. She didn't know her ass from her el-
bow, but she looked as though she knew more
than the Greeks and Ezra Pound had ever pieced
together—and maybe she did. She wasn't sexy-
looking, but she was sex. Do you comprehend
what I'm talking about? In college once—when
I was on the boxing team, Doc—I was knocked
out by a poem by James Stephens about that Irish
queen named Deirdre. I walked into the hotel
lounge in London that afternoon, after just having
had my ass shot at for the first time, and I looked
around for a table—I was with a Texas bombar-
dier named Shorty Spicer—and I found myself
looking into the eyes of Deirdre. That's roughly
equivalent to putting your head into a power
mower. I mean it doesn't stop with one whop.

(Silence)

CONTINUE.

I just walked over to her table and asked if I could sit down. She didn't say anything, so I sat there and there it was. Shorty was more inclined to walk around among the assorted talent asking: "Excuse me, lady, do you fuck?" To tell the truth, I can't remember Shorty after that weekend. Maybe he went home. Maybe he got killed. Any way, he left me with Cybele. There was a crumby trio playing "Tea for Two" and the whole place smelt like orange blossoms somehow. And dusty. I remember that the candlestick on the little tea table was dusty.

WAS SHE A STREETWALKER?

(Expression of anger) She was a girl in London in wartime.

HOW OLD THEN?

Maybe nineteen. I hope to God you have no daughters.

CONTINUE.

Then knock off interrupting with inanities.

I'LL KNOCK OFF, MR. DANZIGER. CONTINUE.

Cybele and I talked well. We laughed at the same things. She had an acute sense of the ridiculous. She'd be laughing if she were here now. We became mental—or maybe humorous—before we became physical. I was just damned excited at meeting a wild-looking female who could talk and laugh. When she liked me a lot she used to touch my broken nose and say with a funny smile: "Danziger-san." Her father had been some kind of minor consul in Japan and she spent a few years there as a kid. It might sound to you like a simple thing, but it was one of the most lovely complicated things that ever happened to me. Danziger-san. I didn't touch her that time, except with my mouth. We necked like college kids and all the great things kept welling up, and I took her in a cab all the way out to Northolt and went back to the hotel broke and involved and ready to take on whatever dragons were looking funny at me.

WHAT WAS THE NEXT TIME YOU SAW HER?

The next day. Every chance I got.

WHICH WAS HOW OFTEN?

Three days about every three weeks.

YOU SOON BECAME INTIMATE?

I fail to see how an ancient screwing can be of current interest to my government.

WE ARE INTERESTED IN CYBELE McCULLOUGH AND IN YOU, MR. DANZIGER. ILLUMINATION ILLUMINATES. THAT'S ALL. YOU CONTINUED TO SEE EACH OTHER?

Yes. She got canned from her job at the ministry, but picked up another a few weeks later, through her sister, doing something at BBC. Cybele has a knack for getting along.

HER DISCHARGE AT THE MINISTRY HAD NOTHING TO DO WITH SECURITY?

No. Unlike me. In those dear, dead days, people could still get fired for not going to work.

HOW LONG DID THIS FRIENDSHIP CONTINUE?

Till almost the end of the war.

WHAT STOPPED IT?

The ravages of time, I guess. I discovered accidentally she was sleeping with a Polish pilot who was attached to one of those expatriate RAF squadrons.

BEFORE YOU DISCOVERED THIS, HAD YOU INTENDED TO MARRY?

Oh, God, yes. We were going to live in Monterey or someplace else where the mountains met the sea, and build a house on a cliffside that faced the sunset, and I was going to write books and films and poetry, and she was going to bear children, and in between we would run on the beach naked and celebrate our sheer exuberance at getting rich and living forever. Like everybody, Doc.

DID YOU STOP SEEING HER AT THIS JUNCTURE?

No. Who ever does? It dragged on as these things do.

DID YOU BEAT HER UP?

Christ, no.

I WAS REMEMBERING YOUR EX-WIFE, STELLA.

Stella was born to get beat up. Cybele was born to make men like me want to commit suicide.

DO YOU, INDEED, HAVE SUICIDAL TENDENCIES?

Sure, Doc, but so far I've managed to contain them. You really are the most naïve man.

INDEED? . . . HOW LONG DID YOU CONTINUE SEEING HER?

Two, three months, off and on.

WHO INSTIGATED THE MEETINGS?

Both. Someone would call. Or write. Everybody would cry and reunite. The war was coming to an end. I was about to ship home. Poignance. You know that word, Doc? It was poignant. Then the next night she wouldn't answer her phone till four in the morning. Poignant.

I AM SURE THAT IT WAS. WHEN DID YOU LAST SEE HER IN THIS PARTICULAR CHAIN OF EVENTS?

We'd made plans for four months to go down to Torquay in August for my seven-day leave. I had a suite at the Queen Anne—a magnificent old barn—and I'd even lined up a pretty twenty-one-foot sloop. Wickered bottles of Chablis, a portable phonograph. The whole bag. So we tried it. It didn't work. It was torture. The last time I saw those precious wicker bottles they were sitting on the beach unopened. Like unwanted kids. I got a letter from her back in the States the next summer, when I was trying to put something together, like everybody else. I recognized the writing and the envelope and the smell, and I did something I've always regretted. I threw it into the fireplace unopened. I saw George Brent or Joseph Cotton do it once, but I never thought I'd be man enough. It turned out to be easy and terrible. A flick of the wrist. Then you wonder for a few thousand nights.

AND YOU DID NOT SEE HER OR COMMUNICATE WITH HER UNTIL 1953?

Correct.

WHO INSTIGATED THE NEW ENCOUN-
TER?

I did.

FOR WHAT PURPOSE?

For the purpose of alleviating boredom. For the
purpose of satisfying my curiosity after all those
years.

WHAT HAPPENED?

I was on holiday for three weeks, and some other plans in England had failed to gel, so I tracked
down Cybele—which wasn't easy.

I IMAGINE NOT. HOW DID YOU DO IT?

A friend of mine who wrote a gossip column in
the *Telegraph* could have tracked down Judge
Crater. He located her in two days.

CONTINUE.

I phoned her. We met for lunch. It was fun.
We were both guarded and older, but it was fun.
She looked better, believe it or not. She's the kind
who looks even better later. Not full-blown, but
kind of magnificent. We laughed and drank and
talked. I asked her what was in the letter. She
wouldn't tell me. The next morning I asked her
to come to Portugal with me, and we flew down
by BEA to Lisbon. I rented a car and we drove
to Estoril, and stayed at a seaside house a friend
had lent me. It was almost like Monterey, except
the food was better. We ate snails and langouste
and each other and never a bitter word. We swam
and sailed and drove by moonlight along the cliff
road. After a week I put her on the plane back to
London and turned away from the passenger gate

wondering what was happening to the St. Louis Cardinals.

DID YOU WRITE HER?

No.

DID YOU MEET ANYONE IN PORTUGAL WHO ALREADY HAS A ROLE IN THIS TRANSCRIPT?

No.

DID YOU TALK TO HER IN PORTUGAL ABOUT CHARLEY HSI?

No. For God's sake.

EMIL CROGER?

Doc, you're losing me.

DID YOU GIVE HER A LETTER TO LOUIS ESTIMET?

I gave her a dozen retroactive orchids for Louis Estimet. When will you admit you're up a dead alley?

WHAT HAPPENED IN NEW YORK IN 1954?

I already told you.

TELL ME THE DETAILS.

The details are nonexistent. She wrote me, then phoned.

AND THEN?

We had dinner. At a French restaurant on West Forty-sixth Street. We drank a lot of wine and talked. She still looked magnificent. I took her to hear a piano player in a place in the Thirties. I took her back to my hotel. We couldn't make love together. As simple as that. She cried. I cried a little myself. Then she got up and left. Don't ask for more details, Doc. That's it.

YOU DID NOT SEE HER AGAIN?

Yes. The last Sunday before she left. For that miserable function called brunch. To say good-bye, I guess. I mean real good-bye. She called and I invited her. At one of those glass and metal places where you're afraid to sneeze. She kept saying: "Dear Peter." I looked at her across the table and thought: I missed it, didn't I? This fantastic woman. This Cybele. Maybe I booted it long, long ago. But we'd used each other up somehow. When I left her on the sidewalk, I kissed her cheek. I felt like a kid who likes candy when his mother says: "All gone." Only the kid is never sure whether it's really all gone or not.

VERY INTERESTING. AND YOU HAVEN'T COMMUNICATED WITH HER SINCE?

No . . . Wait a minute. I sent her a doll.

WHEN?

Just after New Year's. Six months ago.

WHERE WERE YOU?

Saigon, as you know.

WHAT HAPPENED?

I'm thinking . . . I got a little peaky after dinner with some of your cohorts and wandered around and drank a little and eventually bought two hand-carved dolls in the market. Then I went to the Sand House and wrote two notes. I gave a kid some money to mail them. One was to Cybele.

WHO WAS THE OTHER TO?

Someone you wouldn't know.

MRS. PANTELL. YES. WHAT DID THE NOTE SAY?

(Silence) I want to ask questions later about your G-2.

WHAT DID THE NOTE SAY?

It announced the opening of the dolls for dolls movement, or something like that.

YOU'RE A VERY HARD MAN WITH A MEMORY, MR. DANZIGER. PERHAPS EVEN SENTIMENTAL. WHAT WERE THE DOLLS LIKE?

Put me on the rack, Doc. I haven't an idea.

WAS THERE ANYTHING SPECIAL—PERSONAL—IN THE NOTE TO CYBELE?

They were both personal, I imagine.

MEANING YOU DON'T REMEMBER?

Correct.

WAS CHARLEY HSI WITH YOU THAT NIGHT?

Disguised as what?

HAD YOU EVER TALKED TO HIM ABOUT CYBELE?

Negative. Doc, really—

CYBELE McCULLOUGH IS DEAD.

(Silence)

DIDN'T YOU KNOW?

What do you mean she's dead? She can't be dead.

ANYBODY CAN BE DEAD, MR. DANZIGER. HAVEN'T YOU LEARNED THAT YET?

Someone would have told me.

WHO? THE POLISH PILOT? . . . SIT DOWN, MR. DANZIGER. WE CAN'T PICK UP YOUR VOICE WHEN YOU'RE PACING.

(Silence)

When did she die?

FEBRUARY ELEVENTH OF THIS YEAR.

How?

SHE WAS DRIVING DOWN THE MAIN
AUSTRIAN HIGHWAY FROM BOLZANO
TO INNSBRUCK. PRESUMABLY AT A
RATHER HIGH RATE OF SPEED. AT A
POINT WHERE THE DOWNGRADE WAS
FAIRLY DRAMATIC, A CAR IDENTIFIED
BY AN AUSTRIAN MAIL DRIVER AS A
BLUE CITROËN PULLED OUT TO PASS
HER, SWERVED, AND FORCED HER INTO
A GUARDRAIL. WE THINK DELIBERATE-
LY. HER CAR ROLLED AND ENDED UP
BADLY SMASHED AGAINST A ROCK OUT-
CROP. SHE WAS DEAD WHEN THE MAIL
DRIVER ARRIVED AT THE CAR. THE
CITROËN WAS UNIDENTIFIED AND CON-
TINUED ON ITS WAY. FORTUNATELY,
BY HAPPENSTANCE, HER CAR DID NOT
IGNITE.

What difference does it make?

ONLY THIS, MR. DANZIGER. IT ALLOWED
AN EXAMINATION OF THE CONTENTS
BY INTERPOL.

Where did Interpol suddenly come from?

THEY'D BEEN WATCHING FOR SOME
MONTHS.

Why?

POSSIBLY BECAUSE ABOUT A MONTH
AFTER YOU RETURNED HERE FROM
PORTUGAL, IN 1953, SHE WENT BACK TO
THE CONTINENT WITH LOUIS ESTIMET.

Ridiculous. She was taller than he was.

DESPITE THAT, THEY REGISTERED AS
MAN AND WIFE FOR OVER THREE

WEEKS. IN PARIS, IN LYONS, IN GENEVA AND IN MILAN. YOUR FRIEND LOUIS DIS- APPEARED IN MILAN, AND CYBELE Mc- CULLOUGH DROVE TO PARIS IN THE CAR, AND THEN FLEW BACK TO LON- DON.

She was a big, strong, unmarried woman. What's the charge?

SUBSEQUENTLY, SHE ACCOMPANIED ES- TIMET TO OTHER CITIES ON NINE DIF- FERENT OCCASIONS. INCLUDING ONE TRIP TO PRAGUE, ONE TO VIENNA, AND ONE TO EAST BERLIN.

Doc, I don't know what you're trying to prove. Cybele was apolitical.

BUT NOT NONGREEDY, WOULD YOU SAY?

She took care of herself—but not so well as to get killed.

BUTTERFLIES ALWAYS GET KILLED. PLEASURE GIRLS ALWAYS DIE AT A CER- TAIN AGE. USUALLY VIOLENTLY. IT'S THE PRICE OF AFFORDING PLEASURE, I EXPECT, MR. DANZIGER.

What did they find in her car?

TWO THINGS. AN ATTACHÉ CASE FILLED WITH AMERICAN CURRENCY IN HIGH DENOMINATION. AND A PIECE OF PA- PER IN HER PURSE IN LOUIS ESTIMET'S HANDWRITING.

What did it say?

22 HOHENSTRASSE, INNSBRUCK.

Go ahead, Doc. What's at 22 Hohenstrasse? The Chinese Consulate?

A ONE-ROOM OFFICE WITH AN AUSTRI-
AN SECRETARY, MR. DANZIGER. RENTED
AND OPERATED BY A BALTIMORE EX-
PORTING FIRM CALLED CROGER & LAP-
HORN.

(Silence)

I think I'm going insane.

PANTELL: Hello?

DANZIGER: Hello, Esterhazy? Who was on the phone? I've been calling since—

P: Frank. I couldn't get him off.

D: Is he in jail, for Christ's sake?

P: He's in trouble. That's worse to Frank than jail.

D: Good God, woman!

P: Peter darling, it's the price I have to pay. One of us had to make a buck and for the moment you're incapacitated. I can't tell my editor to knock off the phone calls when he's all psyched up.

D: I can.

P: You sound all off-key.

D: An old girlfriend of mine died too young.

P: Do I know her?

D: Cybele McCullough.

P: Poor Peter. I've known for a long time you still loved her a little.

D: Just a little. Not like us.

P: Not like us. I'm psyched up a little today myself. I'm almost finished with the first campus story with guts—you should see the pictures—

and then this morning there was the damnedest newsbreak in history about a major war at another campus, eliminating, of course, the significance of the one where we did all the photography.

D: Real tough. Switch your emphasis. National trend, et cetera.

P: I'm doing so. How did it go today?

D: It's fascinating the way the big mind works. He could be guilty. He probably is guilty. He is guilty. But of what?

P: They'll think of something, old boy.

D: Your optimism is unbridled.

P: I'm not worried. So will you.

D: I damn well better. Can you come to Washington this week?

P: I thought I might, but now heaven forfend. I'll probably get fired.

D: Anything from the boys?

P: That nasty-looking one from NBC—Gilligan, is it?—called and donated a vote of confidence, but he really didn't sound too damn sure.

D: What about Gil?

P: Not a word, so far. I called yesterday and his service said he was in Cleveland. Maybe he's back by now.

D: Why is everyone always in Cleveland when I need them?

P: Why does Danziger always need people when they're in Cleveland? You're a remarkably subjective fellow, Danziger.

D: I love your eyes, your hair, your lips and your et cetera.

P: Likewise, I'm sure. Peter. Will you try to be quiet and sensible and cooperative and get this over with?

D: It's impossible.

P: My plans for our future do not include monthly visits to Leavenworth.

D: If I go to Leavenworth it will be to give a lecture at the Staff and Command School.

P: Sometimes you frighten me. Out there with the dragons, so big and strong, all by yourself.

D: No dragons yet. Just shadows on shadows.

P: Why don't you just shut up and nod and make everybody happy and come home?

D: Here we go again.

P: I'm really not the waiting kind. It's been awhile, Peter.

D: You make that rather clear, Esterhazy, my sweet. It gives me a kind of tug, right here.

P: Now you're angry.

D: Who me? Jesus Christ. How could I be angry with all this *Gemütlichkeit* slopping around?

P: I don't know what to do with you.

D: Your confidence in the condemned man warms the very murmurs of my heart—

P: I can't stand it when you deliberately misinterpret—

KETCHUM: Hello?

DANZIGER: Hello, Gil?

K: I detest being waked up by collect calls, old friend.

D: Yeah. All hell is breaking loose.

K: Give me the gen.

D: It's hard to explain. They're after something different.

K: Different than your stupidity in Cambodia?

D: Not mentioned yet. It's all old girlfriends and college chums and what happened in 1944 and 1958, et cetera.

K: Maybe they're setting you up for something. Who is the guy?

D: His name is Pike. He's good enough to make me think he's good. But I don't know what he's talking about.

K: You're not supposed to know. Did you ever kill anybody or sell the plans for the Norden bombsights or anything of that nature?

D: You sound like Pike. No.

K: Can you stand it?

D: Sure.

K: Do you want a big stink? I can make it. You may be an intellectual asshole but you're still freedom of the press.

D: Then why doesn't Schaefer think so?

K: The public press is a public institution. Hotcakes are things to be dropped. . . . Maybe this foray into other things should tell me something.

D: Good old Gil.

K: What's involved?

D: Not what—who. A guy I knew in college, Chinese, now official. I saw him in the Far East too.

K: When?

D: Early this past winter. The one I told you about.

K: Really, Peter, are you stupid or naïve? I wonder you haven't been run over by a streetcar. What's his name again?

D: Charley Hsi. H-S-I.

K: Would that be Li Hsi, by any chance?

D: Yeah. That's his name.

K: God deliver us. Who else?

D: A guy they say I went through navigation school with. Name of Croger. They think I know him well and apparently he stole the Vatican jewels or something.

K: Who else?

D: My girl in London, years ago. I just found out she was killed.

K: When?

D: In February.

K: What has that got to do with you and all these other people?

D: I don't know, but they keep trying to connect it up. Also a foppish character I met in Europe in '58 and have bumped into here and there. Apparently they were all involved somehow.

K: I don't like the way it smells.

D: Neither do I.

K: Are you clean? Really?

D: Yes.

K: Very interesting . . . What do you want from me?

D: Can you send somebody up to the Landing tomorrow? Esterhazy has the key. I wrote her but it will be too late. There's a footlocker under the bed in the bedroom. In it someplace is a

1943 yearbook called *Celestials* from the navigation school in Coral Gables. We're looking for
a guy named Emil Croger—supposedly in my
flight, Flight One. So help me I can't remember
him. Make stats of all the graduation and group
pictures and legends and get them to me as fast
as you can. I'm at the Shoreham. You hang onto the book. At least I'll find out if my memory
has finally sprang.

K: No problem.

D: Yes, it is, as a matter of fact. I'm in a "when
did you stop beating your wife" situation about
Croger. . . . Also I think my mail is being read.

K: Naturally. You don't think they're idiots, do
you? Where are you phoning from?

D: A booth in a bar.

K: Never mind. They've probably got mine
bugged. My personal feeling at this hour is that
even if you're not guilty of something, your
idiocy should be punished as a sheer subjective
pleasure for us all.

D: Thanks, counselor.

K: *De nada.* I'll have the stats to you by mes-
senger tomorrow night or Thursday morning.
Let me know if it gets stickier.

D: Good night, Gil.

TO: A. J. Katin
FROM: B. Pike

(FORMAL REPORT TO FOLLOW)

As the tapes will indicate, he freely admits
all but one of his associations. I am looking

forward to tomorrow. You will note that he communicates best when angry.

B.P.

Cybele is dead Cybele is dead Cybele is dead.

She said: "So many of you Americans are bullshit artists. Tell me, are you a bullshit artist?"

I said: "I am the pinnacle to which other bullshit artists aspire."

"What is your name?"

"Peter Danziger, although I have always preferred to be called Roger Buckingham."

She said: "You are a pleasantly ugly man. Why did you come to my table?"

"Because you look like an Irish queen named Deirdre and you make my blood race through my veins."

"You are funny, Roger Buckingham."

"I don't want to know your name until I know how badly I want to know you. Do I make your blood race through your veins?"

She said: "No, but you make funny thoughts float through my head."

"That's even better, Deirdre. Are you related to that Irish queen?"

"Actually, I've never heard of her. Would you like to dance?"

"Not unless you insist. I'd rather look across the candle at you. What's your name?"

"Cybele McCullough. I'm here to pick up a rich American and marry him for his fortune and still have my own peccadillos. How rich are you?"

"I own a thing called Illinois. How old are you?"

"Sixty-two."

I said: "Lovely. I'm so bored with these young ones. I think I'll marry you."

"You took a bit of time getting there, Peter."

Eyes and lips and hands and breasts and thighs. Being turned and rolled by a booming surf off the Hamptons.

She said: "Will you be shot at and killed and all that nonsense?"

"Buckingham will be obscenely maimed, but Danziger will parade."

"I'm so glad it's you, Peter. Kiss me some more."

Cybele is dead Cybele is dead Cybele is dead.

She said: "It's so bloody frustrating when you can't get through to someone."

"Turn your head and look at the pigeons in the sun on the slate roof."

"But you love me?"

I said: "Yes, I'm afraid I love you."

Cybele is dead.

In the waist of a parked B-17 in the damp of the fall she said: "I suppose I should tell you I'm formally affianced to a nice man named David Halloway with the forces in Africa."

"I suppose you should. It's cold, isn't it?" And I pulled the scratchy blanket closer around us. The bomber smelled of metal and gasoline and Cybele.

She said: "Peter, is it really proper to be unfaithful to an unrequited fiancé who is being shot at and carries your picture?"

"Perfectly proper."

"You ease my conscience even though you're a dreadful liar. I wish we had some wine."

The call sign of the B-17 was Darklock Q Queen and later for my birthday she gave me a crude lovely ceramic and copper tie clip she'd had made in Soho saying Darklock Q Queen which I still have someplace but the color of the lettering has faded. I hate the way things outlast people.

Cybele is dead.

I said in the M Club: "The Hun has turned tail and now they want me to protect the village of New York against beefsteak profiteers. What is your reaction about joining me as chief taster?"

She said: "Could I have a baby?"

Cybele is dead.

Once I thought I saw you on a British naval arm and the blackout turned dark red.

Cybele is dead.

I had a dream about David long ago: he was blown to bits by a burst of eighty-eight and we both laughed.

Cybele is dead.

On the close inner side of your right breast is a lovely long straight black hair that perseveres and floats so fair on that white swell I could kiss it my life long.

Cybele is dead.

Wednesday

I WOULD LIKE TO GO INTO TWO MAT-
TERS TODAY.

Excellent. That's exactly eight-three less than
yesterday.

LET'S BEGIN WITH CUBA.

All right. What? I know damn well you have
my entry and exit dates, and presumably you've
read the stories I wrote. What else?

WAS THAT WHEN YOU MET MRS.
PANTELL?

Yes.

WAS SHE IN THE BUSH?

God, no!

THEN WHERE?

In Havana.

THIS WAS BEFORE THE OVERTHROW?

This was during the overthrow.

WHAT WAS SHE DOING THERE?

Putting on and photographing a New Year's
fashion show at the Palace for her magazine.

YOU MET HER THERE?

Yes.

HAD YOU NEVER MET BEFORE?

No. Does she enter this inquiry?

ONLY THROUGH YOU, SO FAR.

Let's keep it that way.

TELL ME WHY YOU WERE ALLOWED IN THE PALACE. YOU HAD BEEN FILING SYMPATHETIC BY-LINES FROM THE OTHER SIDE FOR MONTHS.

I was formally invited by Vince Schaefer. The bureau was formally invited by the Cuban Embassy. This way Vince saved an air fare. I don't think they liked my turning up. I was frisked at the gate, but there I was. There was a certain amount of stony-face staring. Then, later, I assumed they were trying to win me over—me meaning the bureau.

I DON'T UNDERSTAND WHY THIS SO-CALLED FASHION SHOW WAS ACCORDED HARD NEWS COVERAGE. AND I CAN'T IMAGINE WHY THE REGIME WOULD INDULGE IN IT AT THIS CRITICAL TIME.

That's why, Doc. To minimize the rumors. It was supposed to be a hands-across-the-sea kind of thing. Gracious civilized behavior while the bearded peons came down out of the hills shooting and scratching. Their only problem was it turned out not to be rumors.

DID YOU SEE BATISTA THAT DAY?

No. He was too busy packing up the family jewels for a getaway, it turned out. That old pack rat never believed in all the schmancy. Or maybe we were really all there for camouflage.

WHO DID YOU SEE FROM THE REGIME?

Madame Batista, almost constantly. And her brother. Or cousin. A colonel, I think. He looked like Basil Rathbone. A few gentlemen in formal afternoon wear.

DESCRIBE WHAT HAPPENED. DON'T MAKE ME DIG.

They showed us through the formal part of the palace, and the gardens, and gave us Bacardis and laughed. There was a Cuban quartet in the garden playing light standards. In the meanwhile, there was sporadic rifle and mortar fire getting closer from out toward Varadero. I had a kid cab-driver standing by who kept running in and leaving notes with the guard for me. After a while the guard started peeling off one by one and I stopped getting the messages. Batista's guard had a terrific instinct for self-preservation. In the meanwhile, there we were in the garden, listening to Cole Porter and drinking Bacardis and hearing the guns getting closer and watching Madame Batista smile and make small talk. She's quite a broad, by the way. Not a flicker of fear. Me, a guy from AP, a guy from UPI, a girl from Fairchild, fourteen skinny models rehearsing on a runway, maybe two dozen assorted international characters like Louis Estimet, a bunch of scared Cuban bankers with fat wives, and Mrs. Pantell and her staff, including two very bored photographers. The garden had been set up with a hundred or so chairs and a stage trimmed with ribbon and gauze and a runway and refreshment tables. At a certain moment, I knew nothing predictable was going to happen there. It was too unreal.

A character in a baby-blue uniform kept handing pieces of paper to the colonel. Just from his face, which was coming apart, I assumed everything else was coming apart. Sure enough, finally an eight-man guard marched in and the colonel suggested in foreboding tones that we depart because of unexpected contingencies. Oddly enough, at that moment I felt sorry for Madame Batista. There were cars waiting at the gate to take us to the airport. Nothing of consequence, you understand, but for our own peace of mind. Local disturbance, et cetera. . . . Something I'll always remember. One of the little magazine girls went beserk. Her fashions hadn't been packed up, and she was responsible. With the mortars sounding a mile away, mind you. This will happen again at the final nuclear moment, and I will be in there rooting for the little girl who wants her fashions back. Aren't people fantastic?

THE ONLY PRESENCE WHICH SEEMS MORE IMPROBABLE THAN YOUR OWN IS LOUIS ESTIMET'S. WHAT WAS THE REASON FOR HIS ATTENDANCE?

Do you want inside knowledge, or a guess?

INSIDE KNOWLEDGE. THAT'S WHAT THIS INQUIRY IS ABOUT.

You'll have to settle for a guess. He was buying something of value for a crisis price.

BUYING WHAT?

I have no idea. Jewels, information, armaments, furniture?

YOU HAD SEEN HIM TWO WEEKS EARLIER IN THE SIERRA, IN ADDITION TO

THE MEETING IN MIAMI YOU MEN-
TIONED?

Yes.

QUITE A COINCIDENCE, WOULDN'T YOU
THINK?

No. Our professions seem to take us where the
action is.

WHAT WAS HIS PROFESSION?

In the Sierra? I'll give you another guess. He
was selling something of value for a crisis price.
What you don't seem to understand, Doc, is that
Louis Estimet is on only one side: the American
dollar. And that only since the pound has been
fluttery. One of these days he'll be trafficking in
marks. That's his ideology, Doc. The crisis price.
I know too that in certain circles this is considered a crime, unless you're listed on the big
board.

I HAVE NOTICED IN YOUR WRITING A
TENDENCY TO SIMPLIFY. I SEE IT IS NOT
ABSENT FROM YOUR CONVERSATION.

Never.

DID YOU LEAVE WITH THE MAGAZINE
PEOPLE?

Against my wishes, yes. I was supposed to cover
the occupation of Havana, if it happened. There
was no question that it was preferred I go. I tried
to bribe two guards, but even their avarice was
down. You could smell death in the air.

DID LOUIS ESTIMET GO WITH YOU?

I didn't see him in a car and I didn't see him
on the plane. I wondered about it later.

PERHAPS HE HAD ALLIES.

If I know Louis he had allies on both sides and a few in the middle. He could easily have slipped away at the airport, too. It was in turmoil. The guards had to get us aboard. All the Batista people were climbing the walls. Not a pretty sight. Their suitcases clinked.

WHY DIDN'T YOU TRY TO GET AWAY?

One beady-eyed little fellow stayed with me lovingly, carelessly flaunting a .45 automatic. I've seen the kind of hole they make.

SO YOU MERELY GOT ON THE PLANE?

So I merely got on the plane.

BUT YOU WERE BACK LATER?

Yes. Better late than never.

BEFORE WE GO INTO THAT, I WANT TO HEAR ABOUT YOUR EARLIER ENCOUNTER WITH ESTIMET IN THE SIERRA.

It was in December, after I got over the flu. A bunch of us went up by truck: a photographer and six or seven news guys. It took forever. They had advanced the headquarters a long way since I was there in October, and everything was a little more military. They were beginning to believe the miracle, I guess. Fidel kept more to himself. The councils of the brave. In the earlier days I remember arguing with him about how to grip the ball to throw a slider.

WAS GUEVARA THERE THEN?

He was there but I only saw him from a distance. No. Once, he gave us a little talk. Mostly about the inevitability of justice. He looked like a guy who had beat me up in high school once, so I never liked him. D'ya see how everything comes together in one piece, Doc?

AND ESTIMET WAS THERE WHEN YOU ARRIVED?

Yes. Once or twice I even saw him emerging from the councils of the brave.

WAS HE FRIENDLY?

Of course. Why not? He had a cottage off the encampment, and I moved in with no misgivings whatsoever.

WHAT DID HE DISCUSS WITH YOU?

Do you really want to know?

WHY ELSE WOULD I ASK?

Girls. Money. The future of Pancho González. And like that.

OF COURSE, IF YOU WERE A PART OF HIS APPARATUS YOU WOULD NOT DIVULGE MORE THAN YOU ALREADY HAVE.

Apparatus sounds strangely like spy stuff.

THERE IS SUCH A THING AS A PROPAGANDA APPARATUS TOO, MR. DANZIGER. THIS IS ONE OF A NUMBER OF ASPECTS TO BE DETERMINED.

You're demented.

I'VE ASKED YOU IF ESTIMET WAS FRIENDLY. HE WAS. WERE YOU?

Of course.

DID YOU PERFORM ANY LITTLE CHORES FOR HIM?

What are you driving at?

ANY INTRODUCTIONS? AS YOU PERFORMED FOR HIM WITH MR. INGEBRITZEN?

No. He knew everyone better than I did . . . But

I would have, Doc. I like Louis.

NO PHONE CALLS, NOTES, DELIVERY OF
MESSAGES?

Repeat no. I told him a dirty joke. Not coded,
by the way.

YOU SUGGEST HE WAS ON FAIRLY INTI-
MATE GROUND WITH THE RULING CAD-
RE. DO YOU KNOW HOW OR WHY?

(Expression of anger) Doc, let me explain
something simple to you about Louis Estimet. He
always acts identically with people he knows and
people he doesn't know. He's Louis. On the make.
On the bounce. All balls and salesmanship. He's a
permanent manic. He's not a plotter, he's not a
spy, he's not particularly devious—he's just a bloody
bouncing manic in search of a buck, and pretty
good at isolating one when it happens along. I imagine his philosophy of life is the law of averages.

THIS IS VALUABLE CORROBORATION,
MR. DANZIGER.

Of what? That he'd sell his grandmother?

THAT TOO. DID HE READ YOUR STORIES
BEFORE THEY WENT OUT?

No. Only the censor.

DID HE SUGGEST SIDELINES THAT IN-
TERESTED YOU?

Incessantly. As with all good conversationalists.
He had a fund of knowledge, and that's what I
live on.

GIVE ME A FEW EXAMPLES.

Sure. Once he told me we were moving to some
village in the morning, and we did. Another time,
he said there was some heavy patrol activity com-

ing in the morning, and there was. Once he brought a Cuban girl back to the cottage and told me she was Carlotta Hapsburg.

DID YOU SEE CYBELE McCULLOUGH IN CUBA AT THAT TIME?

Negative, for Christ's sake!

WILL YOU ADMIT YOU MIGHT RESPOND IN THE SAME MANNER WHETHER IT WAS TRUE OR NOT, MR. DANZIGER?

You're stepping on me, Doc.

OFTEN AN EVASION IS MORE REVEALING THAN FACT. IT WILL BE INTERESTING TO SORT THIS OUT. HOW MANY PEOPLE IN THIS PHOTOGRAPH CAN YOU IDENTIFY?

(Pause)

Me. Louis Estimet. A broad from some network who never stopped talking. Ed somebody— I think from a Chicago paper. A magazine hotshot. I don't know all the hangers-on.

WHO IS THE BEARDED MAN WITH HIS HAND ON YOUR SHOULDER?

I don't know his name. We called him Sancho. He was a little simple.

WHAT WAS HIS FUNCTION?

He had immense responsibility. Like waking up the troops. Making coffee. Doing errands. Building fires. Telling people to shut up when the brass was around.

WERE YOU CLOSE?

Like brothers.

ARE YOU BEING SARDONIC AGAIN?

I don't know how else to handle this nonsense.

WOULD YOU BE SURPRISED IF I TOLD YOU HE IS NOW A PROVINCIAL POLICE COMMANDANT?

Not at all. Type casting. I'm surprised it took him so long to get ahead. . . . God damn it, are you trying to make it that we were blood buddies?

THE THOUGHT HAD CROSSED MY MIND.

We're getting no place.

QUITE THE CONTRARY.

I'd like some coffee.

I IMAGINE YOU WOULD. LEAVE YOUR DISARRAYED THOUGHTS HERE ON THE FLOOR, MR. DANZIGER. WE'LL PICK THEM UP LATER.

NOW. WHERE WERE WE?

Treading water, as I recall.

YOU HAD SUGGESTED THAT MRS. PANTELL WAS NOT IN THE BUSH WITH YOU AND LOUIS ESTIMET?

(Silence)

WHAT IS BOTHERING YOU, MR. DANZIGER?

We shouldn't have bothered with the break, Doc, because now you're upsetting any basis for talk again.

WHY?

You're being too goddamn transparently cute.

TELL ME HOW?

One: Mrs. Pantell was not in the bush with me or anyone. She flew down from New York. I already told you that. Two: I was not in the bush with Louis Estimet. I was in the bush with about twelve thousand troops, about a hundred and fifty newsmen, and about fifty hangers-on, including Louis Estimet. If you can't comprehend that, put me in the federal pen or get me another interrogator with a gift for English.

MRS. PANTELL WAS UNKNOWN TO YOU AT THAT TIME?

I already said so. Check with her magazine.

I DID, THANK YOU.

Then you're simply trying to piss me off. What will I do, Doc? Unload the big secret? Confess all? Implicate William Fulbright?

DID MRS. PANTELL MEET LOUIS ESTIMET AT THE PALACE THAT DAY? YOU ADMITTED THEY WERE BOTH PRESENT.

No.

YOU MEAN YOU MADE PARTICULAR NOTE OF THE FACT THAT MRS. PANTELL AND ESTIMET DID NOT MEET?

No. She was busy doing her thing—arranging to photograph a fashion show—and he was doing his thing—arranging to get rich.

SO YOU ACTUALLY CANNOT SAY WHETHER THEY DID OR DID NOT MEET?

I just told you they did not meet. Why?

BECAUSE OF YOUR FRIENDSHIP IT OCCURRED THAT SHE MIGHT BE ACTING WITH YOU.

(Expression of anger) Acting in what?

THAT'S WHAT WE ARE ATTEMPTING TO DETERMINE, ISN'T IT?

I truthfully do not know how you expect to accomplish anything so long as we continue to play word games. How many points have you scored today? I figure I've got about eleven.

PLEASE NEVER DELUDE YOURSELF THAT THIS IS A GAME, MR. DANZIGER.

You're obviously pointed toward some goal and I haven't an inkling what it is. Maybe if you told me I could help get you there and get myself out of here.

WE'RE DOING FAMOUSLY, AS A MATTER OF FACT . . . NOW, AFTER YOU SAW LOUIS ESTIMET IN HAVANA, WHAT WAS THE NEXT TIME YOUR PATHS CROSSED?

In Saigon.

YES. I WANT TO TAKE THAT UP IN SEQUENCE TOMORROW. YOU NEVER HEARD FROM HIM IN THE INTERIM?

Yes. We sent presents or notes every once in a while. Once a brace of partridge he'd shot in Scotland which moldered away at Customs at Kennedy Airport until they were confiscated for having feathers, or something. Once a fancy corkscrew. Why, I don't know.

WHAT WAS THE TONE OF HIS NOTES?

Scatological.

I MEAN: WHAT SORT OF INFORMATION DID HE IMPART?

Very little. "Just been fishing in Perthshire and off to Vienna on business. Things going swimmingly. Do hope to see you soon, my dear fellow!" Detailed, basic intelligence like that.

DO YOU SAVE THEM?

In an album, Doc. It's red morocco, and I bind

them up myself so the messages won't get smudged.

DID HE EVER COME TO NEW YORK?

Oh, sure. He'd call the bureau every once in a while, but I was usually out of the country. Once he called when I was in town, but I was busy and nothing happened to work out.

WHERE WAS HE STAYING?

The YWCA.

I VERY RARELY HAVE THE OPPORTUNI-TY TO PLAY SQUASH ON A WEEKDAY, BUT I THINK TODAY WILL BE ONE OF THE DAYS. YOU ARE DETERMINED TO BE UNCOOPERATIVE?

I've never felt more cooperative in my life.

THANK YOU, MR. DANZIGER.

PANTELL: Hello?

DANZIGER: Hello, baby.

P: How is it going, darling?

D: Atrociously, I think.

P: Are you bearing up?

D: Yeah, and being as obnoxious as possible. Look, about last night . . .

P: Let's not talk about it. I didn't mean to press you. I wrote you.

D: After we're married I want to have Pike up to the Landing for the weekend. He can show you how to subdue me.

P: We can have Vince Schaefer at the same time and just have a blast.

D: Jesus, I miss you.

P: Me too, Peter. Are you coming back this week-end or do you want me to come down?

D; I'll come there. The dust in this town has dust on it.

P: Will it be AWOL and all that kind of non-sense?

D: No. They may even send a driver to sponsor my private thoughts.

P: Maybe they're afraid of you.

D: I kind of doubt it. . . . Esterhazy? How are you? Really?

P: Oh, worried. I'm so upset by what they're try-ing to do to you.

D: So am I. That's the tactic. To hell with it.

P: Jack Walsh sent you a nice telegram.

D: What did it say?

P: "Continue buck-and-wing on afterdeck. Good luck to both of you." Something like that.

D: I think he's hooked on you. Since that day you wore the tight white pants.

P: I love it when you're jealous.

D: You're an old-fashioned woman.

P: That I am.

D: I feel so damned frustrated.

P: Oh, honey, don't! Welcome to the human race!

D: Maybe I mean confused. I can't even remem-ber who are the good guys. Fortunately, every time he opens his mouth the confusion disap-pears.

P: I knew you'd somehow arrange things righ-teously in your mind at the moment of combat.

D: Do you know what I'd do to you if you were here right now?

P: Describe it.

D: Esterhazy, they think I'm guilty of something.

P: And you know you're not?

D: I'm beginning to wonder. Motivations and all that.

P: Don't do that or you'll rot! . . . What will we do this weekend?

D: I'd like to eat some red meat and hear some piano and not much else except talk and such.

P: Fine. We'll cook here and play Oscar Peterson.

D: Couldn't be better.

P: Up the Middle Ages, darling.

D: All of it.

FROM: B. Pike
TO: A. J. Katin

FORMAL REPORT TO FOLLOW

My feeling is that we accomplished a great deal today, information-wise, as well as drawing out subject's hostilities and ego motivation to divulge. At this moment I would project that when we break him down on Croger, the balance of the involvement will blossom organically.

B.P.

There is a secret to the way dim light shining through red glass onto a polished well-kept mahogany bar oils the psyche. Miami was chill when we got off the plane. Down the wind tunnel from

Lake Wales all the orange trees and sunburnt girls were shivering. Someone had arranged motel accommodations across from the airport. I held out for a single in lieu of a fag photographer and got it, helped by American green. I washed and put on a sweater and went to the bar. The wood reflecting the redness anesthetized me as it had so many times in so many places before. Obviously, I was in the wrong place at the wrong time now. I thought of Ed Newhouse walking down the plaza in Havana, maybe two hundred yards behind the action, mentally writing his story, while Danziger-san sat contemplating red lights on oiled mahogany across the street from the Miami airport. Maybe they had occupied the palace. Maybe Batista was hanging by the thumbs. Maybe they were distributing the fancy fashions to the Fidelistas.

I went to the phone and called Vince Schaefer. His secretary, who even on the telephone looked vaguely like a pelican, said he was out. I said I wanted to talk to him. She said she liked to think Vince could relax on the rare occasions he had a chance to eat. I said the overfed bastard was probably sitting four feet from the telephone. She said the overfed bastard already had a lead story from Ed Newhouse and how were things on the beach? I hung up and went back to the bar. Madame Pantell was sitting three stools away. She seemed like a crowd because no one else was there. In Havana she had impressed me as a tall tawny officious blonde with good breasts and a

Perle Mesta manner. She looked the same, except she was moody, leanly profiled, staring at her drink as lone people do in bars. I sat down and stared at mine.

She said: "Are you all that disappointed not to be in at the kill?"

"It's what I'm paid for, unfortunately."

"Will they shoot him?"

I said: "Batista?"

"The hell with Batista. I mean the cute little colonel."

"Indubitably. Aren't you a little bombed?"

"Yes, I am a little bombed. Aren't you bombed?"

I said: "Not yet."

Later we went into the dining room for dinner. Her eyes were green with brownish flecks.

I said: "I have always had a penchant for girls with green eyes and brownish flecks. Usually they are not as tough as you."

"I'm tough, all right. Do we have to go on with my analysis?"

I said: "We don't have to go on with anything but the shell steaks."

"You're terribly defensive, aren't you?"

"You come on pretty strong."

She said: "Ed Dana told me you were a gentle man."

"Why would he bring it up?"

"I asked him last week when I heard you were going to be covering this ridiculous thing."

"Do you think it's ridiculous?"

She said: "*Götterdämmerung* and false eye-lashes? It reminds me of *Idiot's Delight*."

"I am unsure about how to proceed with a contemporary who attracts me but who is as formidable as you are."

"I have a darling little seamstress on First Avenue who runs off my protective coloration."

Later I said: "Are you a gentle woman?"

She thought for a moment: "I believe I am, *por favor*."

I said: "Who is Mr. Janice Pantell?"

"A lovable bear of a man."

"With what parts missing?"

She finished chewing, and wiped her lips and smiled brilliantly at me: "Do you really want to know, or are you just prying?"

I invited her to my room for a nightcap, not lusting exactly, but intrigued, quite unwilling to let her go with so many things between us unfinished.

She declined quite formally and said: "Come to mine. I have a bottle of Dewar's. We can talk."

We settled in opposing chairs with dim lights and scotch and ice and motel Muzak. Everything she said touched me strangely. I didn't know whether she was opening up her soul or I was. She had seemed to become more grave and beautiful across the dinner table, and now her brain was on still another new wavelength that allowed me to know her more quickly, more deeply, than anyone I had met before. She seemed to take off that First Avenue protective coloration in layers —one thin layer after another, each new layer revealing fresh surprises of shade and texture and mind.

I said: "Tell me about that husband."

"He looks like a god and unfortunately believes he is. But his domain is limited to about ten miles east or west of Gates Mills, Ohio."

I said: "What's his name?"

"John K. Pantell the Third. We're still married and he's still the guiding light in those parts. He played football and all that and it seemed desirable and sort of windswept. Mucho money, I should add."

"What happened?"

She closed her eyes: "Just everything. Mostly my fault, I expect. I was dissatisfied. Everything seemed so trivial. I'm not good at picking the right upholstery. I wanted to know my man, but he didn't want to be known. He flew into rages about things I would say innocently to his mother. I felt I was twenty-two years old phasing out a forty-year marriage. Peck-peck and orange juice." She opened her eyes at me suddenly. "Are you peck-peck and orange juice, Peter?"

I said: "Of course. How long did it last?"

"Three years, the first time. I went back and tried again for five months a year later. More of same."

"Were you good together in bed?"

"I thought so before we were married. Afterward, I don't know. It suddenly became kind of deodorant."

I said: "Who did you think of?"

She said instantly: "Robert Donat."

I said: "Poor mistaken child!"

She said: "Donat wasn't King Kong, you know."

I said: "No, there was a certain difference."

"Mine thought he was King Kong. Also, I didn't get pregnant."

"Personally, in those days I adored girls who didn't get pregnant."

"I wanted to, God knows."

"Something wrong with his hormones, undoubtedly."

"Undoubtedly."

I said: "Why didn't you get it annulled when it was all over?"

She said: "Let's not talk about it anymore. . . . Peter, are you infatuated with me?"

"I am secretly desirous of your mind and body and moods."

"You're so goddamn afraid to commit yourself, aren't you?"

"I'm inclined to overcommit, that's all. Also I've been cut off at the ankles on a couple of occasions."

"So am I. So have I. Will you pour?"

I mixed more scotch and ice. I changed the radio from Kostelanetz to Ray Charles. By now the fifth was getting low.

She said: "You should be in Havana, shouldn't you?"

"I should be, but I'm not. It will all work out according to the ironies of time."

She said: "My right foot gets cramped. If you would rub it just there, above the instep."

"Janice, something important is happening to me."

"That's fine. A little lower though."

I said: "There's something going on here. You know that, don't you?"

"Big old you, Peter?"

"Big old me."

She thought for a while: "I've always been unable to decide whether to cry at injustice and go out and make storms about things or to laugh at absurdities or to fall in love with somebody. I don't think you can do all three."

"I think you can do all three."

"Personally, I've never decided which to do, so I just muddle along."

I said: "Personally, you're J. Alfred Prufrock."

"Personally, I could get hooked on you."

"I'd like you to get hooked on me."

She said quietly: "Do you want me to take my clothes off?"

"Do you want to?"

"I'd rather not, just now."

"Then leave them on. Let's not louse anything up yet."

We kissed for a while and the flecks in her eyes intoxicated me and she suddenly became as precious as she is.

"I thought you'd be a bull-like man."

"Not me. I have to be in love."

"What a tragedy, you poor fool! So do I."

She broke away and went into the bathroom. When she came back she looked as though she had been crying.

She said brightly: "Can we go for a drive in the wind? I can get a car."

"We'd probably better unless you prefer to be seduced."

"What an old-fashioned word. Jesus, Peter."

We kissed some more and she left abruptly.

I accelerated a Plymouth convertible out the curved macadam away from the Moorish architecture. This one had been rented by one of the photographers. She put on a white scarf.

I drove her down the Tamiami Trail and through Coral Gables and past the old University of Miami campus and along Dinner Key and up the line to Miami again through the faded remnants of an intense part of my life. I talked continuously—wanting to communicate and coming alive again with the feel of the wind and the darkness and the lights and the memories and her presence.

She said: "It's the first time this bloody place sounded as though it could mean anything."

"It doesn't mean anything. It's just a part of my disappearing life."

"Are you exactly what you seem tonight?"

"No."

"Bravo!"

"What do we do about that fellow in Gates Mills?"

"Are you serious?"

"I'm afraid so. Let's develop Plan A."

"The problem is, you see, he's a Catholic. So am I."

"That's not as tricky as being half-Lutheran and half-Jewish."

"Is that what you are?"

"That's exactly what I am."

"Peter, that's beautiful. I knew there was something about you!"

"You can take off your clothes now."

"Can't you find a beach? It's so uncouth on the highway with policemen around."

"There are policemen in Lauderdale who are used to it."

She said: "Hurrah! Let's stop in Lauderdale and shock policemen and celebrate Plan A!"

We stopped at a bar down near Bahia Mar and got absolutely stinking on stingers.

The next morning my phone rang and someone read a telegram from Vince Schaefer telling me the way was cleared for me to proceed immediately back to Havana and I'd never once made love to my true love.

Lucky Ed Newhouse covered Fidel and Havana, while I followed the mopping-up in the provinces, local prison camps, the rounding-up of Batista beasts, the unbounded joy of the populace. From day to day my hard news was almost identical, so I relied primarily on color stories.

One of them was about the similarity of brutality, whatever the cause. I tried to describe the sight and smell and sound of fear, and found little philosophic difference. That was the story that got me shipped home. I tried to explain to the press officer in the Hotel Nacionale that I had reported equal or worse truths about the Batista regime, and that perhaps the liberated people were overly enthusiastic due to years of oppression.

I got to New York on March 29. She picked up on the first ring.

I said: "Sitting by your phone waiting for whom?"

"Peter. I heard. Where are you?"

"Idlewild."

"Do you know my address? You haven't written."

"I did write, *por favor*. About twelve. Consult your local censor. Haven't you gotten any?"

"Negative."

"Think what you have to look forward to. Shall I come there?"

"Yes. I have news to report. Did your letters say you felt the same?"

"A little bit more, for an old fellow."

"Good. There are some letters for you at your office too. You disappeared so quickly."

"Shall I check into the Algonquin?"

"No. Come here."

I found a cab and needled through the traffic and I showered and we ate and went to bed from Friday till Sunday night.

After a while she said sleepily: "You have no idea what a luxury it is to be loved again."

"You mean screwed again?"

"I mean loved again."

I gently kissed her nipples and her navel and her pubis and fell asleep almost happy.

She had been to Gates Mills for a devastating two days. John K. Pantell had decided she was a whore and then turned over the card by saying he wanted her back and would never ever allow an annulment, a separation or divorce.

I said: "You sound muted."

"It's hard not to feel guilty with all that righteous power."

"Bow your head, woman?"

"Precisely."

"Do you need permission to go for an annulment? Or we could go to Mexico. Like tomorrow. You don't want the Pantell millions, do you?"

"God, no, but I can't. You don't know about my mother."

"I didn't know she entered into this."

"I'm afraid she does, Peter. She has a heart condition."

"Excuse me. I don't see the connection."

"I can hardly cross her."

"Is she against me or something?"

"She doesn't know about you. She's against violating a sacrament."

"Are you telling me you can't marry me?"

"Not yet, at least."

"What do we do? Wait for your mother to pass on?"

She slapped me as hard as she could, a wild-swinging belt which cupped my ear painfully.

After a while I said: "I apologize. I've got two weeks and then I go to Tel Aviv."

"I'm sorry I hit you. We can have the two weeks, can't we?"

"Does your mother like Pantell?"

"She rather hates him. But we were married by the bishop of the Cleveland Diocese."

"I love the way your breast looks shadowed against the light like this."

"Jesus, what shall we do?"

"I'm willing to go to Mexico tomorrow."

She began to cry: "I can't."

We had driven down from my sister's, near Boston, and stopped finally at a steak place outside Greenwich.

By candlelight I asked her: "I've always meant to ask you your maiden name."

She lifted her glass and drank: "Esterhazy. I thought you knew."

"Are you serious?"

"Of course."

I grinned at her. I loved it. It sounded like a good omen. I ordered a bottle of Châteauneuf. Then I told her the lovely old wartime story of the summit meeting when Roosevelt, showing off a little, casually displayed a fancy silver cigarette lighter engraved: "To Franklin D. Roosevelt from the Dedicated Men of the 101st Airborne." To which Churchill retaliated by casually displaying a fancy gold watch engraved: "To Winston Churchill from the Free People of the British Commonwealth." To which Stalin retaliated by casually displaying a fancy platinum jeweled cigarette case engraved: "To Count Esterhazy from the Vienna Jockey Club."

When she had stopped laughing I asked: "Is it those Esterhazys?"

"Yes, I'm afraid so. A cousin. My mother met him in Europe on one of those tours young ladies used to take. She was beautiful, and still is, but a little difficult."

"I'll be damned!"

"Oh, he left not long after I arrived. I was eight."

"Are you an incredibly wealthy heiress?"

"Of course. The only reason my mother worked as a buyer at Stewart's for nineteen years was because she adored it."

"I thought I had it made with you, Esterhazy."

"I think perhaps you do, Peter."

After that I called her Esterhazy.

I was writing think pieces about the Fidelistas most of my daylight hours. Vince Schaefer took me to lunch twice.

Esterhazy and I had a flare-up one night and I packed and went to the Algonquin. She met me in a neutral bar after work and we went back to her office while she finished a chore and then to the Village for dinner and then back to the Algonquin.

While she was dressing to go to the magazine in the morning she said: "Why don't you go out and talk to my mother?"

I was shaving.

"With you, you mean?"

"No. Just you."

"And ask for your hand? I'm almost fifty years old, for Christ's sake! Are you chicken?"

"Completely. I'm still awed by her. Besides, I'm on assignment."

"What are you lacking: religion or guts?"

"Guts, Peter."

I was angry suddenly: "I'm not the kind to come between a girl and her mommy."

"Dammit, you don't know her! I have to go."

"Edit something wonderful!" I yelled as the door slammed.

I flew to Louisville that afternoon.

She was small and elegant and had cheekbones. She had a small elegant house on the road which led to the country club. Everything about her was understated: her lawn and garden, her clothes, her hair, her decor. The living room was superb, although nobody had ever lived in it. I thought perhaps she was lonely.

She ushered me in with sober graciousness. She had a pleasant Kentucky accent with overlays of British.

"When I received your telegram I recognized your name, Mr. Danziger, but I don't really understand why you are here. Is it something to do with Janice?"

"Yes."

She was very cool: "Is she all right?"

"She's fine, Mrs. Esterhazy."

"Then—"

"It's my intention to marry her. I hope to get your approval."

She took time out to think: "Would you care for some tea?"

"No, thank you."

"A glass of sherry?"

"No, thank you."

After a moment seated: "You cannot possibly marry someone who is already married, Mr. Danziger."

"She's legally capable of getting unmarried, as you know."

"Not against the whole structure of her background."

"I understand her father wasn't quite so parochial."

She looked pale and quite ill: "That was a cruel thing to say. That's what I'm protecting her against."

I stood up: "I'm sorry. I am a bit cruel. She wants to marry me too."

"What does John Pantell say?"

"No."

"Then why are you speaking to me? He lives in Gates Mills, Ohio."

"She values your blessing."

"She shan't have it. Is she trying to torture my last years?"

"She's trying to live a life."

"She didn't even come out for Christmas."

"She had to go to Havana."

"Janice married of her own free choice, I don't think she really ever worked at it."

I moved and sat down across from her: "That was many years ago. People change and mature and learn, Mrs. Esterhazy."

She passed one hand across her eyes, brushing

old cobwebs: "I am not well. My faith is important to me."

"Is Janice?"

"Of course. My darling girl. She's doing so well now. Why should all our lives be disturbed?"

"Isn't it possible, Mrs. Esterhazy, that's what lives are about?"

And I was afraid that was what lives were about, and kind of glad. Disturbed lives are the interesting lives and the livable lives and the loving lives and the others are moo-cow. Not-to-be-disturbed is the most disturbing sign I have ever seen. I suppose it means "Death coming" and that is the time to be disturbed, by God! Consult thy disturbances. Invite lovingly thy disturbances. And if ever there is a time: *be* a disturbance. Go out big. Make them say: When the old fella left he had been completely disturbed in his lifetime, from one direction or another, and he disturbed us when he left, and we will disturb our children, who will hopefully disturb our grandchildren. Resist being a splat on the sidewalk or a figure on the medical reports. Scream at your wife and then get killed in a gunning accident. No one can ever forget. Disturb.

But this perfectly impeccable china doll in her impeccable china dollhouse was not to be disturbed and had never been disturbed and would be so only if I broke the spell or scratched my groin or married her daughter or broke a teacup.

I said: "Mrs. Esterhazy, I'm not here to disturb you, but I am trying to get through to you that your daughter and I are going to be married."

She flicked a mote of dust off the walnut coffee table and looked at me and sighed: "Last year my friend Rowena died, and there was no reason for her to die so young. This year Father Carnoby transferred to another parish. Next year Janice will marry beyond the sight of God. Do you want my blessing?"

"I wouldn't want to beg you for anything, Mrs. Esterhazy."

"Can you make her happy?"

"I don't think anyone can make anyone else happy. I guess I can make her live."

"On whose terms?"

"On the terms that arise."

"Are you so confident, Mr. Danziger?"

"No."

"What solace are you offering me?"

"It's a chance for her."

"Is that solace? I'm her mother."

"She doesn't belong to you any more. She belongs to me. People change hands. Like possessions. They pass on. What are we fighting about?"

"I've given up."

"You give up tougher than anyone I've ever met, because you haven't given up. You want to cry a little in private?"

"I have been, Mr. Danziger. You're a brutal man."

I stood up.

"Are you leaving?"

"Do we have any more to talk about?"

"I can't think of anything, except perhaps that glass of sherry."

I carefully sat down again: "You are a very perceptive woman, Mrs. Esterhazy. I didn't want to go so quickly."

"Not at all, Mr. Danziger. I'd like some too. What's more, I don't believe you're quite the ogre you fancy yourself."

She poured from a cut-glass decanter on the sideboard. When she turned to me again she was smiling. It seemed paradoxical. She handed me a delicate tulip glass: "Here you are. It's Tío Pepe in Baccarat. My husband took me to Jerez when I was very young, and taught me it was the only proper sherry for an apéritif. If you were in dire extremity, I believe he said, you might settle for La Ina. It should always be served in Baccarat. You see, Mr. Danziger, those are the kinds of rules I've grown old with."

I recognized the attack and sniffed that wonderful old aroma and tasted it.

She laughed. For a moment I could see her as a young girl: "You're always at battle, aren't you, Mr. Danziger? I've known unfortunates like you. Poor Janice!"

I laughed with her: "And you're about as helpless as a mamma sabertooth."

"That's not really my objective. To show my claws. Truly, Mr. Danziger. Let me merely say that if she were free to marry I might be refreshed by the change."

She held up her glass: "That's a compliment, Mr. Danziger."

I raised mine and we sipped, gazing at each other.

I realized she was beginning to get to me, flags, guns, galleons, diplomacy and all. In older wars, they used the word "gallant."

She lowered her eyes, then raised them quickly again: "Let me tell you something I remember about Janice when she was about twelve. It might teach you something you'd like to know. . . . It was the Fourth of July. We have parades out here. And picnics. We're really very simple people. Janice was riding a float decorated, I remember, with red, white and blue garlands and with a kind of unrecognizable green papier-mâché Statue of Liberty as centerpiece. They made it in the garage, and there was chicken wire inside. A handsome man on a white horse was riding off to one side, a marshal, I believe, and that night when we got home, Janice said to me: 'When I grow up I want to be married to that pretty man on the white horse. . . .' You're not pretty by any stretch of the imagination, Mr. Danziger, but I presume you have some kind of white horse?"

"I believe I do," I said. "A little swaybacked."

"I knew you did. I should tell you also that I disagree violently with some of your political opinions. You're in the paper here, you know."

"Which ones? Opinions, I mean."

"Most of them, for that matter."

"Do you read me often then?"

"Only since Janice asked me to."

"The worst conspiracy of all is the conspiracy of women," I said.

"She also called me that you were coming out. I believe she thought the combined assault would weaken my convictions. But they're not my convictions, you see. They belong to a great many generations. . . . Would you like another sip of Tío Pepe?"

"Yes, please. I don't understand why Mr. Esterhazy left you."

"He was that kind of man, Mr. Danziger. To leave people. He died very young, and quite willingly."

"I'm sorry."

She fluttered one hand: "It was his kind of performance and he did it very well. He was remarkably handsome."

We spent another hour together, and when I left I knew where Esterhazy had come from. I sent the old girl some flowers from the airport. All I had lost was the war.

Esterhazy and I had a ball-breaking fight: thrust and parry to the head, the heart, the groin, the sensitivity. When I was leaving she said, exhausted: "We haven't really signed anything except our death warrants, you know."

"Tell me how it can be happy and honorable with your mother dead but hideous and unacceptable with your mother alive? It would show no respect for her, among other things! It's not a life value, baby, it's a death value."

Her eyes were still red from earlier: "Peter, you adore to state things in the filthiest way possible."

"Do you want to marry me?"

"Yes. In God's good time. I've said we could live together now and forever. Why are you suddenly so stupidly honorable?"

"I'd feel like a tainted trophy; worth this much but not quite that much. Your mother liked me. . . . I can state that flatly." .

"The men I'm attracted to inevitably turn out to have granite egos."

"I'll dig up a *zofig,* if you'd like one."

She fell back limply on the sofa: "Oh, Peter!"

My blood gushed into my head and I felt suddenly dizzy. For God's sake, I was thinking, I wanted her belatedly: children and Sunday dinners and a lawn mower. Old too-little-and-too-late Danziger. The back of my throat ached. I knew it was finished.

Our eyes unlocked and my hand opened the door and my feet walked out and I died a little more. And blind men peered at mirrors in an empty house.

We wrote occasionally as the years went by. Bittersweet letters. Brown leaves falling in the autumn. Her letters sounded chatty and her life busy. I was jealous still.

How could she not know she was my lover? Yet how could she? Idiocies. Two years later her mother died. I remembered that fragile iron-strong little lady with clarity and felt sorry for her and the age we were losing day by day, and sorry for Esterhazy too. *Weltschmerz.* What happens to Tío Pepe and crystal and gentle manners and five-generation silver service and rustling silk which holds the scent of orange blossoms?

I was working out of Tel Aviv all those years, at the moment doing a series on a kibbutz down in the Negev, and the contrast of subjects was so unimaginable I couldn't decide which was the reality. The truth, of course, is that they were conflicting realities.

The stinking thing to me was that I no longer felt urgency about Esterhazy. Perhaps it was the inexorable years and the quixotic libido and the gradual drying-up of such unsurvival values as sentiment. But I dreamed about her often. She would be serving me ginger cookies in the nude and Monsignor Fulton Sheen would canter in with Stella. Later a black man would chase me down the corridors.

I was transferred to Washington to add my considerable weight to covering the '66 midterm elections. Vince was always decent about breathers. Everybody with an established by-line got invited to everything, so I had my black tie pressed and cavorted with the establishment. Vic Hume and I played squash almost every afternoon late, then showered, switched to black tie and went embassy-crawling.

At the Pakistani reception it happened: I met Esterhazy. She was across a large, ornate room jammed with free-loaders, drinking champagne on the arm of a chair containing one of the handsomest British Guards types I had ever seen. Silvered temples and proper mustache and a crimson sash across his stiff white front which dated from the Battle of Hastings.

I decided I could take him with sabers but not with foils.

I threaded my way through the anchovies.

"Hello, Janice."

She reacted. After a moment: "Admit that's a little shocking, Peter."

"How are you?"

"I guess you didn't get my last letter. To Tel Aviv?"

"Not yet. I came back two weeks ago."

"Oh."

She turned to her escort: "Tony, meet an old dear friend. This is Peter Danziger. Colonel Anthony Yarborough."

He smiled brilliantly: "Delighted! I know your work very well indeed!"

He rose and did all the rituals.

"Tony and I are to be married. That's what I wrote you about."

"How nice. Congratulations, Colonel."

We did the rituals again. I was seething.

To Esterhazy: "I guess I didn't get the message fast enough after your mother died."

"Waiting for you is like watching grass grow. Who said that?"

"Red Smith. I trust you'll be perfectly happy."

The colonel sensed vague currents and seemed distressed: "I think I'll find us all something to nibble."

After he disappeared I said: "You fucking idiot!"

She touched her wrist to her forehead: "This is so confusing. Am I really, Peter?"

"Nibble, for Christ's sake!"

"He's not really like that."

"He's exactly like that. Are you hooked on him?"

"Of course. Why else would I marry him?"

"You were hooked on me too, once. Are you divorced yet?"

"No. Not quite."

"You're just playing games again then."

She sipped her drink, then looked up at me: "Maybe."

I couldn't help laughing. She looked so damned innocent and honest.

She smiled back: "Peter, your letters were so guarded."

"Bandages," I said. "When you bleed you use bandages."

"I liked what you wrote me about my mother."

"I tore up a few others I wrote about you."

"Why then?"

"I felt guarded. Your letters were guarded too."

She put her head down: "Dammit. I wish you hadn't come here."

"Really, Esterhazy?"

"Yes, really. I don't want you to be hurt, oddly enough."

"I think you're picking a British mock-up of John Pantell the Third."

"Don't. Don't analyze so much."

Somebody was playing a zither or whatever, and the crowd was increasing and the colonel was making his way through the press with a plate of nibblies.

I asked: "Had we better talk?"

She thought briefly: "I guess so. Where can I reach you?"

"At the Shoreham. I'll be there by ten."

I grinned at her suddenly: "You see? You're already plotting against him."

"God deliver me," she said quietly as the colonel bore down.

I called the bureau from the hotel to find out who Colonel Anthony Yarborough was. He was the eldest son of a deceased general of distinction from Surrey, widowed, with two children both female. Currently military attaché to the British Embassy in Washington. He had been here for two and a half years and in the normal course would be rotated in another year and a half. It was presumed that he would receive his promotion at some time during this period. He was rumored to have some family money, and at one time had a certain reputation as a gay blade in various capitals. His name had been linked once with that of a blonde British film star.

And what meant this to Esterhazy?

She called around ten thirty.

I asked: "Why don't you come up here?"

"I'd rather meet you on neutral terrain."

"Where? Downstairs?"

"How about the Bistro?"

"Fifteen minutes?"

"Good."

"Don't bring his majesty."

She hung up.

I arrived first and got a table in the bar.

Except for the flickering glow of the candles the place was murky dark.

Her face and hair and fur and white dress

emerged floatingly out of the gloom. She seemed somber.

After we were settled and had ordered scotches, she finally looked at me: "This isn't going to be pleasant."

"So long as it's truthful."

"I always have been truthful with you, haven't I?"

"Do you love the guy?"

The candlelight gently illuminated her face and hair. There were a few more laugh lines around her eyes. She looked magnificent. Finally: "I don't know. But I want to marry him. He's so —serene. So easy to be with. He's secure, Peter. Not chasing off after ghosts or dragons. He accepts the world as it is, and me, and acclimates, and I've really always wanted that kind of security. That kind of ease. That kind of nonpressure."

I added: "That kind of nonrelationship."

"I knew you would say something like that. But perhaps you're right. That kind of nonrelationship."

"How do you go about going to bed with a nonperson?"

"None of your damn business."

The thought of it made me want to vomit. We sat in silence for a moment. A pudgy blonde laughed shrilly at the next table. Two men passed by—one a Congressman who looked as though I should know him. I tried to remember his name, but all the time I was imagining my Esterhazy making love to that vegetable of a colonel.

"Do you get along with his daughters?"

She flashed her eyes angrily at me: "You've been doing your homework!"

"Of course! What do you think I am? A *nebbish?*"

"I don't know what you are, Peter. I almost said darling. But you've been gone too long. Why did you walk out? . . . No, let's not open that up again."

"I wanted to come back."

"I wanted you to come back."

"I wanted to say I was sorry. I wanted you to bear Peter Danziger the Third. I wanted a lot of stupid things, so long as they were with you."

She said brightly: "But you went out and closed the door and never came back, didn't you? Didn't you, Peter?"

"I never told you I acclimated to the world as it is. I carry anger."

"Anthony calls all that the garbage of the past."

"I didn't think he was that bright. At any rate it equates with the garbage of the present. What's his position on the garbage of the present?"

She looked down at her rings, and sipped some scotch and glanced at her watch. Off in a corner someone started playing the piano.

I realized that I was finding some perverse enjoyment in torturing myself.

I softened my voice: "Why did we meet here, Esterhazy? Dearest Esterhazy. Would you like my blessing?"

"Give me a cigarette." (She never smoked.)

I lit it for her.

She said, through the smoke: "I had some such

thought. I wanted you to understand, for some ridiculous reason. I cared about you so much, and for so long, and then it just dissipated. Not enough nourishment, I guess."

"I don't have to understand. God bless you, Esterhazy."

She stood up abruptly: "I'm going to leave, Peter. This is brutalizing. Good-bye."

She vanished head up, into the darkness. After a while I paid the bill and got my coat and walked out into the street thinking about the garbage of the past.

Over the mantelpiece is a slab of highly finished walnut with words deeply carved in and gilded: DANZIGER'S LANDING. It looks like a boat transom because it was carved by Jack Walsh. Walsh thinks everything should have a transom plate.

It identifies the Landing: the place you always come down. Three-and-a-half uphill acres of granite and white pine. There's a brook by the house that makes a lovely noise at night. The cedar house sits on a rise and in the winter there is nothing between it and the North Pole but a barbed wire fence. One of the granite pieces on the front of the fireplace is loose, and you can hide love letters or pot behind it. The place smells musty when you come in after an absence, but you open all the doors and windows and light a fire and boil some coffee, and after a little of that it smells like home. The furniture came from here and there. You can put your feet up on anything. The style is Jewish Renaissance. In the fall you get an influx of field mice, and then you arrive for a weekend and create an outflux. You can swim in the deep part of the brook down by the road. You're an honorary member of the Fire Department. There's a lilac bush twenty-five feet high and a hundred years old. There's no lawn to cut. You can see Polaris through the high window from the bed. When the skim ice forms on the brook in the morning, the wild geese start moving south and you think of a boy walking in the autumn with his father.

After the elections were over, analyzed and re-analyzed, I went to New York for reassignment and to dig out a missing paycheck. I disciplined myself for those two weeks not to dial that well-remembered number. I picked up a few bucks being a panelist on one of those Sunday political shows on TV, and finally rented a car and drove up to the Landing for a week of fine December weather.

I told myself I was improving the place by scything down some brush and chopping some wood and scraping and painting the kitchen cabinets which had blistered for no apparent reason. The place smelt musty so I left all the doors and windows open on Saturday when I drove down to pick up a steak and some salad stuff, staples, cigars and a bottle of booze in the little Connecticut town.

There was a Thunderbird in the dirt driveway when I got back. Esterhazy was sitting in front of the cold fireplace with her coat on.

We looked at each other enigmatically. I didn't

know what to say, so I walked past her into the kitchen and began putting groceries away.

She came to the door: "Is there any rule against a fire?"

"Not at all. I'll build one. The cold air is bracing, isn't it?"

"Not particularly."

I laid a fire and lit it. Then I closed all the doors and windows, got an electric heater out of the bathroom and plugged it in in the living room. The radio was playing *"Arrivederci, Roma."*

I said: "You'll be able to take your coat off in about four hours, now. How did you find the place?"

"You drew me a map once, remember?"

I said: "There's a new road. You must have come the old way."

"It was a very pretty drive. I didn't know it was so far."

"Yeah, those things out there are Berkshires."

She took a deep breath. Her face was still expressionless. I sensed suddenly that she was embarrased.

I asked: "Do you want a cigar or anything?"

"No. I want a small glass of straight hooch and I want to take off my shoes."

I was confused, as usual, but about as happy as I could remember being.

We stayed on the couch in front of the fire all afternoon, under a hundred-year-old handmade quilt. I remember awakening once or twice and hearing a football game on the radio in the kitchen and thinking it was funny as hell.

I grilled the steak in the fireplace. Esterhazy made fried potatoes and a salad and I found a bottle of Beaujolais. She lit candles and we ate in front of the fire.

As we were eating: "I always wanted to get you up here."

"I got me up here. Never forget it."

The wind was picking up outside, whistling through the pines. The radio said snow.

"Peter, don't you want to know what happened?"

"Not especially. You're here."

"He turned out to be such an ass: I knew it the night I met you at the Bistro. That's why I left in such a hurry. I didn't know where to go from there."

"I don't want to talk about it. Now that I know you put onions in your fried potatoes, you're okay by me."

"I'm glad you're angry about things."

"Esterhazy, I'm not angry about anything."

"I mean, that you're not acclimated."

"What about divorce?"

"It's all settled. Quietly and properly. I get my decree in early February."

I set down my wineglass and slowly lit a cigar.

"What's the matter?"

"Somebody's following us," I said. "I leave for Saigon on December 26."

Thursday

LET'S BEGIN WITH MR. CROGER.

I don't know him. Still.

YES, YOU DO.

Relentless pursuit, Doc. Prove it.

EXAMINE THIS PICTURE.

(Pause)

Okay, examined. I've seen it before.

IS THAT YOUR CADET CLASS?

Yes. That's me in the second row. The good-looking one.

WHO IS DIRECTLY BEHIND YOU AND SLIGHTLY TO THE LEFT?

This one?

YES.

Mike Chiapa. On his left, Tully Cartwright.

THAT MAN IS EMIL CROGER.

Bullshit. That man is Mike Chiapa. Is this picture from my lawyer, by the way?

NO. WE FOUND OUR OWN.

You're definitely off it, and we're wasting time.

WE HAVE ESTABLISHED IT, MR. DANZIGER.

Let me put it this way. For ten weeks at Selman Field, Louisiana, and a much longer time at Coral Gables that man answered roll call to the name of Mike Chiapa. The last time I saw him, a few years ago, he still answered to Mike Chiapa. Your intelligence goofed.

BUT YOU ADMIT YOU KNOW THIS MAN?

I already did.

HIS NAME IS EMIL CROGER.

So you said.

AND YOU HAVE NEVER HEARD THAT NAME BEFORE?

No, god damn it!

YOU KNEW HIM ONLY AS CHIAPA? MIKE CHIAPA?

Right.

I WANT TO READ BACK A SENTENCE YOU USED TWO DAYS AGO. "I BUMP INTO MIKE CHIAPA EVERY THREE OR FOUR YEARS HERE AND ABROAD."

What is it with you, Doc? Research or infallible memory?

INFALLIBLE MEMORY, MR. DANZIGER . . . NOW, DID YOU SEE HIM OVER THE YEARS A TOTAL OF SIX TIMES, TEN TIMES, TWENTY TIMES?

If I remembered I'd be glad to confess.

WE'RE GOING TO RECONSTRUCT WHERE, WHEN AND WHY.

You're getting into the root canal again.

GOOD. LET'S BEGIN AT THE BEGINNING. WHAT WAS THE LAST TIME YOU SAW CROGER AT CADET SCHOOL?

Let's call him Chiapa, okay? I never heard

of Croger. Is that especially hard for you to comprehend, Doc?

VERY WELL, CHIAPA.

(Pause)

I guess at the party after graduation. Everybody had a girl or a parent. I told you about this. I can't remember him that night because we weren't that close. Undoubtedly, if he had a date she was some kind of monster. We all had small intime tables under Japanese lanterns and I wasn't looking at Chiapa, I was looking at Spence. But assume he was there.

DID YOU SEE HIM THE NEXT DAY?

No. I bummed a flight from Boca Raton to Chicago, and thence by bus to Muskegon.

WHERE DID CHIAPA GO?

Ask the Pentagon. I have no idea.

I ASSUME THIS WAS A LEAVE OF SOME SORT?

Yes.

WHAT HAPPENED AFTER THE LEAVE?

I reported to Avon Park AAC for crew assignment and operational training.

WAS THAT IN FLORIDA?

Yes. Third Air Force.

WAS CROGER—WAS CHIAPA ASSIGNED THERE?

No.

WHERE DID THE OTHERS GO?

Three or four with me to Avon Park, the others all over the map.

WHAT DETERMINED THE DISPOSITION OF ASSIGNMENTS?

You had a limited choice when you graduated: air transport, combat, instruction, et cetera. I chose combat because I knew Avon Park had B-26's, and it was close to Spence. When I got there they'd phased over to B-17's and that's what I got. On the approach you could see the skeletons of 26's on the bottom of Lake Arbuckle, so maybe it's just as well.

DID YOU SEE HIM AFTER THAT IN THE STATES?

No.

HOW LONG BEFORE YOU WENT OVERSEAS?

A couple of months—maybe three.

AND YOU DID NOT CHANCE ACROSS HIM IN THAT INTERVAL?

I did not chance across him.

DID YOU FLY ACROSS?

Yes.

FROM WHERE?

Hunter Field, Savannah, Georgia, then to Bangor, Maine, for supplies and gear. Then to Gander, then Wales. We flew our first mission three days later. Mentally, we were still over Charlotte, North Carolina.

TELL ME ABOUT THE FIRST TIME YOU SAW CHIAPA IN ENGLAND?

Why don't you just ask me if I did see him in England, Doc. Someday you're going to get so tricky you'll get wound up in that tape machine and they won't find you until morning. The answer is: about a year later.

SO YOUR MUTUAL PRESENCE IN THE

PARK LANE HOTEL ON JULY 14, 1944, WAS
NOT SHEER COINCIDENCE?

Yes, it was. If he was there at all.

I ONLY DEAL WITH FACTS, MR. DANZIG-
ER.

What did he do on this infamous day?

HE HIRED OUT TO LOUIS ESTIMET, FOR
ONE THING.

Doing what?

AS A FRIEND OF BOTH, DON'T YOU RE-
MEMBER?

I'd never met Louis Estimet, remember? We
keep going around and around.

AND WE WILL CONTINUE SO LONG AS
YOU CONTINUE THE ROLE OF THE IN-
JURED INNOCENT.

Just for the hell of it, Doc, what if I were innocent of whatever it is?

I WILL BE GLAD TO GIVE YOU MY OPIN-
IONS ON ABSTRACT JURIDICAL MAT-
TERS AT ANOTHER TIME AND PLACE.

In that case I'll continue the role of the injured
innocent. I kind of like it.

MEANING YOU DECLINE TO DISCUSS
CROGER—CHIAPA—IN DETAIL?

Not at all. Just fade out the innuendos and
we'll go ahead swimmingly.

WHAT WAS THE NEXT TIME YOU SAW
HIM?

In London. At a private club.

BY ARRANGEMENT?

By accident.

WHAT TRANSPIRED?

Hello, hello, have a drink transpired.

DID HE PRESENT ANY PROPOSALS?

No.

WAS HE SEEKING YOU OUT?

No.

THEN WHAT WAS HE DOING THERE SO COINCIDENTALLY?

Seeking out Armagnac or a girl or general recreation, I suppose. Your questions are kind of naïve.

WHEN DID YOU SEE HIM AGAIN?

A day or so later. A lot, after that. Two or three times a month. For general recreation.

YOU NEVER THOUGHT IT ODD HE PURSUED YOU?

No. He didn't.

WHY DO YOU SUPPOSE HE FOLLOWED YOU ABOUT?

Pure charm and friendship, Doc. If I knew what you were driving at I might be able to help you more.

I NEED NO HELP, THANK YOU. DID YOU LIKE HIM?

Very much. He kind of grew on you.

DID YOU SEE HIM AT THE SAME INTERVALS THROUGHOUT THE WAR?

No.

EXPLAIN THAT.

I saw him often for four or five months. Then no more.

DIDN'T THAT STRIKE YOU AS ODD?

Not at all.

WHY NOT?

I assumed he'd finished his tour and gone home, or got transferred, or married, or got himself killed.

THAT'S A RATHER CALLOUS ATTITUDE ABOUT AN OLD FRIEND, ISN'T IT?

Not in those days, Doc. People came and went. Where were you: in Culver Military Academy?

WHEN DID YOU SEE HIM AGAIN AFTER YOU CAME BACK STATESIDE?

(Pause)

I'll have to think about that one.

PERHAPS I'VE FINALLY STRUCK THE EX-POSED NERVE.

Don't be so goddamn smug. I can't remember.

COULD IT HAVE BEEN PERCHANCE IN GALVESTON, TEXAS?

You keep surprising me, Doc. Indeed it was. Now how the hell did you know that?

DON'T YOU REALIZE, DANZIGER, THAT SERVICE RECORDS ARE PERMANENTLY ON MICROFILM?

Lordy be! I thought it was your astrologer!

WHAT HAPPENED IN GALVESTON?

Nothing happened in Galveston. You flew weather ship once or twice a month to get in your flying time. Otherwise, you went to the beach or played dice. Everyone was waiting to get out.

DID CHIAPA SHARE THIS IDYLLIC EXIS-TENCE?

I suppose so. He stayed in a hotel in town. Being Jewish, I was trying to save money so I lived on the base. We only saw each other three or four times.

WERE YOU CONFIDANTS?

You know, this idiotic language must signify more to you than it does to me. What the hell does that mean: confidants? Did he unleash his innermost secrets and desires? Did he tell me how he wanted to dynamite the First National Bank of Galveston? Did he rue the day he met the sweet girl on the beach who turned out to be a hooker? Did he—

YOU ARE DETERMINED TO BE UNRESPONSIVE.

Not a bit. I can't respond to questions I don't understand. No, Doc. In your sense we were not confidants. We went to the beach together a few times and gambled a few times. Once we went to Houston and met some girls and got smashed. I never saw him sell a single secret, or pass a microfilm in a Zippo, or shine up to a Kraut PW. He never tried to interest me in the Ukraine. He was pure, man. He never said too much of anything, for that matter. I liked him. What is he supposed to have done?

DON'T YOU KNOW? IT'S INCREDIBLE TO ME THAT YOU DON'T, AS A NEWSMAN.

Take it that I've been elsewhere. What did he do?

A GREAT DEAL, MR. DANZIGER. SURELY, YOUR BUREAU WOULD KNOW.

I don't have a bureau, thank you kindly.

WHEN DID YOU SEE HIM NEXT AFTER GALVESTON?

What the hell did he do?

YOU'RE ANGRY. THAT INTERESTS ME.

Was it under the name of Croger or Chiapa?

THE NAME HE USED IS NOT PERTINENT.

He bollixed you with it!

NOT FOR LONG.

It damn well is pertinent if I'm supposed to identify with him.

DO I UNDERSTAND YOU TO MEAN THAT YOU DO IDENTIFY WITH HIM, WHAT- EVER THE NAME?

Jesus Christ, we're back where we started!

NOT QUITE. YOU SEEM REMARKABLY HEATED IN VIEW OF THE BLAND NA- TURE OF MY QUESTIONS.

That's why, you dumb son of a bitch!

SHALL WE TAKE A BREAK AND COOL OFF?

No. We're wasting time. How do I get my clean bill of health and what does it have to do with Mike Chiapa?

A GREAT DEAL, AS IT HAPPENS. YOU ARE ONE OF THE ONLY PEOPLE WHO HAS A TRACEABLE TIE WITH HIM OVER SEV- ERAL DECADES.

I've known a lot of people that long.

SO I HAVE OBSERVED. WE'VE DISCUSSED SEVERAL OF THEM, HAVEN'T WE?

You sound as though you just scored a point, but I don't know what it is.

DID YOU EVER MEET CROGER IN FRANCE, AFTER THE WAR?

If you mean Mike Chiapa, yes.

WHAT WERE YOU DOING AND WHAT WAS HE DOING?

It was years later. I was covering the French elections because some guy in the Paris Bureau broke his leg skiing. They sent me down from Bonn. Do you want his name or X rays or anything?

WHAT WAS CHIAPA DOING?

I don't know. It was in Marseilles. The mayor was one of the candidates. I'd gone down there to do background and interviews. Mike had written one of his oddball cards saying he'd be there for a few months. I hadn't seen him since Galveston.

DESCRIBE THE ENCOUNTER.

It wasn't an encounter. I phoned him and walked over to this seafood shanty and there he sat. We ate and talked. He called me at the hotel a couple of days later and persuaded me to take a day off before going back to Paris. He'd chartered an auxiliary yawl and thought we should enter some point-to-point race and have a bash afterward. Anyway, I did. We broke the headstay shackle and finished next to last. But we had about a half-case of chilled white Beaujolais aboard, and pheasant sandwiches, and an elusive girl in a white bikini named Biscuit and the whole thing worked out. One of those days, Doc. If he passed any secrets to anyone he heaved them over the side bit by bit in empty Beaujolais bottles. Next question.

I SEE WE'RE REALLY NOT GETTING ANYWHERE.

We're not getting anywhere you want to get,

apparently. It's sticky how unmalleable facts can be, isn't it?

WHAT A PITY FOR YOU, MR. DANZIGER, THAT YOU SEEM TO HAVE SOME DEEP BLOCK ABOUT ALL BUT THE MOST SURFACE ASPECTS OF YOUR MEMORY.

What a pity for you that I'm not Marcel Proust. The prose I write gets fish wrapped in it the next day.

I REFRAIN FROM COMMENT.

That's a funny, isn't it, Doc?

WHAT DID CHIAPA TELL YOU HE WAS DOING IN MARSEILLES?

I don't recall that he mentioned.

MR. DANZIGER, BE SENSIBLE! YOU ARRANGE TO MEET AN OLD FRIEND IN A SEAFRONT RESTAURANT IN MARSEILLES, AND YOU DON'T SAY: "HEY, MIKE! WHAT THE DEVIL ARE YOU DOING HERE, OF ALL PLACES?" NOW WHO IS BEING NAIVE?

(Silence)

Business and pleasure, I believe he said.

WHAT BUSINESS?

I'm trying to recall.

TRY HARDER.

Nothing illuminates.

MIGHT IT HAVE BEEN EXPORT-IMPORT?

Might have been.

BUT YOU'RE NOT SURE?

No.

PITY. IT WAS, AS IT HAPPENS, WHERE

DID HE SAY HIS HOME WAS THEN?

Baltimore. Before that I think he lived in New Jersey. Who did he kill?

NO ONE, TO MY KNOWLEDGE. BUT ISN'T IT INTERESTING HOW YOUR MEMORY REJUVENATES ITSELF? LET'S CONTINUE. WHAT HAPPENED AFTER YOU BROKE THE HEADSTAY SHACKLE?

What do you suppose happened? And why would you want to know? We were going to weather so the boom came down in the cockpit and the sail bagged. We all jumped out and swam to Leningrad.

DID YOU REPAIR IT YOURSELF?

What possible difference could it make?

DID YOU?

Temporarily. We needed a replacement shackle and I didn't happen to have one.

THEN HOW DID YOU FINISH THE RACE?

We rounded up and I looped it with wire. When that broke, a spectator boat came alongside to see what was the trouble. They wanted to put us in tow, but we borrowed a shackle and finished the race on our own, just for the joy of it. Our engine didn't work either.

DID YOU GO ABOARD THE SPECTATOR BOAT?

No. I was fending off. So was Miss Biscuit, with occasional eye-filling results.

SO CHIAPA WENT ABOARD?

Yes. They had a box of fittings to choose from.

HOW LONG WAS HE GONE?

He wasn't gone at all. He stepped into their

cockpit and diddled through a tin box and jumped back with a shackle and a *merci bien*.

WERE YOU WATCHING HIM WHEN HE CAME BACK ABOARD?

Naturally. Major, why are we bothering with all this? It wasn't a Russian submarine, it was a beat-up old French cabin cruiser. There was a fat lady in a halter on the transom.

WAS THE SHACKLE IN HIS HAND?

How could I remember?

TRY TO.

(Silence)

No, it wasn't.

HOW DO YOU KNOW?

He grabbed a stay with each hand as he jumped aboard. We were three or four feet apart at the stern. There was a little sea running.

WHAT WAS HE WEARING?

White pants and a yellow waterproof.

VERY INTERESTING.

Very not. By pure deduction, was that when he transferred the microfilm?

I'M MERELY TRYING TO DEMONSTRATE TO YOU THE REWARDS OF ENLIGHTENED OBSERVATION. WHAT HAPPENED AFTER YOU FINISHED THE RACE?

We went into some club and picked up a friend of Biscuit's and drank and ate and danced. It was a mob scene, so finally we sailed back to Marseilles by moonlight, running before the wind all the way. Chiapa was playing the guitar. Badly. We had a rain squall. I got off at the dock and found a taxi and dropped the two girls at Biscuit's apartment. I went back to my hotel and to bed. I had to fly to Paris in the morning.

NOW WE WILL TAKE A BREAK. NOT FOR YOU BUT FOR ME. SHALL WE SAY: FORTY-FIVE MINUTES?

Make it an hour and a half. I want to go back to the hotel.

FOR ANY PARTICULAR REASON?

Jesus, you're nosy!

MY PLEASURE, MR. DANZIGER. DO YOU RECALL THE GIRL BISCUIT'S LAST NAME, BY THE WAY?

Of course. It was De Gaulle. Biscuit De Gaulle.

THANK YOU. IN AN HOUR AND A HALF, THEN.

ALL SET?

Yes. I'd like to ask a stupid question.

STUPID?

I'm sure you'll consider it stupid. Being who you are and all that.

PROCEED.

You harangued me for a couple of days about not knowing Emil Croger. Now it has developed that his name in fact is Mike Chiapa. Clarify this for my simple mind, Doc.

CERTAINLY. IT WAS A NATURAL ENOUGH MISTAKE. LET'S SEE ... HE WAS BORN EMIL MICHAEL CROGER IN NEW-ARK, NEW JERSEY, IN 1923. HIS FATHER WAS OF GERMAN DERIVATION; HIS MOTHER A RECENTLY EMIGRATED

ITALIAN, A SINGER. THE MARRIAGE BROKE UP VERY QUICKLY. YOUNG CROGER WAS A TROUBLEMAKER, BY THE WAY. HE ENLISTED UNDER HIS OWN NAME, CROGER. UNFORTUNATELY, EARLIER HE HAD TAKEN LEGAL STEPS IN A PHILADELPHIA COURT TO CHANGE HIS NAME TO HIS MOTHER'S MAIDEN NAME, CHIAPA. THIS WAS GRANTED WHEN HE WAS UNDER AAC AUSPICES AT NASHVILLE, TENNESSEE, AND HIS RECORDS WERE SENT ON TO SELMAN FIELD, LOUISIANA, AND CORAL GABLES, FLORIDA. IN THAT NAME. UNFORTUNATELY, THE MASTER FILE, DUE TO OVERSIGHT, CONTINUED TO CARRY HIM UNDER HIS ORIGINAL ENLISTED NAME, CROGER. TODAY, HE USES BOTH INTERCHANGEABLY. THE IMPORTANT FACT IS THAT YOU KNOW HIM, AND HE IS STILL A TROUBLEMAKER.

Sure, Doc. You know everything about him but his name. Tell me: to get into Intelligence or whatever you call it, what do you have to do? I mean, I've got this nephew in Boston who's a dropout, and he got fired from the drugstore and my sister's worried sick and I thought if you put in a good word for him . . . the kid's a whiz on names . . .

VERY FUNNY, MR. DANZIGER. MAY WE PROCEED?

Sure, Doc. Just asking.

YOU DON'T IMAGINE THIS SATIRE IS

EASING THE PROCESS FOR YOU, DO YOU?

I certainly do.

LET US SEE . . . WE DISCUSSED CHIAPA'S AND YOUR ACTIVITIES IN MARSEILLES . . .

A sailboat race is not an activity.

DON'T BE SO SENSITIVE. LET'S DEPART FOR A MOMENT FROM THIS OBJECTIVE EXERCISE. TELL ME WHAT YOU THINK OF CHIAPA AS A MAN? HOW DO YOU ASSESS HIM AS A HUMAN BEING?

I truly do not understand what you're trying to do. What the hell difference does my opinion of Mike Chiapa make to this awesome department?

BEFORE YOU LEAVE HERE, IN A FEW DAYS, MR. DANZIGER, I PROMISE YOU WILL KNOW ANYTHING ABOUT THE INQUIRY YOU WOULD LIKE TO KNOW, WITHIN CERTAIN LIMITATIONS, OF COURSE.

The limitations, of course, being the things I actually want to know.

ARE YOU NORMALLY SO CANTANKEROUS? I HAD HEARD YOU WERE BASICALLY AN AMIABLE MAN.

If I don't want to talk subjectively about Mike Chiapa, I sure as hell don't want to talk subjectively about myself.

WHAT KIND OF MAN IS HE?

I'll introduce you sometime. He's a fairly hard guy with a tremendous talent for pleasure. He's a faker, in some ways. About hardness, I mean. The kind of role John Garfield might have played.

Heart of gold beneath. All that. Is this honestly helping you clear me?

ANY INFORMATION IS OF VALUE.

To me?

THE INFORMATION MUST BE SIFTED BEFORE ITS RELEVANCE CAN BE DETERMINED.

One of the trickiest ways of saying no I ever heard. I suddenly get the sense that I'm not here to clear myself but to help Uncle in some unknown way. Is that right?

IF YOUR INFORMATION IS OF VALUE TO US, NATURALLY WE WILL USE IT. AND IT IS NOT OUR FUNCTION TO CLEAR YOU, MR. DANZIGER, BUT YOURS. AS THE NOTICE SAID: "IF YOU WOULD LIKE TO CLEAR YOURSELF OF ANY TAINT." UNQUOTE. THE BURDEN IS YOURS, NOT MINE.

And you're after something else, obviously.

I'M AFTER ANYTHING THAT CLARIFIES VARIOUS UNDERTAKINGS THE GOVERNMENT HAS AN INTEREST IN. INCLUDING YOURS.

Talking to you is like reading Merriam-Webster out loud.

THANK YOU. TELL ME ON WHICH OCCASIONS YOU MET CHIAPA IN CUBA?

I love that plural you stuck in. I saw him once.

DESCRIBE IT.

It was fairly early in the game. Before I got the bug. I came down from the hills and was staying in Havana, catching up on the other side and coughing a lot. Mike was in the same little hotel, Los Cygnes—that means "swans." I saw his name in the book when I registered and left a note. Later, he left a return note to meet him at a club in Varadero at eleven that night. I was feeling lousier and lousier, but I pulled my frail self together and went out there. He was at a table in back when I walked in. He had a girl with him. They were talking hard. When he saw me he stood up and swarmed all over me. We had one drink, alone, and then I told him I thought I had chicken pox or something and asked if he wanted to go for a walk. I wanted out. We walked a couple of hundred yards to the beach and sat on the sand and looked off toward Key West. There was a warm breeze blowing offshore and not much surf. We talked about God-knows-what-all, mostly the war, I guess. Then, later, he got me a cab and I went back to the hotel and woke up in the morning with a hundred-and-four-degree fever.

WHAT WAS HE DOING THERE?

If the girl's looks were any indication I'd be embarrassed to tell you, Doc.

YOU KNOW I MEAN HIS BUSINESS ACTIVITIES?

I didn't ask. As a matter of fact, he didn't ask mine. Sometimes people have friends who don't ask all these questions, you know. I suppose you ask your kids to describe their stool when you get home at night.

YOU'RE BECOMING DANGEROUSLY CLOSE TO THE MARK OF BEING OB-

SCENELY PERSONAL, MR. DANZIGER.

What do you think you've been?

I CAN DO NOTHING WITH YOU IN THIS MOOD.

See you tomorrow, old cock.

Darling Esterhazy:

Another day gone. He dislikes me now. I can almost always get off early. I don't know yet what he's getting from me, but he seems increasingly smug. This scares me a little.

I called you a couple of times, but probably too early. Then I went out to Alexandria with Vic Hume, and we charred some lamb chops in the backyard and swilled ninety-seven-cent Chianti. And talked about the olden days. His wife Alice—I've told you about her, once so beautiful—has gone on some kind of mystic kick. No makeup, weaves her own clothes, eats nothing but birdseed or whatever, and breathes in and out deeply all the time. A couple of times she asked Vic when he was going to stop contaminating himself and he kissed her absently on the cheek and said, "Tomorrow, honey, first thing tomorrow." I didn't know whether she was talking about me or the Chianti or the cigarettes. In the meanwhile the lamb chops were burning.

Everybody seems to have a theory about what I'm doing down here but me. I'd tell you some of the theories, except that they might

make you as irritated as they do me. Vic
says Vince Schaefer flatly refuses to discuss
the Danziger matter: it doesn't exist. However,
I do.

All of it,

P.

TO: A. J. Katin
FROM: B. Pike

FORMAL REPORT TO FOLLOW

He is tied in closely with Croger by his own
admission.

B.P.

Nostalgia is an incomplete emotion, but when
you meet someone from an earlier incarnation it
seems important. He tapped me on the shoulder
one night at the New Magyar Club. I turned and
looked up at him. I had just been arguing rather
pointlessly with Cybele.

He said: "Lieutenant Danziger, I presume."

"Hello, Mike. Where did you locate the mustache?"

I introduced him to Cybele and asked him to
sit down. He had always had a quality of interested
quietness. That night he drank nothing but beer.
She responded to him in some way—perhaps to
dramatize to me that I was not the only fella in
town, and became animated, the best of Cybele. I
caught my usual creeping jealousy.

After finding out who he was, where he came
from, and whether he liked Brahms, silk pajamas,

Labrador retrievers and such, she began picking his memories about me. Her theory that night was that I was basically a kind man who, when exposed to her, by some inexplicable alchemy of personalities, became a brute. It was an interesting theory and perhaps there were seeds of truth in it.

I became brutish as a result. I made a date with Mike for lunch the next day at the Grosvenor, and quickly shagged him out of there.

Cybele was bitchy but marvelous.

Next day, while we were drinking martinis at the Grosvenor bar, a round-faced terribly young American glider pilot vomited on Mike's shoe. Then the boy began to cry. We left shortly and walked down Park Lane and across into the park. GI's were playing baseball, and overhead the scud wind was working on the cables of the barrage balloons. The oblongs cast weird shadows across the outfield. Some kids and their nursemaids were watching stonily the bizarre activity on the field. A vendor was selling buns. Beyond it all were flak batteries tended by bored Tommies in flat helmets. It was sunny but chill.

Mike said: "This country touches me. It's simply amazing how many things touch me these days."

We bought some buns and sat down near the home plate side of third base.

He went on: "I keep thinking something terribly important is happening to me every moment. This grass. Jesus, look at it! Feel it! Look at the sun on that blonde nurse! Look at that idiot on third base! Those are the best faces I ever saw!"

I said: "For your information, my girl is off limits."

"Who the hell is talking about your girl?"

"You are, whether you know it yet or not."

"No, Peter, I'm not!"

"Go on about the grass, Mike."

"I felt sorry for that poor slob in the Grosvenor, that's all."

"I don't think you should feel too sorry for him."

He said: "You like to pretend you're a cold-hearted bastard, don't you?"

"I just think you should have bounds for your sympathy."

"Same thing."

"I have no sympathy for this bun, for example."

"Hey, Danz. Where did it all go? Where did everything disappear to?"

We watched the ball game for a while, and then went back to my room and got mildly swacked on a bottle of sixteen-dollar scotch that was light green in color.

The tannoy speaker blared my name across the squadron area and the surrounding farmland, and a voice announced I was expected instantly at Group Operations.

I borrowed a bicycle and went down there. They wanted a crew to fly a bunch of medics into newly liberated Paris. We were selected because

I had had four years of French.

Chiapa showed up that afternoon on one of his sojourns and I invited him along as special observer.

We landed at Villa Coublay and located a ride into town and ultimately found a few rooms in a tiny hotel on La Rue des Enfants Qui Crient, just off the Palais Royal. Then at refreshing rates we cashed in pounds sterling for francs and spent the afternoon wandering the places we had read about for so long.

After London, it was unique seeing no other American uniforms, although no girls were kissing us as they did to our people in tanks. Chiapa complained about this.

A girl at the next table at the Dôme looked like Cybele with blond hair.

"Mostly we bomb kids and pregnant women well away from the industrial sectors," I told her carefully.

She smiled and joined our table. She understood no English.

Later she took us to the place where she worked, which was the most magnificent whorehouse in the world, called the Sphinx. It looked like the lobby of the Radio City Music Hall and the girls ranged from four-feet-eight to six-feet-four. Chiapa selected one of the former, and for appearance's sake, I chose one of the latter. I didn't have guts for the Cybele one.

Mine had a tiny angry red scar on the inside of her thigh.

"Ceegarette," she said brightly, adjusting her long self.

It seemed perfectly logical.

There were no taxis when we left. Chiapa and I walked here and there with impeccable senses of direction.

Chiapa kept saying: "Peter old boy."

We kept shaking hands.

I woke up on a bench in a tiny green triangle of a park with schoolchildren and sunlight glazing down into my eyes. Chiapa was asleep on his belly on the next bench.

"Bon matin," I said hoarsely, and as the kids ran off I was thinking: Cybele, Cybele, my crazy Irishman. Here I am, all balls and disdain. I might as well have been a *Luftwaffer*.

We found our way to the street of the crying children in pain. Chiapa groaned and laughed and groaned. His crinkly face kept crinkling. I still see that face crinkling in the morning sunlight, Major Pike.

The next day I walked the Seine until dark. The bookstalls were gone. I discovered a new kind of sausage. It was white. There were kids everywhere. I gave one of them the insignia off my hat. Demoted, I walked back just before dark. I couldn't decide whether I'd had penance or enjoyment. We flew back on Thursday.

It must have been a few years after Marseilles, just before I went to Tel Aviv. I stopped over in London for a few days for the usual briefing. The new European manager's name was Manners. I didn't like him particularly, simply because he was more concerned with the bureau's lineage flow than with its quality. He was emaciated and always wore a black suit.

The first day he bought me the usual expensive lunch at the Bagatelle. Over capon and asparagus and a half of dry white he asked me if I knew Mike Chiapa.

"Yes," I said. "Do you?"

"Not yet."

"How did you guess I did?"

"Just a thought."

"What about him?"

"He's in London. Would it be natural for you to call him?"

"Sure, but why?"

"He's an interesting man."

"Manny. Stop the bullshit. Why?"

"He's making a lot of money."

"Knowing he's here, I'd call him anyway. What do you want to know?"

"Maybe how he makes it. There is some interest in that question. Without causing any ruckus, you understand."

Manny always hated ruckus. Like World War II was a ruckus.

"Okay. Would it be okay if I just asked him?"

"I've known for years that was the Danziger definition of research."

"Where does he stay?"

"The Dorchester. Fourteenth floor. The door to the left."

"You sure are knowledgeable, Manny."

We lit cigars and escaped each other.

I walked over from the Square and found him in his suite, dictating to an owlish British secretary. It was something about the rate of exchange between pounds sterling and Spanish pesetas. The suite was late Queen Anne with early cigar butts added. He looked more formidable. He had put on weight, and a little hardness. He smiled at me when I walked in, then finished his dictation. His suit cost four hundred dollars. The secretary wiggled into another room.

He said: "Peter Fahnstock Danziger."

"Hello, Mike. How did you know my middle name?"

"It came to me."

"Jesus, that's beautiful!"

We shook hands.

I said: "I came over here to cadge a drink."

"How did you know I was here?"

"It came to me."

He laughed a little falsely and started to mix drinks: "I'm not even registered."

"It's okay, Mike. I didn't even ask for you."

He looked hard: "No kidding, Danz, where did you hear?"

"I didn't as it happens. I saw you crossing the lobby . . . What the hell's the big secret?"

He handed me a drink and we sat down and made the usual saluds. Now there was a falseness in the whole performance, both ways.

"Where are you off to now, Peter?"

"The Middle East."

"Boy, could I use you. The way you get around."

"Use me for what?"

"As a contract agent. I can't cover all my markets."

"What's the product?"

"It varies."

"So do I, Mike . . . What are your plans for this evening?"

"Negative. But I've still got some work . . ."

"Pick you up at eight thirty."

"Beautiful."

"Dinner?"

"Dinner."

He went back to work and I went out to buy a suit and get my camera fixed. London was lovely for a change: a soft blue-gray afternoon with a hint of late spring. The leaf buds were bursting out in that fresh apple green. I thought about Cybele for a moment. Then I had trouble finding a Leica dealer.

That night, first we went to the White Castle on Percy Street which, unlike various namesakes, is one of the great restaurants of Europe. The maître d' even pretended to recognize me. We sat banked off from the kitchen by potted palms. I thought of the quixotic truth that nothing changed while everything was changing. Here we are: me, the White Castle, Mike Chiapa, the potted palms, the smells from the kitchen, the cabs outside, the silhouette of the city, the ancient memories, the same old pleasures, the same old horrors. And someplace sat a man with a red button. Instant Auschwitz. When I was a kid the scratchy old record of Mr. Gallagher and Mr. Sheen made me uncomfortable because Mr. Sheen might have been a sheeny, and that was a big word in western Michigan those years. I ordered the Dover sole.

I managed to forget what Manners was prying for—having known Mike much longer than Manners and liking him better despite all the camouflage, and having the whole question of corporate loyalty a little unsettled in my mind anyway.

I remember this: in Bonn a few years earlier I had had a scoop on the up value of the mark handed to me across a breakfast table by Inge-britzen—no accident—and filed it accordingly as a lead story, and found out later it was held up for two days and then by-lined by my bureau chief. Nothing to do with the aspirations of man and the disposition of soul, but it unsettled me.

Narrowly, I hope, I am a professional. But the personal parts get invaded; the sensitivities become aroused; the body grows older; the brain cells diffuse; the chancres multiply. And then the battle is touched off to combat the inclination to say: I *was* . . . Fuck thee . . . Fuck everything . . . Then you are dead.

I wasn't dead yet and Mike Chiapa had breasted the bulwarks with me many years ago.

We went to a club in Chelsea called His Own and had brandy. We had been talking about politics and World Wars II and III and a girl in Washington he was enamored of when a dandy gentleman in a dinner jacket came up to Mike.

He was a little tight. He wore a hairline mustache and much cologne.

"Michael! What a surprise!"

"Hey, Philippe! Shake hands with Peter Danziger."

He ordered us all a Hennessy and talked intently to Mike. His problem was simple. Michael knew his sensitivity. He was to escort a recently widowed American woman to a gambling casino. She had a slight reputation as a man-eater, and he, Philippe, did not desire to be man-eaten. On the other hand, she would make a highly desirable match. In short, he wanted to score, but she undermined his confidence. He and Mike seemed to be old pals.

Mike said: "You are fortunate tonight to have Peter Danziger here. This is his type of problem. . . . Would you advise Philippe, Peter? He is one of my dearest friends."

I said: "Certainly. Philippe, exactly how big is your penis?"

He looked at Michael.

"I believe that's your problem," I said.

Mike said: "I never thought of it that way."

Philippe said: "I am a man of forty-two years with the normal successes."

"Aha!" I said. To Mike: "Should I tell him?"

"I guess you better tell him," Mike said.

I turned to Philippe: "Let me see your ankles."

He looked perplexed.

"It's the thickness," I said.

"The thickness?"

"American women can tell. They like men with

thick ankles. Ankles indicate a vital equivalent thickness. Need I be coarse?"

He admitted I need not be coarse and displayed his ankles. They were rather pathetic as ankles go.

"They won't do," I said. "Mike, do you think his ankles will do?"

Mike peered at them: "I'm afraid not. Not for an American woman."

Philippe looked half-dismayed, half-distrustful. He gazed uncertainly at his ankles.

"Handkerchiefs," I said suddenly. "Lots of handkerchiefs."

"Handkerchiefs?"

"To bulk them up," I said. "They've got to be bulked up."

"About a half inch each," Mike said.

I said: "That should do it. Inside the socks."

"Do you really think so?"

"I know so. Look at Mike's ankles. Women *know*."

Mike said: "Women in Baltimore have commented time and again about my ankles."

"You see?" I said to Philippe.

"I'd best go back to the hotel first," he said distractedly.

I never found out whether or not Philippe bulked up his ankles, and occasionally I wonder about it.

Mike and I went back to his suite after a few hours. He made coffee. We listened to a few of his new records, which I didn't like particularly because they were sort of pseudo-pseudo. Dramatic treatment for no discernible reason in the music.

Not the old Mozart-Danziger purity. The view from his window was superb. I could see almost all the way to Northolt and Cybele. It wasn't the miles but the years that were spectacular. Due west was Esterhazy. Vincent Sheean used to write about the long view.

"Mike, are you a successful type back home?"

He laughed. "A dollar here, a dollar there. You know, Danz, I've known you longer than anybody else in my life except my mother."

"That's because you don't keep up with people."

"I suppose I don't. Do you?"

"A few. I try to bump in, here and there."

"I never even knew my old man. They told me he was a bastard, but maybe he wasn't. Now he's probably dead. But maybe he was a nice guy."

"Personally, I would have found out."

"I would too. Now. But not then. Do you like your job, Danz?"

"Within limitations. It's what I do. I get involved. What do you get involved with?"

He got up and walked over to the window for a moment: "The buck. And women. I'm absolutely crazy about women."

"How do you make your buck? I always thought you would be easy come, easy go."

"Not me. That's one thing I learned about."

"Never ask a question in the first sentence," I said.

He laughed: "I operate a little. That's all. Baltimore's a big port."

"Big for what?"

"Commission buys. Whatever it is."

"Like rice? Like steel? Like fertilizer?"

"Yeah. Like that. All you need is a warehouse and a telephone book and a few contacts."

"Sounds stifling."

"It is. Then you branch out. Then you set up your own shipments. Then you count the green."

"Jesus Christ. Mike Chiapa the Operator."

He laughed again: "Yeah. Mike Chiapa the Operator."

On the BEA flight out, I sat next to a youngish American brigadier on his way to undisclosed places east. He wore tweeds, and by the time I learned he was a general I liked him—which was counter to my normal inclinations. His name was Sam Arrow. He was familiar with my work and thought my opinions were far out on certain matters. I couldn't get him to specify which. I asked him if he were an Indian and was not surprised to hear he was, indeed. His family had left the reservation when he was a kid, and his father had made it with a garage in Devil's Lake, North Dakota. Sam had worked his way into Dartmouth on that old Indian clause they had, and then transferred to the Point after his freshman year, with a little Congressional help.

He had immense strong teeth and a flashing smile and spoke in short hurried sentences. He began talking about the impossibility through history of regulars and irregulars on the same side having any military affinity, based on their necessarily disparate military states of mind. The question was not important to me then, but it became vital in later years. I've wondered a few times what I owe him.

He based his case on adventurers from Custer to Pancho Villa, Carson's Raiders, Commandos, the Stern Gang and the Ergun, although his own specialty was the War Between the States.

I told him I once had heard a pukka British colonel curse out the Commandos with bulging veins, for breaking every civilized rule of warfare built up over the centuries.

He laughed and said he had studied under him.

At Rome, while we waited for our respective flights, we shared greasy eggplant parmigiana in the terminal dining room, and agreed that Europe was almost ready for Howard Johnson, after a few more eggplant. He drank off his three martinis in one gulp each, with a fast throw of his neck, as though they were stomach medicine.

We swapped cards before he ran for his flight. I found his card years later, and wondered whether the first unreconstructed Indian had ever earned his second star, or been killed, or merely buried in that nifty eight-sided slab on the Potomac.

I knew instinctively that under duress, or in the lonely late late hours, he still hoarded a small private pleasure in the battle of the Little Bighorn.

There was a letter from Esterhazy at the hotel in Tel Aviv—her first letter to me, really, filled with unstated regrets, not recriminations. It was a bit chatty and surface-oriented, but it was long, and it had traces of blood in it. I was still too freshly hurt to appreciate, but I still have it. I wondered if she were trying inarticulately to break through. It's what I would like to have done, but didn't know how to begin any better than she did. So I never started . . .

Somehow it activated my chemistry enough so that next morning I had the necessary audacity to jam my way through into permission for a private interview with Dayan on the border two days hence. When his Oxford-accented secretary finally capitulated with the news later that morning, she sighed and said: "Very well, Mr. Danziger!" Then to herself: "These Jews . . . !"

I laughed like a Yiddische baby. It was that kind of country. I thought how nice it would be if they ran Muskegon.

An old friend of mine named Jeff Cowan had left the bureau and gone to work for a magazine with a specialty he had developed called "The Way It Was." It was a flashback of familiar names and places and events, and it worked for him. He was younger than I am, actually, but his province was the past—and what he could evoke from it. In time, I expect, the actuary tables will phase out his audience, but in the meanwhile, he's had a run for it. Like the boy and the book about penguins, he could tell me more about yesteryear than I really wanted to know.

I bumped into him at a symposium on the Middle East at the American University in Beirut later that year. It was all very professional and well meaning, except for one firebrand from Syria, and it was with high relief that I saw Jeff coming out of the men's room after the first session.

We lunched wetly, and talked about olden days and agreed to meet that night. He was covering the event for a sick friend, being unfortunately near the spot. I dozed through the afternoon session. Everyone agreed that it would be terrible if there were any more trouble, and everyone agreed there would be more trouble.

I met Jeff that night in a restaurant called Haguib, and as we walked down the short steps into the place, I saw Mike Chiapa talking to a man by the kitchen door.

He saw me coming, froze for a moment, then quickly slipped through the door into the kitchen. It was deliberate and stupid—whatever his motive—simply because he knew that I had seen him.

When he knocked on my hotel door that night —I had been trying to draft the ultimate letter to Esterhazy—I discovered that I was still irritated.

"Hello, Mike. What a surprise. I didn't see you sneaking into the kitchen at Haguib," I said flatly, without letting him in.

"I thought the man you were with was somebody else."

"Bullshit."

"Can I come in? I'll explain."

I opened the door: "I don't want to hear about it. You look like an unsuccessful pickpocket."

He began to laugh: "Me and my ego."

"Get it over with," I said. "Who was he supposed to be? J. Edgar? IRS? Interpol?"

He sat down, squinted at me. That old Chiapa squint.

"Well?"

"I thought he was a man I recently took a lot of money from. Legally."

"Then you saw me and figured I was following you."

"No. I just panicked. Jesus, Danz, didn't you ever panic?"

"Not in a Lebanese kitchen. What have you been stealing?"

"Buying is the word."

"So you're selling guns and buying hashish. I don't like to see my friends blow their poise."

I heated some coffee on my plug-in and we lit cigars and talked about London. He didn't know what had happened to Philippe either, but wagered he had struck out—either way, just from worry.

After that night we were never very close again. I wonder now, after all these years, if my casual comment about guns and hashish hit some kind of target.

Friday

GOOD MORNING.

Good morning.

LET'S TALK ABOUT THE FAR EAST.

Now we get down to it.

THIS DAY'S CONVERSATION IS NO MORE NOR LESS IMPORTANT THAN ANY OTHER DAY'S.

You bewilder me.

I SEE IT WAS REPORTED IN A HANOI NEWS BROADCAST AND IN THE HANOI PRESS THAT YOU ENTHUSIASTICALLY BACKED THE EFFORTS OF A VILLAGE HEADMAN NAMED CAI.

Enthusiasm is a little strong. I merely said his village seemed to work.

HE HAPPENS TO BE A RATHER NOTORIOUS SPECIMEN OF VC.

I'm sure he is. My personal opinion is that he's not dangerous.

YOUR PERCEPTION OF DANGER IS RATHER RUDIMENTARY, THEN. SOME OF OUR TWO CORPS PEOPLE CALL HIM

THE BUTCHER. WERE YOU FRIENDLY?

I didn't bust him in the snoot, if that's what you mean. Nor he me.

SO YOU WERE ON A SOMEWHAT FRIENDLY BASIS?

We were on a reporter-host basis. If that's friendly.

HE'S SMILING HERE IN THIS PICTURE WITH YOU.

It's not a smile, it's a rictus. He always looks like that.

BUT HE SEEMS PLEASED TO HAVE HIS PICTURE TAKEN WITH YOU.

Don't you believe it. His village had just been bombed. What difference does it make?

THE TUMULT OF YOUR WELCOME IS A LITTLE THOUGHT-PROVOKING, WOULDN'T YOU SAY?

Vince Schaefer would hire me back and double my salary if he knew I ever provoked a thought. This conversation is inane.

WHAT EXACTLY DID YOU MEAN WHEN YOU WROTE HIS VILLAGE SEEMED TO WORK? FOR WHOM?

For the inhabitants, which I presume is the proper judgment of a village.

DO YOU INCLUDE ENEMY VILLAGES IN THAT NEAT CATEGORIZING?

Villagers live in villages. The village either works for them or it doesn't, whether anyone else likes it or no. Think of Fiorello LaGuardia.

I FIND THAT ARGUMENT HARD TO AC-

CEPT WHEN THE VILLAGE SUPPORTS AN
EVIL CAUSE.

What should I have done? Zap them? Who de-
cides who is evil? They acted as though me and
my B-52's were pretty evil.

THERE ARE ETHICS WHICH FORM PART
OF A GLOBAL PICTURE YOU OBVIOUS-
LY CANNOT UNDERSTAND.

I obviously cannot. I never saw a global ethic
in my life.

AS AN ASIDE, MR. DANZIGER, MY SUPERI-
OR REMARKED AFTER READING THE
FIRST SEVERAL DAYS OF TRANSCRIPT
THAT HE FELT RATHER SYMPATHETIC
TOWARD YOU, THAT YOU WERE OB-
VIOUSLY LACKING SOME SMALL LOBE
OF YOUR BRAIN WHICH MIGHT RELATE
YOU FAVORABLY TO YOUR BACK-
GROUND AND YOUR COUNTRY.

I'm sure I would enjoy meeting your superior
immensely.

HAPPILY, HE IS MORE CONCERNED
WITH LONG-TERM CONSPIRACY THAN
YOU ARE.

I guess he is. I only see with these old eyes.

HAVE YOU EVER CONSIDERED THAT
THE ALACRITY WITH WHICH YOUR BU-
REAU DROPPED YOU MIGHT REFLECT
ON YOUR OWN CAPABILITIES AS A RE-
PORTER RATHER THAN ON OUR OPIN-
IONS ABOUT YOUR ACTIVITIES?

I never have, as a matter of fact.

YOU MIGHT TRY IT ON. THERE WAS VERY LITTLE PRESSURE BROUGHT TO BEAR ON THIS END.

Doc, I don't believe you. Also, I know Vince Schaefer. Let's try another tack.

VERY WELL. BUT THINK ABOUT IT. WHEN DOES ONE KNOW WHEN ONE IS OVER THE HILL?

One smells it . . . Can we get on?

I BELIEVE I TOUCHED A NERVE, MR. DANZIGER.

You probe long enough, you have to.

DO YOU DOUBT YOUR OWN REPORTAGE?

Of course. Let's get on with it.

YOU ARE SAYING YOU DO NOT SUPPORT YOUR OWN JUDGMENT?

Christ, no! I only worry that my infallibility may be as specious as yours. It's not likely, but I worry.

AN IMPORTANT ADMISSION, MR. DAN-ZIGER.

De nada. I wake up with it every morning of my life. Don't you?

ACTUALLY NOT. BUT YOU DO ADMIT YOU ARE INSECURE ABOUT YOUR OPIN-IONS?

I certainly am, and hope to remain so. What are you: a fucking know-it-all?

WE'RE NOT TALKING ABOUT ME, MR. DANZIGER.

I'm talking about you.

WE'RE DISCUSSING WIDELY DISSEMI-NATED INFORMATION FROM A SOURCE

WHICH NOW QUESTIONS ITSELF.

That's the best kind, Doc.

HAVE YOU EVER BEEN WRONG?

Once when I was about eight. I can't recall the circumstances. . . . We're not going anyplace with this infallibility thing, Doc.

ON THE CONTRARY, WE'VE ALREADY ARRIVED. I FIND IT PROVOCATIVE THAT YOU CAN FILE STORIES WHICH SUPPORT THE ENEMY AND HELP POLARIZE PUBLIC OPINION IN YOUR OWN COUNTRY, AND NOT BE QUITE SURE THE NEXT MORNING WHETHER YOU AGREE WITH YOURSELF.

What am I being grilled for: conspiracy or fallibility?

SIMPLY FOR THREAT, MR. DANZIGER, WHETHER YOUR MOTIVATIONS ARE TREASON, CONSPIRACY, DELUSION OR MONEY.

It must be wonderful knowing the lines in advance, and having the whole denouement in your briefcase. I assume that space behind your eyes is a briefcase?

CAPTAIN ANDERSON IN SAIGON REPORTED THAT YOU HAD AN INSTINCT FOR INVECTIVE.

If you think that's invective you went to a sissy school.

DO YOU THINK THE VC ARE RIGHT?

What does right mean? They're murdering people. So is Saigon. So are we. I think they've got a legitimate gripe. It's their country too and they think the government stinks. I think it stinks too.

THE SAIGON GOVERNMENT WAS ELECT-ED BY THE POPULACE, I UNDERSTAND.

With a helping hand by Uncle. Also, I didn't notice that the VC were enfranchised.

WHY SHOULD THEY HAVE BEEN? THEY'RE THE ENEMY.

That's what we're talking about.

YOUR THOUGHT PROCESSES AND YOUR CONVERSATION GO AROUND IN CIR-CLES.

Yes, they do.

LET'S TALK ABOUT SAIGON. HOW DID YOU GET IN TOUCH WITH YOUR FRIEND CHARLEY HSI?

I didn't.

YOU DIDN'T? YOU WROTE THAT HE AND HIS SUPERIOR WERE INSTRUMENTAL IN GETTING YOU ACROSS.

I found it out later. I had no idea at the time everything was set up.

BUT HE ADMITTED TO YOU LATER THAT HE HAD IN FACT SET UP THE EN-TIRE TRIP?

Yes. At least he indicated it. He was sort of hesitant.

WELL, DID HE OR DIDN'T HE?

The answer is: both. He did and he didn't.

THIS KIND OF INTERROGATION IS MOST FRUITLESS FOR ME, MR. DANZIGER.

I guess you should manufacture people who have no uncertain areas.

WHAT WAS HSI'S FUNCTION WHILE YOU WERE IN ALIEN TERRITORY?

He was kind of a host.

HE ACCOMPANIED YOU ALL THE WAY?

He and a happy handful of others. I was up to my ass in accompaniers.

I'M SURPRISED THE VC ALLOWED A CHINESE INTO SUCH AN INTIMATE AND POTENTIALLY EXPLOSIVE POLITICAL SITUATION.

I was surprised that Hanoi would. With all their Russian arms, et cetera. Do you know anything I don't know?

ABOUT WHAT?

About political shadings?

I PROBABLY KNOW A GREAT DEAL YOU DON'T . . . WHO WERE THE OTHERS ACCOMPANYING YOU?

A VC captain named Nuy. And an aged Hanoi gentleman, a political adviser, I believe, called Nguyen Than. All this is pretty well detailed in my releases.

I KNOW. BUT I ASSUME THERE WILL BE, AS YOU SAY, SHADINGS WHICH MAY DIFFER BETWEEN YOUR TESTIMONY HERE AND YOUR CHURNING OUT FOR A MASS PUBLIC.

Not at all, as it happens, Doc. I don't churn out.

I'M TALKING ABOUT SHADINGS YOU MIGHT NOT EVEN KNOW WERE SHADINGS.

You're calling me stupid, I do believe. A minute ago I was an international plotter. One of us has got to be schizo. Plunge ahead.

I WANT TO KNOW EVERY DETAIL, FIRST, OF HOW YOU ARRANGED THIS THING. I ASSUME IT WAS ONE OF THE BUDDHISTS.

I'll tell you that: yes. But I won't tell you which one.

DO YOU MIND TELLING ME WHY NOT? NOW THAT YOU'RE THROUGH WITH HIM?

By some coincidence he might get his throat cut very gradually. And he's a gentle man.

WE WILL PROBABLY BE ABLE TO GUESS, AT ANY RATE. HE IS UNDOUBTEDLY UNDER SURVEILLANCE.

Of course he is. Bad surveillance, by the way. There are more civil servants peeking from behind bushes at every Buddhist temple in Saigon than there are people inside contemplating the absolute.

WOULDN'T YOU, WERE YOU IN POWER, OBSERVE THE ENEMY WITHIN THE GATE, MR. DANZIGER?

I might try to establish myself first so that he had no reason to be my enemy.

THIS IS NAÏVETÉ. HOW MANY BUDDHISTS HAVE SUPPORTED THE SAIGON GOVERNMENT?

I have no idea. How many Buddhists has the Saigon government supported? Your Saigon people keep sticking Buong and a dozen others like him in jail at the drop of a hat. I don't know what it is. We keep driving neutrals into the enemy's hands, almost deliberately it seems, and then we start looking around for villains and yelling conspiracy. I'm serious, Major. Is it policy? Or just dumbness? I expect it's dumbness. John Foster said that neutrality was immoral. Try to sell that to a Buddhist, or to anyone not entirely demented. Most people know in their bones that being neutral in another man's guerrilla war is the only way to save their ass—at least until we made it cost their ass. Why is my country so goddamn subjective? Love me, love my idiocies? Major, this infuriates me.

YOU ARE AN AUDACIOUS MAN TO COMMIT THAT TO THE RECORD AT THIS TIME, IN THESE CIRCUMSTANCES. PERHAPS YOU HAVE SAVED US HALF A DAY OF PROBING YOUR INTENT.

Good. My intent is very unwholesome about this kind of inquiry and probably wouldn't stand much probing.

HOW DID YOU GET TO YOUR BUDDHIST? SIMPLY WALK IN AND ASK?

I kept putting the word out to assorted people that I was interested in doing a story about the VC from the other side. Then I waited.

WHAT KIND OF PEOPLE?

Bartenders, storekeepers, newsmen, waiters, hotel managers, cabdrivers, B girls . . .

WHAT HAPPENED?

I waited around a couple of weeks. In the meanwhile I picked up a government tail, so I knew the message was floating around out there somewhere. Then, late one night, a little man came to my room.

WHO WAS HE?

I don't even know his name. He spoke no English, but in French we arranged that I meet him the next night outside a restaurant about a mile northeast. I was to take pains to lose my tail first. I would be observed, and if no one met me within twenty minutes it would be because I still had the tail.

DID YOU MEET HIM?

Yes.

THEN WHAT HAPPENED?

He took me to a house where another man questioned me in English.

ABOUT WHAT?

About my intent.

WHAT WAS YOUR STATED INTENT, IF I MIGHT ASK?

I thought you might. I'll tell you what I told him. Here is half the enemy and no one knows who he is. What he thinks, how he feels about Hanoi, how he feels about Saigon, what he eats. Salisbury went to Hanoi, all very legally, and did the series from there and opened up a lot of people's eyes. I wanted to make the VC my bag.

VERY PLAUSIBLE.

It was and is.

WHO WAS THE SECOND MAN—THE ONE WHO SPOKE ENGLISH?

He was Vietnamese. Well dressed. It was a pleasant, fairly expensive house, but I don't know that it was his. He was quite bright, I thought. I couldn't tell how old he was.

WHAT WAS HIS NAME?

He introduced himself as Niem.

WAS HE A VC?

A sympathizer, at least.

WHERE WAS THE HOUSE?

I didn't notice. The cab went around the horn four or five times en route.

WHAT WAS THE FINAL DISPOSITION OF YOUR DIALOGUE?

I was to wait and word would be got to me within ten days. I would meet someone first, the Buddhist, it turned out, then I must be prepared to leave on an hour's notice.

DID YOU HAVE THE FEELING CERTAIN CONSULTATION HAD GONE ON?

Of course.

DID THE PLAN WORK OUT THAT WAY?

It did. The efficiency was kind of amazing.

PROBABLY A COINCIDENCE. WHO WAS TAILING YOU FROM THE GOVERNMENT SIDE?

A gorilla. They stuck a shantung suit on it. It kept looking away if I glanced at it.

FOR CURIOSITY'S SAKE, HOW DID YOU LOSE HIM SO EASILY? APPARENTLY YOU LOST HIM THREE OR FOUR TIMES.

I'm an old mystery reader. It was a cinch.

HOW?

I enjoyed it. First, let me tell you that my hotel had three public entrances, plus one through the kitchen and one through the laundry. That happenstance took care of a couple. The men's room at the Sand House opens into both the bar and the dining room. I set up a ritual during the ten days of going into the bar and having exactly one drink, then going into the men's room, then coming out into the bar again and walking to wherever I would have dinner. The important night, I just walked through.

CHILDISH, REALLY, IF YOU'D HAD A PROFESSIONAL TAIL.

Yeah. I had other plans, if needed.

EXACTLY WHAT PART IN ALL THIS DID LOUIS ESTIMET PLAY? I KNOW FOR A FACT YOU SPENT AN EVENING WITH HIM ABOUT THREE WEEKS BEFORE YOU DISAPPEARED. DID YOU TELL HIM YOUR PLANS AND ASK HIS AID?

Of course. I told everyone in Saigon my plans and asked their aid. Including your Press Office.

WAS ESTIMET THE ONE WHO IN FACT PUT THE OPERATION INTO EFFECT? WAS HE NOT YOUR ACTUAL UNDERCOVER MAN IN THIS ENTIRE EXERCISE?

No. To both.

HOW DO YOU KNOW?

How would he make a buck out of it? He's in a different business.

TELL ME WHAT HAPPENED THAT NIGHT. HOW DID YOU MEET HIM?

There was a note when I got back from the Press Office.

WHAT DID IT SAY?

Would I have dinner.

AND YOU DID?

I did.

HOW DID HE KNOW YOU WERE THERE?

Everyone in Saigon knows when anyone is there. Also, my presence normally conveys a little scuttlebutt, Maje.

WHERE DID YOU MEET HIM THEN? . . . CAN'T YOU SIMPLY DESCRIBE WHAT HAPPENED WITHOUT MY HAVING TO PRY YOU OPEN FOR EACH SENTENCE?

You're paid to pry . . . I met him in the lobby around eight. He was dressed like a successful rock singer. We went immediately to a restaurant called the Lotus where he had reserved a table in one of those private dining areas. It was in a window alcove with blinds all around. It was a good idea too, because the place was jammed with compatriots and they get a little noisy. The air conditioning worked, the food was good, the wine was superb, and Louis was his usual effervescent self. Next question.

WHAT DID YOU TALK ABOUT? DID HE TELL YOU WHY HE WAS THERE?

You've started to double up on your questions, have you noticed that? Naturally, I asked him. He said that Saigon had become the world center for informal trading and that many fortunes were being made. He wanted me to come to a party he was going to throw when he made his, which would be in about two months' time. In short, he hadn't changed.

WHAT DID HE PROPOSE TO TRADE?

His usual, I guess. Money for merchandise for more money.

WHAT KIND OF MERCHANDISE?

How the hell should I know? Whatever was around at the proper price, I expect. As in Cuba. Hand grenades, helicopters, brocaded silk, Napoleon brandy. It's not the merchandise, it's the market that motivates Louis.

DID YOUR FRIEND CHIAPA JOIN YOU THAT EVENING?

Negative. You mentioned he was in Saigon, but I still don't know it.

HASN'T IT STRUCK YOU AS INTERESTING THE EXTRAORDINARY AFFINITY OF THE BUSINESS PROCLIVITIES OF CHIAPA AND ESTIMET?

Why would it? I don't fall over in a dead faint when I meet two shoeshine boys in a row. Or two majors. At any rate, everyone in Saigon is in buying and selling, one way or another. Including majors.

HOW DID ESTIMET REACT TO YOUR PROPOSAL TO GO OVER WITH THE VC?

He thought it was charming.

WHAT PRECISELY DOES THAT MEAN?

"What a brilliant idea, Peter! You do have such thrust! I have always envied your directness." That sort of noncomment. Inside, Louis isn't really interested in anyone else.

DID HE MENTION ANY OF HIS BUSINESS ASSOCIATES IN VIETNAM?

Are you mad? Louis never gives anybody anything, and that includes information. He did buy the dinner, I might add. He isn't stingy in that sense.

WHAT HAPPENED AFTER DINNER?

We talked some more, and then two Eurasian girls came in. He had arranged it, I suppose. They were hookers. I'd seen them around. With Esterhazy on your mind you don't need that kind of anesthesia, but we did take them dancing in one of those little places that seem to grow up overnight like mushrooms. The music was so loud you couldn't even hear the beat. So we went back to the hotel for a nightcap, the four of us, and I finally said good night to everybody. I remember, my date smiled finally, as I was leaving. She was tall and willowy and quite good-looking, but when she smiled she was missing a top incisor. Do you know about things like that, Doc? Do you know how virtuous that can make you feel?

WHO IS ESTERHAZY?

A lady I know.

WE'LL MEET HERE AFTER LUNCH. IS TWO HOURS ENOUGH? I GATHER YOU DON'T APPRECIATE OUR CAFETERIA.

I don't, and I'd just as soon stay hungry and keep going so I can finish in one session and get back to the shocking exposé I'm writing about your shoddy practices.

EXCELLENT. WE'LL CONTINUE THEN . . . YOU KNOW, IN PLAYING BACK THE TAPES LAST NIGHT I WAS SLIGHTLY

AMAZED AT THE LACK OF CREDIBILITY IN MANY OF YOUR STATEMENTS TO DATE.

You're probably right. Nowhere is the credibility gap greater than in this room at this moment.

ON THE OTHER HAND YOU HAVE OPENED UP AREAS OF INTEREST I HADN'T EVEN BEEN LOOKING FOR.

Such as?

YOUR POLITICAL STANCE. YOU SEE, YOU WEREN'T INVITED HERE FOR AN INVESTIGATION OF YOUR POLITICAL COLORATION.

That's the first hard news of the day. Then why?

FOR OTHER COGENT REASONS.

Which shall remain nameless, no doubt. Also, I assume my political coloration is hardly government business.

DEPENDS ON WHAT YOU DO ABOUT IT, FOR THAT MATTER.

Demonstrations make my feet sore, if that's what you're worrying about.

OH, IT'S NOT CHARGEABLE, I'M AFRAID. BUT YOUR GENERAL ATTITUDE OF DENIGRATION ABOUT OUR NATIONAL GOALS WOULD RAISE QUESTIONS IN MY MIND, I'M AFRAID, IF I WERE RUNNING AN INTERNATIONAL NEWS BUREAU.

I don't think that's your bag, Doc.

NO, BUT YOU'VE BEEN WORRIED ABOUT MR. SCHAEFER. HAVE YOU CONSIDERED THE POSSIBILITY THAT YOUR ATTI-

TUDE MAY HAVE DISILLUSIONED HIM ABOUT YOU TOO?

He's disliked my attitude for years without doing anything about it. He also dislikes yours. Do you know one thing he asked me to look into in Vietnam? You'll be surprised. It's about teachers. Civilian teachers. A few of them have written books. It gives one pause, Doc. How many volunteer American teachers and agriculturists have your bloody military thrown out of occupied villages? You see, you guys react—you don't act. If the VC or Hanoi teach grammar or planting to five-year-olds, then you don't. You automatically assume it's a Communist trait. But it's great to teach five-year-olds!

DEPENDS WHAT YOU TEACH THEM, I EXPECT.

Okay, teach them your way. But why throw out the teachers? Why make it a confrontation between academics and military?

PERHAPS THEY WERE TEACHING BADLY. THERE HAVE TO BE CONTROLS IN THESE SITUATIONS, YOU UNDERSTAND.

Talk about controls to Vince Schaefer, if you like, but don't try to frighten me that he's worried about my disrespectful attitude. His attitude makes mine look like David Eisenhower's.

I WAS SPEAKING ABOUT THE LACK OF CREDIBILITY IN SOME OF YOUR STATEMENTS.

So you were.

YOU SAID, I BELIEVE, THAT YOU HAD NEVER SEEN LOUIS ESTIMET IN THIS

COUNTRY EXCEPT FOR THE GRATUI-
TOUS INFORMATION YOU GAVE ABOUT
A WEEK IN MIAMI. IS THAT CORRECT?

Yes.

PERHAPS YOU'D BETTER REFRESH YOUR
MEMORY.

Scratch it.

CHICAGO. 1967. THE PALMER HOUSE.

My life is a series of hotels. But you're right.
Write down that I almost got away with it. Would
you like to know all the nefarious details?

AN INDICATION, AT LEAST. I KNOW
MOST OF THEM. WHAT WERE YOU DO-
ING THERE?

Stopping over from the coast at bureau request
to look at some opening of space-age products at
the Merchandise Mart.

WHERE DID YOU MEET ESTIMET?

In an exhibition room.

WAS HE CORDIAL?

He's always cordial. He introduced me to a
couple of men he was with. He was madly excited about the idea of the Merchandise Mart.
He'd never seen it before.

WHAT WAS HE SHOPPING FOR?

Missiles. He wanted to buy an Apollo missile.

YOU MERELY WASTE TIME WITH THIS
TYPE OF REMARK, YOU KNOW.

It's the only type of remark I can think of.

HE GAVE NO INDICATION TO YOU OF
HIS PARTICULAR INTEREST IN A PROD-
UCT?

None whatsoever.

DID HE SEE YOU ALONE AFTER THAT?

Yes.

DESCRIBE IT.

We had lunch alone at that terrible restaurant downstairs. We talked about stealing space equipment. He had steak and I had chicken with goop on it. We decided Sargent Shriver was on an ulcer diet. We made plans to play tennis the next morning with the two men I had met. They belonged to a club in Winnetka. It was okay with me. I'm not that wild for space-age products. Before we left in the morning, I had to go to the Palmer House arcade and buy a complete outfit including tennis shoes. I borrowed a racket from the host, whose name was something like Milligan. His company made some kind of plastic excretory device for astronauts. A thing to pee in, in other words. If you ever need one you'll know where to go. He was very proud of it. Maybe that's what Louis was planning to smuggle behind the Curtain. God knows they could probably use something like that over there. Milligan and I beat Louis and the other guy two sets to one, mainly because of my tiger-quick reactions at the net. Then we had lunch at the clubhouse. Mine was corned beef. I remember I had beer with it, because I don't like beer. I can't remember what Louis had, but if you really want to know I suppose I could check with Milligan. The other man had something to do with money and didn't say much. He also played tennis with absolutely no trace of a backhand. You can never tell about these bankers. A car took Louis and me back to

the Palmer House that afternoon. He was bubbling with cheer and asked me to have dinner with him that night, but I went to O'Hare Airport instead. You see, I wanted to get this plastic pee-bag back to Vince Schaefer before something burst. You see . . .
YOU MAY LEAVE.

TO: A. J. Katin.
FROM: B. Pike

FORMAL REPORT TO FOLLOW

Increasingly disagreeable, as you will hear. But it is coming together. Will consult legal department over weekend. Permitted D. to go to New York.

B.P.

The high fluty monotone said in French: "We all assemble at eleven o'clock at this identical location. It is in your own interest to be unobserved."
I said: "My care shall be as extreme as the urgency of my assignment."
Eyelids closed over narrow eyes as a benediction.
It was raining later. By flashlight the mud underfoot erupted in tiny geysers. I left my cab half a mile away and did all the devious things I had learned from Saul Panzer. Sudden reflections in rain puddles of dark hooded figures waiting under the terrace. The small dark car was a shape to match them. Maybe a Renault. Doors slammed in-

conclusively and headlights flickered yellow. Incipient generator problems like the Model A parked in front of the Muskegon High School spring dance eons before Buddhists and VC penetrated minds like mine. The gears made a ratchet sound. Nothing to see but puddling mud in front, occasional yellow lights to each side. Once, a flaring white light. We went north out of the city, then west. The barrel of a handgun glowed dully across the front seat, pointing roughly at my clavicle. Windshield wipers wapped back and forth ineffectively. From the back seat the driver and guard looked neckless in their hoods and I wanted to vomit from fear and disorientation.

The gun barrel disappeared before city lights faded. Darkness was heavy but palatable, like a dinner at Luchow's. I slept for a while. Low voices awakened me from in front. Electronic music with overtones of clack-clack. We were turning left; south or southwest. There was no place to go southward but the river. From the map I had studied earlier I decided we were giving Tan Son Nhut a wide miss and heading for the Mekong.

The skinny little monk on my left in the back seat was just a tiny black shape lost in dreams of elsewhere. I asked in French: "May I light a cigarette?" Silence. Then from the front seat: *"C'est permis."* Tête-à-tête voices continued. I had a certain conviction they were speaking of me.

I said to the little black shape beside me: *"Si j'avais su que vous veniez, j'aurais fait un gâteau."*

The shape stirred and leaned its head comfortingly on my left shoulder.

We went through potholes and finally into a crater. The little monk woke up and we all got out and pushed. Beside the others I felt like a giant. I started to giggle as I set my feet uselessly in the mud and my shoulder against the spare tire. Who are you, big thing called Danziger? What are you doing here? There was a sound of spasmodic artillery far off to the right. The guard from the front seat pulled his hood down to push. Full head of hair. No monk he. I could not stop laughing. They looked at each other and we pushed some more and the car moved out. They smiled at me as though I were an idiot or a child, and we climbed back inside, brothers under the mud. Smiling, the little monk's face reminded me of an Irish bartender I knew once in a pub in Marylebone. It became a pleasant journey.

Later, the highway picked up. Bulldozers had been working. The top was crowned. It looked like an American road to me, a heavy equipment road. I began looking through the wet windshield hoping not to see any heavy equipment. Then after five or six miles the road resigned.

When the shooting began we stopped abruptly and left the car and dived into the bush. Dawn was breaking. The rain had turned into drizzle. I still felt half-asleep. The mud was cold as it penetrated to knees, elbows and belly, but the air was already beginning to heat up. My escort made no answering fire. After a moment, a voice chattered a hundred yards away and my three escorts stood up, chattering back. I waited, then rose. I could see no one but us. I followed the black shapes across the road to the headlights again. The front-seat guard peeled off his robe to show a faded semi-uniform. He smiled at me over his shoulder as if embarrassed at being discovered, but too hot to care. A tiny mustached VC lieutenant was waiting with a burp gun beside the far door of the Renault, smoking. Much chatter which I could not understand. They kept looking at me. Finally the VC smiled and nodded at me. I nodded back, wondering why everybody was so goddamn jolly. He gestured for me to get into the car. As I did, he got into the front seat and the fake Buddhist crawled behind the wheel. The monks simply disappeared: one moment bowing good-bye, the next moment a few leaves rustling. I lit a cigarette and said in a Colonel Blimp tone: "Move out!" and we did. They were both laughing at me. I had never been so funny before, or so unsure of myself. My bladder was emitting little screams of pain.

I stared out the window. It might have been the boondocks of southern Florida thirty years ago except for the lack of scrub pine and the exotic blossoms which somehow looked like the insides of chickens. We went through a few empty paddy villages. I figured we were more than halfway between Tan Son Nhut and the river, heading southwest. Once, looking back, I saw people coming out of huts after we passed. We were on a two-track trail now. Now and then we skidded by armed troops, mostly barefoot, ambling aimlessly along the trailside in twos and threes.

Usually they waved. They all looked about twelve years old. One of them jumped out in front of the car as we approached and did a kind of crazy jig, jumping out of the way just in time. His two companions were helpless with laughter. It was not a Karl Marx kind of thing. The lieutenant appeared not to notice. He talked and smoked almost incessantly; his cigarettes smelt disagreeably rank. I wondered if it was pot. I opened the window. After a while the rain stopped and everything began to steam, including me. I stripped down to my T-shirt. From the front seat the lieutenant pointed at it and said something in Vietnamese. I nodded, wondering to what I was committing it or myself. My stomach was complaining a bit so I pulled out a candy ration and handed it around. The lieutenant chewed in tiny bites with his front teeth, frowning curiously at the chocolate before each new nibble. He nodded his head at it from time to time.

There was a sudden series of heavy explosions ahead of us and to the right. Whomp. Whomp. Pause. Whomp. The kind of whomp that vibrates the brain inside its casing. The driver slowed instantly and looked at the lieutenant, who made a fluttery little gesture with his fingers. The car stopped and we got out. Now I could hear the jets. It sounded like five or six. Then one came into sight between the trees, high, glinting as it disappeared into stratus. A 52. There were a few more whomps and four more 52's appeared, racked up and wheeling into a cloud. A little flak

followed in trail, well below and behind. I used
the occasion to pee.

About ten minutes later we got in the car and
continued. The lieutenant looked worried; the
fun and games were over. I hoped the 52's hadn't
changed the arrangement. If I had been the lieutenant I might have told Danziger-san to go screw
and take unpleasant messages back to his compatriots. I could see a pillar of black smoke
through the front windshield. I considered offering the lieutenant my T-shirt.

Suddenly he began to chatter excitedly. We
abruptly accelerated, veered off the trail through
a ditch and into leafy bush. The two in the front
seat instantly disappeared, leaving their doors
hanging open. I tightened up, slid to the floor,
grabbed my jacket, opened the right-hand door
and crawled out on my hands and knees. The
vines enveloped me almost immediately. I
crawled thirty or forty feet and stopped. I was
sweating hard. I wondered what had queered
them. I wondered where they were. I wondered
what I was doing there. A bug slowly orbited my
eyelid. I moved to brush it off, and stopped.
Heavy feet were crunching toward the car. It was
like the bad part of a dream just before you wake
up. I stopped breathing for two hours and twenty
minutes. Voices came from the far side of the
car. First: "The little bastards disappeared." Second: "Shall we look?" First: "They'll be halfway
up the river by now." Second: "Or maybe they
got a bead on us." First: "Let's get the fuck out
of here." Second: "Zap the car first." Silence; then

the footsteps bolted away noisily. I held my ears and sank my face in the swampy growth, waiting for the car to blow, but it didn't. As so many times before, my identity seemed scrambled. I wanted the good guys to get away safely so the other good guys could come back safely and take me to their leader. My whole life I've had trouble choosing sides. Sometimes I wasn't even on Danziger's side. A psychology professor at Michigan told me once I was unable to make commitments. A journalism professor told me the same week I had an open mind. Balance them out and you hold a pair of treys.

The footsteps were gone now, but snatches of voices trailed. Bad jungle warfare. Must tell someone, I thought. I wondered if the lieutenant would use his burp gun, and what I would do if he did. God, how confusing nationality is! I began to count slowly from one to sixty. After the fourth cycle I heard movements in front of me. I raised my head slowly. The lieutenant was standing, lighting a cigarette. I stood up. He glanced at me, then concentrated on his match. Finally he beckoned me to follow him. I did not see the guard at all. I never saw him again. I was afraid to go back and get my gear from the car. We started off through the soggy bush on foot. The vines were like honeysuckle. He kept turning and motioning me to be silent, but it was difficult with fifty feet of honeysuckle in tow. Besides, his head cleared the overhang and mine didn't. I remembered going rabbit hunting with my father and an old hound named Diane in

Pentagon. No American belonged in his country—a country of underprivileged people, not of American-backed puppets in Saigon. One day they would welcome us back as benevolent tourists, perhaps . . . Had I noticed the bodies outside? The machinery and the men who created those bodies were products of my country. For all he knew, I too was a puppet of his enemies, trying to ferret out information about the security of his sector. I should know that to the last men the Liberation Front would throw out all renegades of any nationality. The war was going well beyond belief, because Western training was not adaptable to Liberation tactics.

I lit a cigarette. To my surprise, the colonel and Nuy each accepted one too. I lit them all with the Zippo.

If I, perchance, turned out to be beyond confidence, it was unfortunate that I would have to perish in some abrupt manner. If not, as his superiors suggested—men in very high places—if I were indeed searching to report both sides of the question, the hoped-for peace, and the futility of injustice, then we were on the same side, men of goodwill, and the hospitality of the sector was mine.

In the meanwhile, because he was a hardened military man who took no chances, I should acquaint myself intimately with Captain Nuy, who would be my constant companion and escort so long as I remained in Liberation territory. He would also be entrusted to return me safely to Saigon, from which rodent nest I might report my

Michigan and Father's muttering, "Bumblefoot!" I thought maybe they should have defoliated after all. I thought of Vince Schaefer's round impassive face having lunch at Costello's. I thought of Esterhazy's round impudent breasts. I wondered if I would be shot. I wondered why everything always went haywire. Murphy's law. We walked for a couple of hours.

The camp was a shambles, still smoking. There were eleven small bodies laid out in a line in front of one hut: four uniformed, seven in paddy clothes. I could not tell the sexes. The burp gun was behind my back now, nudging. I kept walking. The smoke was from the remains of a long low shed across the square. Mobs were still running around it. It stank of diesel. The smoke was still pillaring up about a thousand feet to where it shredded and swirled off in the wind. I felt a lot of eyes burning at me as we crossed the square to a Soviet command car that seemed to be temporary HQ. Someone was talking into elaborate radio gear; others clustered around. There was a spiky cluster of mobile antiaircraft dug into the brow of a hill beyond. Beyond that, the woods were smoking. The burp gun was still in my back; I figured we were making a brave entry for the troops. A young man detached himself from the group and moved toward me. He wore dark-rimmed glasses and a muddy denim jacket open over his thin chest. He was tall for a Vietnamese. When he spoke I could see one gold incisor.

He said in Oxford English: "You arrive too late for the picnic, Mr. Danziger."

I couldn't think of a sensible answer.

He smiled vacantly and said: "My name is Nuy. Come with me, please."

I followed him past the command car. The cluster of troops instinctively moved away from me as I passed. I remembered reading that to Oriental nostrils we meat-eating Westerners smell to high heaven. Maybe their deal made me smell even worse. I looked over my shoulder at the lieutenant once, but he pretended he had never seen me before and joined the group by the radio. We stopped by a thatched hut, relatively untouched.

Nuy said: "Come in, please."

We stepped up into a large plain room with a slatted floor, a planked table and two benches. There was an ornate black-and-gold high-backed chair at the end of the table. The table was burdened with transmitting equipment, Japanese. There was a pile of colorful charts alongside which looked as though they had been drawn by a child—but that kind of judgment is a mistake we always make. The floor was covered with unrolled bamboo which crunched when you stepped on it.

A short muscular man had his back to us, talking musically to a pretty young woman in white. When she left through the back I saw that she was astonishingly beautiful and terribly young, like so many Vietnamese women before the sudden moment when everything comes apart. The man turned to us. He wore baggy khaki trousers and a faded-blue tunic, like Nuy's, with insignia. He looked like a small Oriental version of Erich

Von Stroheim, without the menace. Whe spoke to us his voice was still musical, resonant tenor. It was short, but apparently an order.

Nuy said: "Colonel Nimh would like empty your pockets please."

I did so methodically, onto the table. Ke Sinus inhalant. Lighter. Cigarettes. Handk Pen. Address book. Bills in various cur Passport. Wallet. Card case. Nail clipper. Nuy pawed through the pile and looked questioningly.

I said: "The rest was abandoned with the

He nodded and studied the inhalant, un the end, sniffed, put it back. He glanced card case, studied the picture of Esterha tured for me to return the gear to my pocket

The colonel began to speak in Viet then switched to strongly accented Frencl alized he had no English. I said to Nuy: "I colonel I speak no Vietnamese, and I lear French under bad auspices."

Nuy said: "I will translate. Kindly be seate

I lowered myself to a bench. The colo mained standing. It was stifling under the I had a sudden fear of falling asleep. The began to talk in musical bursts; squinting with friendly intensity at the end of each and quieting Nuy with one hand as he w and on.

It was certainly not his idea to have an alien in his security area. I had no more there than he would have in the councils

learning to a world which was filled with too many lies from the other side. If, on the other hand, by misadventure I displaced Captain Nuy, or he me, it would be assumed that the displacement was deliberate on my part. I should remember, should that happen, that Liberation justice was as straight and as swift as a bullet.

He smiled at me after finishing.

I said: "I understand and appreciate the colonel's comments, and I will make it my prime objective to remain as close to Captain Nuy as though he were my new bride."

The colonel nodded politely and left. I hoped it was after the pretty girl in white. He looked like a sad man. He looked a little like a Marine colonel I had met three weeks before up in Da Nang. Jesus, hadn't I been meeting a lot of sad men. I thought of the bodies outside and the bodies two weeks before outside the cement apartment building in Saigon and the bodies in the infirmary at the 388th Bomb Group in Knettishall, England, in 1944, and I realized I was a sad uncomprehending man myself.

I said to Nuy: "Onward and upward."

We stepped out into the sunlit square.

I said: "He is a Hanoi man."

Nuy smiled and rubbed the back of his neck.

"Why do you assume?"

"He seems rather disciplined."

"You think we are children down here?"

"I know you're not."

He smiled meaninglessly again.

We crossed to the Soviet Command car, deserted now. The fire at the head of the square had diminished, but people were still standing around. Someone had removed the bodies.

Nuy said: "I am from Saigon. The university." He looked at the last remnants of the smoke webbing in the wind.

"Where did you learn English?"

"Where you learned French, in Paris, but under better auspices."

I laughed while he was adjusting his glasses again, and decided he was of value.

We ate in a clearing in back of what was apparently a mess hut. Bowls of rice and meat in a highly seasoned sauce with slices of melon.

I loaded up. Nuy said: "One of our tactical advantages may be that we do not have to provide field rations for men of your appetite."

"I am in reality sent over to consume your rations and frighten you out of the war in disbelief."

"Are you considered to have a large stature in the United States?"

"You mean physically?"

He nodded.

"Bigger than average, but there are men who play basketball who make me look like a baby."

He said: "I know about basketball. Are you a supporter of Marshal Ky?"

"No."

He thought and I ate for a while in silence. The other men eating were watching us, but when I looked up they glanced away.

He said: "Ky is ambitious for himself."

"In my country, every politician is ambitious for himself."

"That must be very demeaning."

I said: "It's hard to explain, but occasionally it works out fairly well."

"Was it in fact the ruling cadre that had your young President shot?"

"I don't think so. The President himself is almost always the head of the ruling cadre."

He said: "Then it was senseless for someone to kill him without a power rationale."

"There were people who did not like him."

"Then why did they elect him?"

I said: "They liked the other man less."

"I would like to speak to you again of this." He looked at his wristwatch and said: "We will remain in this village until almost darkness. Then at a certain time I will come and we will proceed to the river. Would you like to rest a few hours?"

"Yes. Could I get some writing paper?"

He said: "I will obtain paper and implements."

We went to a hut near Colonel Nimh's cottage.

"Would you mind if I worked outside in the air?"

He smiled and adjusted his glasses on the bridge of his nose and made a slight gesture at the ground: "There is little area for you to disappear." Then he walked down the line toward the colonel's cottage to tell him how much I ate, I suppose.

After he had brought paper I settled down to write my notes, but I didn't really feel like it and everything that had happened was burned into my memory as usual, so I wrote a letter to Esterhazy instead. Maybe I was putting out rescue lines.

I remember thinking it was a little mawkish, but folded it into my pocket anyway. It is so easy to run your own variations on: "Little did I dream while sitting in the midst of the VC in a burning village that your image would float up before my eyes."

I ran three or four variations on the theme before I quit: There is such a terrible difference between telling someone you do love that you love her, and someone you do not. A literary friend of mine told me once that the pathos in the very best writing is due in part to its inarticulateness, the things it tries to communicate but cannot. In this light I had just written a helluva letter.

The sun was unbearable so after a while I went inside the hut and kicked off my shoes and sprawled on a mattress tick full of dry leaves which had a certain fragrance.

I dreamt about my father and a ballet dancer and an air-raid shelter.

Nuy woke me up. Gently. It was early twilight.

We drank sweet tea across the compound, sucking the dregs from our cups, then followed a small elderly man in ragged shirt and trousers up a trail leading off behind the diesel shed. It was still smoldering.

Nuy was wearing a bandolier and carrying a carbine with a long clip. He walked in a gangling loping fashion, adjusting his eyeglasses on his nose every few steps. He smiled vacuously when our eyes met, and his gold tooth picked up the setting sun, but I knew I was under loving care. I wondered if he knew how much trouble I'd expended to get there.

I had tentatively girded myself for another stumbling jungle trek, but the trail this time was broad and well marked. From time to time before dark we heard jet engines overhead and once a racketing chopper, but the old man never slowed his pace.

We rested after an hour. I offered Nuy a cigarette.

He smiled his diffident smile: "Someone on your side told me they disease the lungs."

"It is probably true. At the moment, I am concerned with other things. How do you meet others on my side?"

He had a way of turning off his attention so that remarks would simply drift over his head unheard, and this he did now. He reminded me of a Columbia professor I played bridge with in New York who mentally disappeared into quantum from time to time, usually when I was working toward slam.

I said: "Why don't you perspire?"

His attention came back. He looked at me, then down at his chest: "I do not perspire as easily as you, apparently."

It was growing dark. The old man got up and went on his way without looking back. We rose and followed.

Nuy said: "We are almost at the river."

We weren't almost to the river at all. About forty-five minutes later we entered a knee-depth swamp transected by deeper gullies.

I imagined myself carrying the portable and handbag I had left in the Renault.

Then we fetched up on a shelf and waded through pond lilies and reeds to a kind of island. An there, on the other side, was the river. Broad and flat and smelly as the Mississippi. I sensed fish dying on the flats. There was some boat traffic on the far side, tiny yellow lights moving mostly downriver. Distant sounds of small engines chugging. Bird cries. A warm breeze touched my face. I felt as I had as a kid when the *Père Marquette* wailed through western Michigan in the night on its way to someplace unimaginable. I always thought Cab Calloway was in the Pullman.

Nuy said: "Quietly now, Mr. Danziger, we will board in a few moments."

I waited in silence for a river junk or cargo barge, but when a boat without lights burbled quietly up to the two-plank dock on the end of the islet it was a dark-painted lapstrake skiff—about twenty-two feet—like a Morgan or Ulrichsen that you could see speeding across Great South Bay any Sunday toward the flounder grounds.

Our little guide disappeared into the reeds, and Nuy and I boarded. Almost instantly the shadowy skipper throttled up and turned into deep water upriver. The engines settled at about 1,500, branches disappeared overhead, and then wind came up in our faces and we were in mid-river.

I said: "I thought the river was patrolled?"

"Very badly. Would you mind seating yourself so your head cannot show?"

I sprawled down in the stern and cradled my head on my hands and looked at the sky while Nuy went forward to consult with the helmsman. Everything seemed unreal.

After a while Nuy came back and squatted beside me: "Are you familiar with the films of Catherine Deneuve?"

"Is she the blonde?"

"Very blonde."

I said: "I have seen her twice, I think."

"I have seen her twice also, but nothing recently."

"I saw her a few months ago in a film in which she was a loving housewife in the morning and worked enthusiastically in a bordello in the afternoon."

Nuy said: "I imagine she would do that well."

"Very well indeed."

"Is it true that you are an important person in journalism?"

"Yes."

"And you think to find a different brand of truth now?"

I said: "I hope so."

He sat back and adjusted his head on something. Finally he said: "Everything becomes strange ultimately."

I didn't know what he was referring to so I shut up and tried to revive my fading memories of first- and second-magnitude stars in the same sky but a different hemisphere and for that matter, a different world. I wondered if I was the same Danziger.

A while later a searchlight swept over us, lighting the shelter top. Nuy touched me in a kind of warning but I was not about to go anyplace. I heard a heavy engine alongside; then it picked up and accelerated past us as we rolled in the wake, and its beam flicked off.

I said: "She fell in love with a young criminal who had all gold teeth."

"I had this one installed in Paris by an expensive technician. It needed repair and I thought it would give some distinction."

I said: "I can't remember whether she got shot in the end or not."

"I would imagine she got shot by the husband."

"I guess I would have shot her too."

"She is very pretty."

About an hour later we throttled down and moved inshore toward the starboard bank. Nuy and I were leaning against the railing now.

I said: "We must have been close to the border."

"Now we are well upstream of the border."

There were people waiting. I thought they were waiting for us, but after we tied up the men boarded and went into the shelter cabin and began handing out bags. Nuy and I stepped onto a soggy bank. He said: "Now we are on tight discipline again, Mr. Danziger."

"Captain, you could not leave me if you tried."

The air was alive with swamp sounds. We walked east about three or four miles: Spongy at first, then leafy hard ground, and finally into heavily forested low hills. The bags had been placed in woven shoulder harnesses which creaked along behind us. There was no special attempt at security. Nuy talked freely about motion pictures he had liked in Paris: He had seen several American pictures and admired Paul Newman, Sidney Poitier and a girl I had never seen named Ann-Margret. Whenever I asked a question about the terrain or the river or the logistics he reverted to his semi-hypnotic security status. At that moment his mind was in Nuy country. I thought it was a helluva device.

After a while I was tired again. If I had had a son he would be about Nuy's age. I kept remembering a line from some book: "This deck don't fit my feet."

We came down finally into a dimly illuminated village. A dozen or so window apertures glowed yellow. I could hear a few generators throbbing as we descended. There must have been seventy or eighty trucks and carriers trailing back into bush.

Two sleepy men in uniform checked us in at the gate. They may have been Cambodian, stiffly formal in khaki uniforms with red epaulettes. At least they looked unlike anyone else I had seen.

Nuy was still in his silent period. We went through with no apparent problems. He took me to a compound in the center of the activity which had its own inner ring of VC guards. This might have meant that the VC or North Vietnamese did not trust the Cambodians, although using them, but that is the way my mind works when sleepy. I chalked it up, though.

Again we passed through and then stopped by a canvas-covered two-and-a-half-ton truck. Light showed through here and there.

Nuy spoke to someone through the tailgate slit. Then he said politely: "This way, Mr. Danziger."

He led me to a flat area away from the vehicles. It was dotted with sleeping figures.

He said: "Are you hungry?"

"I can eat."

He went away and came back with two bowls and two tin cups. Rice and fish and hot sweet tea. We sat on the ground and ate.

"This must be the lower end of what they call the Ho Chi Minh Trail."

He said: "I have been requested not to comment on political matters."

"Okay, what do you suppose this unpolitical fish is called?"

He said simply: "I would prefer not to know. Did you ever eat at an establishment in Boulevard Raspail called the Porte d'Or?"

"No, but I have passed it often."

"It is interesting to me how in conversation the world diminishes."

"My favorite restaurant in Paris is called De-Regny. It was only eight tables in a cellar and they charge you the war debt but the cooking is impeccable. A woman and her husband run it. He is a cripple who works magic in the kitchen and she is an administrator who should be employed by one of our governments."

"Is that on the Rue de L'Opéra?"

I said: "Just off it. It's been there since 1946 and it gets dowdier and better every year."

"It is extremely unsettling to sit here near the Mekong and converse with an enemy about things I remember."

"Nuy, you don't really know if I'm an enemy yet."

"I was extremely fond of Paris."

I said: "I am surprised that you were allowed to become fond of Paris."

"Before all this. I was in France when my father was killed. It was an interesting place to observe."

"Would you like to go back?"

"Not now. There are too many matters requiring my attention here."

I asked: "Where did you learn your English? It's very good."

"I went to a school for six months and afterward I studied with a tutor named Monsieur James for one year and a half."

"He was undoubtedly English. Your accent is excellent."

Nuy looked pleased: "The old gentleman had a certain intellectual style, although to my surprise he tried to seduce me on several occasions."

"That's an occupational hazard for expatriates

who fall back on teaching the mother tongue."

He said: "He was a nice man but extremely decadent."

There was a hut set aside for us, with cots. I fell asleep almost instantly.

The man who interviewed me in the morning might have been a retired professor wearing sailing clothes as a kind of lark. He had a scraggly white beard, deep laugh lines around his eyes and a tiny potbelly on a thin frame. He waited for me in a large airy hut with netting, a wooden floor and wicker furniture. There were books here and there and a lithograph of Ho on a cabinet at the back. There was a strong smell of spices.

Nuy went into his protective trance as we all shook hands. The professor said in strongly accented Berlitz English: "Welcome to the Liberation, Mr. Danziger. I hope to open your eyes. Will you be seated?"

I said: "How do you do, sir."

He said: "I am a senior political adviser to the Liberation, Mr. Danziger. I came here expressly to feed your quest. My name is Nguyen Than."

I said: "How do you do, sir."

We studied each other for a moment.

He said: "I understand from my superiors and your writing that your status is of a noncommitted seeker of facts?"

I thought for a moment. Nuy was regarding me closely. I said finally: "I am noncommitted about the wisdom of my country's presence. I am not sure I am noncommitted about what your people are doing or what my people are doing."

He laughed for his own reasons: "Excellent. So it is merely a question of exposing a valid viewpoint to a reasonable man."

I said: "I am not positive I would recognize a valid viewpoint if I sat on one. Which, sir, of the two opposing forces do you speak for?"

Nuy stirred. Nguyen Than looked puzzled: "Two opposing forces?"

I said: "Yes, sir. Hanoi or the NLF? As a journalist I like to identify the subtleties of my source."

Nuy interrupted: "Our objectives are identical, Danziger."

Impatiently, Nguyen Than waved him into silence: "This is an interesting schizophrenic approach. Do you suggest our objectives are divided?"

I said: "Of course. What was the bond between the Maquis and the French government in exile once the shooting stopped?"

"But the shooting has not stopped."

I said: "I am just so bored with mutual bullshit."

An old familiar voice behind me said: "If I may be allowed an epigram, Peter, everything about our cause—including its bullshit—is mutual."

I turned and smiled at the squat Chinese man in the sunlit doorway. I said: "Hello, Charley. You're getting fat."

Charley Hsi looked like a cherubic philosopher who had been boiled in linseed oil. We drank tea for an hour and talked about other times. Nguyen Than picked at his chin reflectively. Nuy went to the doorway and gazed out, his posture a little dejected. I thought his assignment was a little unsettling for him. Charley still rocked silently when he laughed. By unspoken agreement we limited the conversation to ancient memories and bridge games and jokes, each trying secretly to comprehend the happenstances of the years. He said: "Do you still keep the plaque we gave you?"

He cocked his head, trying to remember, then smiled: "To Peter F. Danziger. Noble, strong and subtle. The deuce of clubs."

I said: "It's all rusted. Jesus, you guys bought a cheap plaque. . . . I guess you knew I was going to be here, Charley."

"I was, you might say, instrumental. And instrumental, too"—he nodded—"in gaining the so valuable services of the eminent scholar Nguyen Than."

I assumed it was a signal to begin again. I said: "Is Kosygin sending a man, or is this the whole party now?"

Charley laughed, Nguyen Than looked pained and Nuy merely looked outranked.

Charley said: "Why do you think we went to extreme trouble, lasting many weeks, to arrange your visit, Peter?"

"I suppose the fact of my presence, itself, may be a plus of some sort."

Nguyen Than said: "Yes, we let you come and open all the doors."

"I presume I'm at the terminus of the so-called Ho Chi Minh Trail?"

Than said: "There is no such legendary trail in Cambodia. We bring down our transport as we must."

Charley said: "There is no security question about your knowing it. General Abrams, I am sure, knows it intimately through daily aerial photographs, so we expect it cannot hurt if you know it also."

"What if the Americans decided to bomb it out?"

Charley said: "And violate a neutral state?"

"You have already established that as a possible precedent."

Nguyen Than was smiling secretly: "Neutrality is a silly concept, Mr. Danziger. Your own Mr. Dulles announced that neutrality was immoral, and we are inclined to agree with him."

Charley said: "Unless, of course, the neutrality is on our side . . . But certainly you are aware that your people have bombed in Cambodia on many occasions?"

I said: "Then why not here?"

Charley said: "This is a Cambodian village. The subtleties, as you implied, are confusing. It is less embarrassing to drop by accident on a truck trail a mile inside the border."

I said: "Charley, you are still a dead pan with a questionable hand."

He said: "It has been difficult finding a foursome the last few years."

I said: "You'd clobber yourself out anyway. You never understood defense."

He laughed silently: "All that has changed drastically, Peter. Also, fortunately, I have remained on the offense."

Nuy interrupted: "When did you want me to have the car ready?"

Nguyen Than spoke rapidly in Vietnamese, and Nuy left. Then he turned to me: "I think Mr. Hsi is more cynical than I. The Cambodian government knows who will be its permanent neighbors. It is a natural decision."

Charley said dryly: "It is a natural decision because there is no alternative decision."

I said: "I trust this isn't entirely a lecture course, gentlemen. Why don't you show me the noble, strong and subtle transport troops at work?"

Nguyen Than said: "Perhaps you would enjoy a little lunch before we depart. Mr. Hsi informs me that you partake of spirits?"

We drove fifty or sixty miles up the trail in the afternoon in an open command car, mostly in low gear. Nuy was at the wheel with Nguyen Than beside him, Charley and I in back with equipment. The trail was all dirt, just wide enough for two vehicles, with corduroy in the soft spots. There were numerous plank bridges, several of which looked as though they might have been zapped and hastily repaired.

There was not too much coming down that day; mostly nondescript medium transport. A few of them carried troops, armed but not uniformed, which meant VC, I suppose. I saw nothing I hadn't been briefed about half a dozen times by Saigon press officers, with the single exception that the operation was simpler, smaller and more amateurish than the synchronized *Red Ball Express* which had been described. I did not discount the possibility that the amateur night might have been arranged for my benefit—but I was after a political story anyway.

I had always been particularly intrigued about the ultimate disparity in objectives between Hanoi and the VC, and I wondered again about mutual sensitivities.

When we passed a random pack of troops in black pajamas I said innocently: "Are these troops Liberation or Hanoi?"

Charley Hsi picked it up instantly: "The important thing for you to know is merely that they are dedicated Liberation troops, whatever their origin."

But Nguyen Than had started to interrupt and loused up his act: "Irregulars. We divide our functions between Liberation guerrillas and trained, supported Hanoi troops, you see. Both groups work in unison."

I grinned at Charley. He smiled back and shook his head.

I said: "I'll be goddamned, Charley. So you guys are backing the southerners."

"You were always wont to leap to conclusions, Peter." He looked out at the scrub inconclusively.

In late afternoon we stopped at what looked like a former plantation. A large manor house with a screen porch surrounded by outbuildings, with sleeping huts down the hill to the west. There was a beautiful little well-pagoda in the center of the square in front of the big house.

When we went into the big room behind the screened porch we were greeted by three Vietnamese who were obviously there for the purpose. Can't remember their names, but only one was formidable: a tiny grinning death's-head of a man in plain khaki. Nguyen Than addressed him deferentially as General Dinh. He was one of the few men I have ever met who could speak without moving his lips. Beyond an opening nod to me after Than's lengthy introduction in Vietnamese, his eyes avoided me scrupulously. The other two looked like officer's club hangers-on. I had the subtle impression that Charley Hsi was ill at ease. We were allowed to wash and relieve ourselves in baroque old bathrooms, and then we went back to the main room and filed in to a curry dinner which was quite bad.

The dinner conversation was conducted completely in Vietnamese, with the exception of Nguyen Than's occasional questions to me: "Would you care for additional rice, Mr. Danziger? General Dinh is giving me information which will be of considerable interest to you."

Wanting an interpreter, I suddenly realized that Nuy was not with us. Charley kept smiling and eating, eating and smiling. I got the impression he was pretending that he was not quite sure who I was or why I was there. I wasn't too sure myself.

I had a longing for old Nuy and a little conversation about Parisian restaurants.

It was an unrewarding meal for me, and the three North Vietnamese disappeared in sync with General Dinh's last bite. Nguyen Than disappeared after them, making fluttery motions of farewell at me. I had the tight little feeling that everything was getting loused up again.

Then Charley Hsi stood up and walked through the door into the kitchen, leaving me alone. Jesus, I thought. But the door swung open and he came back with a dirty grin on his face and a tray with a bottle of amber fluid and two glasses.

I followed him out onto the veranda, saying: "You are Mao's answer to Charley O., my good man."

"Let us quietly converse awhile," he said.

We sat and drank and talked as openly as two old friends could who had taken widely divergent paths for a generation. There were provinces neither of us could grasp, and we left them uninvaded. I knew that Charley believed quite sincerely that every journalist was in some subtle way an agent of his government, just as he was, openly, of his own. Charley had always been mentally an a priori man—as witness his meticulously planned bridge game—while I had always preferred to feel the wind, watch chips falling and start from there: cavalry into the breach, foot into the mouth.

I said finally: "What were they talking about at dinner?"

"They were discussing the various possibilities of your visit. From your point of view it is unfortunate you do not comprehend Vietnamese."

"Do you?"

"Oh, yes."

"They didn't trust you, though."

He laughed silently: "You dramatize again."

"You might have translated for me—or let Nuy along."

He sipped his Japanese scotch for a moment, thoughtfully. Then he said brightly: "Our paths have been rather different, Peter."

"And now here we are, trying to use each other."

"Am I using you? Or creating an opportunity?"

I said: "There's something you'd like my visit to reflect, certainly, and I used you, unknowingly, to get here for a story."

"Will it be a major story?"

"Yeah, Charley. If not, I'm wasting a lot of time."

"Will it reflect what you see?"

"It will reflect my opinion of what I see."

"Which is?"

"Which is the meaning of a bunch of incomplete impressions which haven't been developed and printed yet."

"So cautious. Let me clear up one point. I had nothing to do with the permission to allow you into Liberation territory. That was strictly the accomplishment of my superior and his contacts in the National Liberation."

"Oh? I thought you said otherwise."

"That was for the benefit of Nguyen Than."

"What is the name of your superior?"

"Tsen Wu Cheng of the Central Committee. His arena of responsibility is this corner of the world."

I said: "And you are—"

"His deputy in residence."

"You have always been so damn tricky, Charley. Why me?"

Charley thought for a while: "You were selected, I believe, because of certain writings which indicated your distrust of the Saigon opportunists as well as of your own country's objectives."

"He doesn't think that puts me on *his* side, does he, for God's sake?"

Charley laughed silently and held up his hand: "Quite the contrary, quite the contrary. I believe his phrase was: 'His mind has not completely hardened and perhaps his eyes are open.' "

"Does he know you know me?"

"Naturally. He knew it when I joined him in 1952."

"Jesus, I was practically still writing sports."

"And quite excellently."

I became a little angry: "You pour. I feel like an unpublished yearbook entry."

"Would you like more of this atrocious liquid?"

I said: "You bet your ass."

After I cooled down, I asked: "What are you all hoping I'll report?"

"What you see."

"Just that?"

"Whatever you see."

"Names and places?"

"Why not, Peter? Our people aren't jeopardized, and we cannot pick up and move facilities, which your people know about, at any rate."

"And you have no single objective?"

"Merely to show you that dedicated people work together also on this side of the conflict."

"Regulars and Liberation?"

"Regulars and Liberation."

"*Ciao*, Charley."

"*Ciao*, Peter."

We sat in silence for a while. The moon was scuttling across some low-flying clouds. I saw a small dark animal nosing busily in the moonlight across the square.

Charley said: "Do you hear from anyone in our class?"

"Not too many. I see Wong maybe once a year in New York. He's with a brokerage, lives in New Jersey. Ted Bieulieu is a friend, still. An engineer with some space company out in Westchester, and married to the most gorgeous female who ever breathed. I keep hoping she secretly hates him, but if she does she has a helluva camouflage. Ed Montrico works in London for J. Walter

Thompson and I probably see more of him than anyone else. It's hard to keep up when you flutter about like I do."

"Or I."

"We both have occupational hazards. I understand from Wong that most of the Chinese ended up in Taiwan. You probably know more about that than I do."

Charley drank deeply and looked at the moon and changed the subject: "Did you ever go back?"

"I stopped by once in the fifties after I covered a convention in Chicago."

"What was it like?"

"The football team was in early practice and a few graduate students were hanging around and there were new buildings all over the place and I met an aging girl I remembered in that bar downtown and I felt like the little doll from Shangri-La who suddenly turned into an old lady."

We were each silent. The moon was going to set. I wondered what I was doing with Charley Hsi on a moonlit veranda in Cambodia in the forty-fifth year of my life.

I said: "What ever happened to Philip Wu?"

"He died, Peter. About ten years ago. Consumption, I believe."

"Where?"

"Outside Peking. He was manager of an electrical supply plant. But he was always sickly, you remember."

I said: "Except for his bidding. Remember that six notrump doubled and redoubled?"

"You were attacking me, Peter."

"No. Wu was attacking you. I just held on and watched."

"How curious our memories are."

I said: "I could replay that hand this instant."

"I could also, my friend."

"But sometimes I can't remember what my father looked like."

"Our memories and our actions are linked or unlinked, I wonder?"

"I wonder too."

Charley squinted at me: "Are you married, Peter?"

"No. Soon though. After this trip."

"I congratulate you."

"I suppose you have the large family you were always talking about, Charley?"

"Yes."

"You used to say it was our only opportunity for immortality."

Charley laughed again: "I've discovered other opportunities. But it is comforting. Six boys and three girls."

"And all in the Red Guard, I'll bet."

He laughed again: "Youth follows its own lead."

"If you were in America with teen-agers, I'd feel sorry for you. I hope they're all properly reverent."

"Yes, I think so."

"We always thought you'd marry that Margie—what's her name?"

"A mutual passing fancy. Can you imagine her bearing nine children quietly?"

"Not even loudly. Charley, you know, you're a big fake. You're homesick for the University of Michigan."

He said: "That is a mistake you must never believe. Tomorrow we go to some Liberation villages across the border."

I said: "Nguyen Than told me we were going up the trail toward Laos."

He said: "You will find that our professorial friend is occasionally in error about tactical matters."

I stood up: "I can understand why these Hanoi people give you a pain in the ass."

Standing up with me, he almost collapsed again in silent laughter: "You are such a dear man, Peter. Why must you always telegraph your psyches?"

Nuy was waiting impatiently in my double room, pacing, wearing a black cotton miniskirt wrapped around his skinny waist. He turned as I walked in, his glasses and his gold tooth slashing in the yellow lantern light. I liked Nuy, and perhaps that is why I felt fleetingly like a disloyal comrade.

He said with intense irritation: "I was ordered to accompany you whatever your destination, but the general's orderly said I could retire at my convenience."

I said: "You didn't miss a thing. The conversation was in your language, between the general and the old fellow. There was hardly any meat in the curry."

He was still angry: "I have read about Prussians.

Many of these stiff-backed people are Prussian in mentality."

"Charley Hsi agrees with you. But they say you need these types to maintain the discipline."

Now he was furious: "We kill with imagination and we occupy terrain and we disappear again. What other discipline? Hanoi people did not create our discipline."

"Maybe they think you're a bunch of wild dilettantes, Nuy. After all, they beat the French in open battle. Maybe they think about you people as the German General Staff thought about the Hitler *Jugend,* handy to throw into the breach, but not of the real essence."

Nuy looked at me suspiciously: "Perhaps you encourage this thought for your own purposes."

"How would you know? The fact is: It hit me in the face. Even my old friend Charley Hsi cannot paint it over."

"What does that mean: paint it over?"

"If there is a flaw on your wall, you paint it over and it disappears."

Nuy sat down on his cot: "You should know, Danziger, that I look for the cunning motives behind your conversation. I am required to report them."

I took off my shirt: "Okay, Nuy. All of our assignments here seem to take us in opposite directions. My office works the same way. This is like old home week."

"And you truly do not support the Saigon regime?"

"God, no. I support myself, and would be happy to support Catherine Deneuve."

He almost laughed. Then he took off his glasses —which left his face looking like a child's—and said: "Good night, Danziger."

The next morning we were pinned down by mortar fire before we reached the village I was supposed to observe. Instead I observed that their side was as confused and indecisive under duress as anyone's side. I was frightened and indecisive myself. We dug in and hung on: Nuy, two VC's and myself. From the sounds, I guessed the village—a half mile or so ahead of us—was shot up but answering back with enthusiasm. Nuy kept cleaning his glasses and shaking his head at me sadly. I wondered if Charley Hsi had begged off because he knew the village would be zapped. Then I wondered if *I* was supposed to be zapped. I was soaking wet from perspiration and swamp water and kept sucking tea from the canteen someone had handed me.

We dragged back to the plantation house in midafternoon. By foot and staff car I estimated we had traveled no more than twenty miles in each direction, although it had seemed longer. There had been no way to recognize the border.

Charley was expansive, which Nuy and I rather resented.

He said: "For your information that ammunition came from Bridgeport, Connecticut."

I said: "The return fire was from Sinkiang. Am I supposed to be surprised that this is a shooting war?"

"You're tired and hungry. Come, we will eat and I will arrange something more informative for tomorrow."

Changing our clothes in the room, I asked Nuy: "Why did we not enter the village after the assault was repulsed?"

"We would have been shot."

"By whom?"

"By whoever remained."

Nuy was immediately dismissed from our presence at lunch, which apparently was the new tactic. Our eyes met as he left the foyer. He made a small gesture with his mouth. I responded in kind to show my sympathy.

I spent an hour and a half with Nguyen Than in a large dusty room which smelt of mold and still had a billiard table in the middle with its felt obscenely ripped. He was a nice old gentleman, more concerned with how he made his point than why. He had studied for some years at the Sorbonne. Mostly he told me about Hanoi's political program in the villages: reading and language programs which began with five-year-olds; cottage industries; regional medical officers who made weekly treks for inoculations and treatment. I deduced after a while that Nguyen Than was the instigator of the program. I took a lot of notes, which seemed to please him. It sounded like a helluva program to me. I wondered if it worked.

I said: "I knew something like this was happening in the North. Are the villages south of the DMZ receiving the same care?"

"When circumstances permit, the Liberation activates the same philosophy."

"That is important news. Perhaps I'll be able to observe this admirable program in action tomorrow."

"Perhaps."

We went on the veranda for tea and lemon cookies. The sun was slanting in and large irridescent insects circled our teacups.

I asked: "Who is the eminent general we dined with last evening?"

"General Dinh is one of the gifted strategists who are so successfully confounding our enemies with quickness and unexpected tactics. His specialty is transport and supply."

"What are his antecedents?"

"As a captain he made the decisive final tactical move at Dienbienphu. He is elevated in our planning now. An amusing note: He was General Big Minh's student commandant as a youth."

Charley Hsi joined us. In Nguyen Than's presence he always seemed a little obsequious: "Well, Peter, have you been learning anything?"

I said: "Most instructive."

"I have arranged a visit to a secured village tomorrow. I will accompany you myself."

"That's like handing me a life insurance policy, Charley."

Nguyen Than said dryly: "Your irony has been communicated, Mr. Danziger."

We visited three bombed-out Liberation villages in the next two days. They were similar to the pathetic villages the other side had liberated. These were the real pawns. The villagers seemed equally shy and the headmen equally noncommittal. One of them was Cai. He was small and uncommunicative and ageless, the kind of man I think of as "a survivor." His village had recently suffered a bombing attack in which many children and old people had been killed, and their new school flattened. I agreed with Cai that it was an outrage. Of course it was an outrage. Everything was a fucking outrage. We had our picture taken together.

I asked Nuy to ask Cai about the political program. He was awaiting it, but it had not arrived yet. They got medicine from the VC, but no food.

The third day we drove north again, for hours. I asked if I could continue north into Laos. Nguyen Than explained that I was not cleared to journey north of Ban Tasseing. They shared an agreement with the Pathet Lao which could not be infringed upon. I would spend a day in Ban Tasseing and the next morning be released to the American Two Corps in the vicinity of Dak To. Captain Nuy would personally accomplish my safe crossover. In the meantime I was free to inquire in any direction my curiosity led me.

The old gentleman ultimately tired of my questions and fell asleep, curled up like a rag doll. The transport coming down from the North was heavier as we approached Laos. I wondered whether I was learning anything of importance, and tried to form the rudiments of a story in my mind. Charley Hsi smiled at me and I smiled back and closed my eyes. As I drifted off, I wondered why Charley did not want me to think he had arranged my trip. Or why he did.

There was loud *chazzerai* at the Laotian border, and much jabbered explanation about the presence of the white gook. At one time I had to get out of the car and put my hands behind my neck and submit to a search. The inhalant again came in for its share of attention. Charley was withdrawn and quiet, but old Nguyen Than threw his hands around and carried on like Queen Victoria. Nuy folded his arms across his chest and disappeared on his regular tour of Paris restaurants.

We passed through, exhausted and hungry, and came at last to a vast staging area outside Ban Tasseing.

There was a bucket-shower behind our three-hut combine, which was a little apart from the activity and had its own guard. I luxuriated in the tepid water, shaved and even washed out my shirt, which was beginning to develop a life of its own.

Nuy yelled finally from outside: "Greedy American press lord!"

I succumbed to the demands of the underdeveloped nations and got out.

Charley Hsi came into my hut while I was dressing: "General Dinh respectfully invites you to dine with him tonight."

"Okay. Who's got a sixteen-and-a-half shirt?"

"He is anxious for you to comprehend the

complexities which they have been surmounting."

"Okay, Charley, I'm anxious to hear the general, but not in a wet poplin shirt."

Charley disappeared and came back with a neatly pressed white silk bush jacket, which was slightly short but which looked not unlike some of the outerwear creations I had seen recently in the window of a men's store on Second Avenue in the Fifties.

Nuy came in while I was trying it on. He stopped, and his eyes told me he found it amusing.

I said: "Shut up, you little dago. This is for the general."

Then I said to Charley: "Listen, old friend, is Captain Nuy invited to this so-important dinner?"

He looked embarrassed: "I think not."

"Charley, tell the general for me that I would deeply appreciate Captain Nuy's presence beside me to translate efficiently the subtleties of his remarks."

Charley's face was enigmatic for a long moment: "If you wish."

After he left, Nuy looked troubled: "Are you trying to create some kind of awkwardness?"

"Not at all. I was quite sincere."

"This dinner is not of importance to me, you know."

"The hell it isn't."

He smiled almost awkwardly and straightened his glasses: "Not as important as the Porte d'Or, at any rate."

The general still spoke without moving his lips, but this time his eyes held mine steadily while he was talking. He spoke in short staccato bursts, then paused and ate while Nuy translated. Occasionally Nguyen Than threw in a clarification. The basis of the remarks was statistical. I knew suddenly that this meeting was the reason for my trip. The rationale was like this: Despite the tonnage of high explosives dropped above the DMZ during the period July, '67, to January, '68, and increased unpublicized bombing in neutral countries ever since, there was an increase in supply and troop movements during the same period of 31 percent. (Facts supplied in carefully charted graph sheets.)

I interrupted before he went too far into it: "Ask the general to excuse me briefly so I may make notes on these interesting comments."

With paper and pen we started off again. It went on for about an hour. Its essence was that beyond killing defenseless children and civilians, destroying hospitals, schools and villages, the bombing succeeded only in hardening resolution and endeavor.

Now, the recent cessation of bombing was being treated in the Western press as a humanitarian gesture. It was not. It was instead a confession of failure. Political repercussions around the world—as well as in my own country—had demanded a cessation in the name of humanity. Also, the economics were lopsided inasmuch as each bombing did negligible strategic or tactical damage, while, at the same time, hardening the determination of the Liberation forces.

A press colleague of mine had been allowed to see the truth of this from Hanoi, and had reported it factually. Now it was hoped I could accomplish no less from my interior look at the logistics of both North Vietnamese and Liberation forces, which no enemy journalist had been privileged to see before. I had been selected out of many possibilities because I had reflected an open mind. It was hoped that my open mind would carry back and communicate the realities I had observed.

Over tea, I thanked the general and requested answers to three questions. He went into consultation with Nguyen Than before Nuy told me to state the questions.

I said: "One: Does the general anticipate foreseeable ground victory with the present lineup of forces? Two: If there should be such a ground victory, who would determine the political future of South Vietnam: Hanoi or the National Liberation? Three: If instead there were a negotiated peace which included the National Liberation, would Hanoi insist on its own voice, or would it feel represested by the National Liberation?"

I thought it would be sticky, but General Dinh only chatted briefly with Nguyen Than before addressing himself to my eyes again.

The answer to my first question was: Of course. It was already happening. In addition, they had a powerful ally I had probably not considered, called Time.

Answer two was the same as answer three: The NLF was not their ally; it was their brother.

If I reported these facts alone, I would perform a service for humanity . . . a word which many of my countrymen did not have in their lexicon.

Would I enjoy good luck on my walkover and a welcome reception by the world on my reactions to this unguarded exposure.

The general leaned across the table to shake fingers with me. Then he crooked one hand subtly at Nuy, who immediately lapdogged after him out of the room.

Charley handed me a cigar with no wrapper. It smelt like Havana. Nguyen Than picked at his chin. Someone started to clear the table.

I lit the cigar and said: "I have never met a general of any persuasion who did not make a forceful presentation."

Nguyen Than said softly: "You are privileged to hear the very inner thoughts of a country."

There wasn't a helluva lot to say to that so I smoked for a while. Why do military men, I was wondering, always think everyone else is so bloody stupid?

Charley Hsi said finally: "You can see the close relationship between Hanoi and the Liberation Front, I think, Peter."

I was thinking: It was all so much bullshit. If you spend your life listening to bullshit from opposing sides and believing it, you become bullshit. Westmoreland and Abrams and Dinh had more in common with each other than they had with me.

I stood up: "Will I see you in the morning, sir?"

Nguyen Than said: "I will be dealing with other matters, although I have enjoyed your character."

We shook hands.

I said: "I hope your children's program works out."

He left with dignity.

I sat down: "Charley, what a farce you have arranged."

"Do you discount everything? Have you learned nothing? You enjoy your cigar, at any rate."

"I learned, I discounted, I am disappointed."

He laughed silently: "You have always been such an impatient fellow."

"Where do you go from here, Charley?"

"Back south for a meeting. Then home for several weeks. It's a shame in this crushing of men we cannot find a third and a fourth."

I said: "You've probably forgotten the opening conventions."

"Probably. Good luck, Peter."

We shook hands solemnly.

He said: "Possibly we shall not meet again."

"Tell Tsen Wu Cheng I appreciated the opportunity."

"He will be delighted to hear it."

We walked outside together. The guard watched us in the dim yellow light from atop the hut.

"Good-bye, Charley. Thanks for arranging everything."

"You overestimate me. Good-bye, Peter."

I turned right and went to my hut. Nuy was sitting on the threshold holding his knees.

I said: "Why don't you either get glasses that fit, or a bigger nose, Nuy?"

This struck him as terribly funny.

I sat down beside him: "Did the general tell you to maintain security and remain vigilant?"

"Yes. Also not to repeat some of the nonsense Nguyen Than stated to him."

"The fact is: I have always spoken and understood your language with complete fluency."

"It would not surprise me. The smell of the Hong Kong cigar is beyond comprehension."

"Any young man who cannot distinguish between Hong Kong and Havana has a doubtful future."

Music was coming from around a cooking fire off to our left somewhere. It sounded like a broken mandolin. We wandered over after a while.

About a dozen troops were cooking and eating. One of them, back in the shadow of a hut, was playing the instrument. Occasionally he would sing a few bars in a high stretched voice with its own subtle nonrhythm. I guess you would call it undemanding music, but it seemed to fit in with the faces and the fire and the smell of the cooking and the tropical night.

I asked Nuy: "What is the song about?"

He said: "A lady waiting for the soldier to come home."

Nuy awakened me with tea before dawn. He

had changed into black VC pajamas. I dressed quickly and gulped down the hot sweet stuff, wishing it were coffee. My stomach was a little unnerved. I felt as though we would be taking off for Merseburg in a beat-up B-17 in about twenty minutes.

"Will it be tricky, Nuy?"

"Should not pose any problems. My people know we will be passing through, so there is no danger ·from that direction. You must walk the last kilometer yourself."

"Okay."

He seemed to sense I was worried: "It will be all right, Danziger."

"Has there been much activity in the area?"

"Not for several weeks. That is why the general chose Dak To. Would you like to eat?"

"No, thank you. I've got a lot of stored-up fat to travel on."

The sky was just beginning to lighten when we left the hut. The same old staff car was sitting in front, a sleepy driver at the wheel. We threaded our way through endless transport parked at random. A few people were awakening and building fires. The huts disappeared in rows up into the high ground. We seemed to be following a flat natural valley saucered between foothills. A shallow muddy stream meandered alongside the dirt roadway. You could sense already that the day would be hot and breathless again.

We left the staging area and took a narrow but heavily used trail east. In the gathering light I could see massive hills in front of us on either side, silver green now with the night fog just dissipating.

Nuy handed me a pack of cigarettes.

"Where did you get these?"

"From Charley Hsi."

"Thank you."

I smoked and thought about Charley as we rattled along. Whether it was his personality or my instinct, I felt somehow I had been used for some purpose beyond my ken. Nguyen Than was, I thought, exactly what he seemed. Charley was the cipher.

We drove in tranquility for over an hour. Some of the views were superb, like the Berkshires around Pittsfield.

Nuy said: "In a short while we will approach a Liberation village. Do not alarm yourself."

There was nothing to be alarmed about. The village seemed deserted until we came to a stop. Then VC piled out of the huts and the bush, and an official-looking gentleman approached the car. He looked perturbed. Nuy leaped out and spoke earnestly to him, then turned back to me: "If you would wait momentarily."

They disappeared inside the center hut. The VC driver glanced over his shoulder at me as though I were a marauding black Angus. Suddenly everyone I had been spending time with the last few days began looking like enemies again. I wondered what the hell Nuy and the chairman of the board were talking about. I lit another of

Charley's Hong Kong Camels and rubbed the gathering wetness off my neck and thought I would see Esterhazy in another month if I were lucky.

Nuy came back: "We are returning you under an alternate plan."

"Why?"

"There has been traffic which we do not yet understand along the original route."

"To Dak To, you mean?"

He sprawled down in the front seat and swiveled to face me. His glasses blankly reflected the bright sky: "Perhaps we will deliver you slightly south. I am instructed that no chances can be taken with your large body."

I said: "My large body agrees with you. That would put me near Kontum, I suppose."

"Perhaps a little to the north and west of Kontum."

The driver was looking bored and hungry.

I said: "Who is supposed to make the decision?"

Nuy flashed his tooth at me: "That is presumably my tactical decision, but I would welcome your collaboration."

"Okay. What is the nature of this traffic?"

"Ground patrols and air activity. It is thought that hostile forces may be building up for some unwholesome purpose."

I threw away the cigarette. A little kid was staring at me from a doorway, his thumb in his mouth. The sun was hotting up.

I said: "My solution is let's eat something. Do you have so sophisticated a thing as a map."

He grinned: "We have the only true maps."

"Let's eat and study the only true maps. I don't particularly want to be shot by either side."

He spoke hurriedly to the driver, who nodded repeatedly. Then the driver got out and trotted into a large hut ajoining the chairman's.

Nuy alighted more leisurely. He seemed to be coming into his own out here where the pressure waits.

We went into a hot elevated room under thatch. Nuy was expansive as he introduced me in Vietnamese to the chairman. I wanted to ask if I hadn't met him once in the Oyster Bar at the Racquet Club. He had the look if not the seersucker. Then he disappeared by degrees.

Nuy said: "Observe our alternatives."

We pored over a chart which, freely drawn, showed every trail and path in the vicinity. I'd already decided to avoid Dak To like lung cancer. I was feeling spooky again.

After a long moment I said: "Can we drive to this point? I can walk from there."

Nuy thought about it. He looked worried. Finally he said: "I must investigate. There may be four or five kilometers of trail under uncertain influence; partially Liberation and partially Two Corps."

He went out as the driver came in with bowls of hot food. Rice, of course, with some kind of meat and a chopped green which looked like okra and was quite delicious. The driver observed me cautiously while we waited. He acted as though every bite I sneaked was depriving Nuy.

The chairman came back with him and they opened up the map again.

Nuy splayed his finger out on the crossroad I had suggested: "There is certain activity in this area also, but it is suggested I may safely release you at approximately here, near the limits of our influence."

The chairman spoke briefly, running his finger along the same trail.

Nuy said: "They will send out runners to prepare Liberation people for our arrival at a certain hour. You are in more danger from your own people than from mine, Danziger. Does that amuse you?"

He spoke to the chairman again, who answered back, bowed and ultimately left.

We ate.

Nuy said: "If I understood the magnificent purpose of your visit I might more easily understand my responsibility."

"If I understood the purpose of my visit I would tell you. I suspect it is to report the facts the general divulged last night."

"I have heard him make the same announcement on numerous occasions to our own people."

"What the hell do you expect from a general? He's like a cannon. You point him in the right direction and he goes off."

"I would like more forewarning on when and where he goes off."

"Nuy, the instant either of us understands a general, let's get in touch."

He glanced at his watch: "Shall we go? I am not utterly without apprehension." He added: "It has been pleasant for me, Danziger."

We pulled south into the foothills after a few miles and the sun got hotter and the tension increased with the humidity. Mostly we followed contour trails with here and there a wooden bridge across a highland stream.

The driver was a cretin. He seemed to search out glacial potholes. Once a flight of 52's went over, high and spread out like a bunch of lost geese.

Half an hour later we stopped midway in the descent of a steep hill. Nuy leaped out and quickly found a path into deep foliage. I lit a cigarette and waited. When he emerged he seemed to be his old swingy self.

He said: "We leave the car here and proceed by foot."

Then he spoke to the driver in brittle fashion. The car reversed and turned and crawled back up the hill.

Carrying my case, I said as we started down: "I wish you had brought me an extra pair of black pajamas."

He said solemnly: "You would not need them. At the bottom of the hill you will see a stream. I will take you to it. You will cross it and proceed directly up the hill on the far side. Ultimately, you will find a trail north-south. Turn south and within several kilometers you will find an American advance encampment."

We were nearing the turn by the bluff at the bottom of the hill.

"Perhaps I will meet you one day in one of those restaurants, Danziger."

I had opened my mouth to answer when the automatic firing broke out ahead of us.

I dove to the side of the road and rolled.

After that there was a great deal of firing, overhead.

I pressed against the bottom of the rain ditch, wondering whether Nuy was just behind me.

A Midwestern voice bellowed from below: "All right, big fella! Rise and shine with your hands up!"

I waited, finally rose to my feet. Cautiously. I could see about six GI's at the ready below me on the side of the road, half in bush.

"Easy mellow down the hill now!"

I looked back across my shoulder. Nuy was a skinny black-and-red splat on the dirt road. He was virtually cut in half. His glasses were broken.

"Hurry now! Hands behind the neck!"

I heard myself screaming: "You zapped him, you filthy sons of bitches! Why did you have to zap him?"

They kept me in a tin-roofed warehouse-type structure for about thirty-six hours. In the meanwhile it had started to rain. There were two sets of guards: four hours on, four hours off. They gave me cigarettes and GI food and coffee on demand, but no conversation.

The next morning a medic came in and lis-

tened to my heart. Mostly, I slept. I would wake
up and hear people yelling across the compound.
Three or four times copters came in and departed. I went into a kind of sleep-drugged apathy.
When I was awake I worried about my stories and
mentally planned them. Everything was right
there in vivid clarity: Nguyen Than clearing his
throat and his thoughts; the sense of intricate
subtleties; the smell of the cooking; the sound of
the singing; the feel of the dust; the way Nuy
bashfully kept pushing his glasses back up on his
nose.

Toward the end I felt disembodied and un-
analytical and didn't care too much.

We flew down to Saigon early in the evening by
helicopter. They had allowed me to shave, shower and change into clean chinos somebody found.
The only good thing about the ride was that nobody shot at us.

Two VC handcuffed together were on the floor.
They kept their heads down. Everyone else kept
staring at me. The chopper smelt of metal and oil
and warm bodies and disinfectant.

We landed at Cholon. They made me wait
while armed guards took off the VC. When I descended, a staff car, a second lieutenant and two
MP's were waiting. The whole thing was ridiculous.

I got into the car and we tore off. Vince Schaefer would have been walking into Tim's about
then. There were guard points at intervals along
the freshly topped road. It was hot. I gathered

from remarks that the VC had been raising hell at night in the area. In all the heat there was a little cold fright floating around that car from head to head.

We stopped at a cement block building in Saigon almost directly across the square from my hotel. For just a moment I thought about the fifth of Dewar's in the gladstone in my closet. I waited on a bench in a bare pea-green foyer. Once inside there were no signs and no guards except for one career sergeant heavily disguised in a Hong Kong rayon suit.

I said: "Pal, is there a telephone?"

He shook his head briefly.

"What the hell am I here for?"

He read a paperback for a while and finally cocked his forehead and stared at me as though I were speaking Yiddish.

"As a civilian, I'd like something a little more oral, friend."

He looked at the door, then at me, then back at whatever he was reading.

I was thinking: First Precinct, Muskegon, Michigan, 1937. And kept remembering Stella and me aged too young in traffic court caught necking and without registration in probably the first station wagon ever built. Same sergeant, same jowls, same eyes. Oh, vain is man who glories in his joy and has no fears, while to and fro the chances of the years dance like an idiot in the wind!

A door opened and a young accountant stepped out.

"Peter Danziger?"

"Yes?"

"Captain Anderson can see you now."

I followed him down a corridor to a small office. The air conditioning was operating loud and clear. The captain was my size but had gloating pig eyes instead of virtue. He was in civilian clothes.

"Peter Danziger? Sit down. Your press clearance is revoked and your office has been so advised. You are also under arrest."

"Why?"

"For violating your press clearance, for consorting with the enemy, and for grossly insulting American military personnel who were acting under orders."

"You know we're going to the Supreme Court with this if I'm not out of here in about five minutes, don't you?"

"Not in a war zone. Read your briefing booklet."

"Who could possibly read a briefing booklet? I have a story to file."

"Let me see it."

"Are you the new press officer?"

"Certainly not. This is a security office. Show me the story."

"I don't have to, if you recall."

He stood up, paced around, looked out the window, lit a pipe, sat down again. I thought he looked like a Southern sheriff who hadn't run to fat yet.

Of course I had written no story, but I had the sense and the feel of it. Apart from the physical aspects, and the personalities, there was another story: a tiny crack in the cement between the North people and the VC, a few power subtleties on all of the sides. I wanted to do a piece about Nuy someday too—but not until later. He wasn't quite dead enough.

He pulled a pad out of a desk drawer: "Will you consent of your own volition to being debriefed on military aspects you observed?"

"Not if I'm under arrest."

"Of course you're under arrest! Did you have clearance from the press officer to go across?"

"No. I applied and he implied it would be granted and then the machinery got stuck."

"So you went anyway?"

"Yes. The occasion arose."

"Who arranged it?"

"I did. With the encouragement of my bureau."

"Through what sources?"

"Through many sources. You can ask in the street and find sources."

"Tell me about them."

"My God, where do you spend your spare time? In the officer's club billiard room?"

"No. I'm too busy with soft-nosed patriots like you, as it happens."

He looked hard and square into my eyes in the manner of Steve McQueen, and pointed the stem of his pipe at me: "Let me tell you one thing, buster. You are not filing one line about your illegal trip across until it has been cleared by everybody from me up to the Pentagon and back. If I have to keep you in a blockhouse from now till 1999."

I lit my last cigarette and looked at the ceiling, wondering what had caused all the fuss.

After a moment he said quietly: "How many enemy troops did you observe in Cambodia?"

"A lot. I didn't count."

"A thousand? Ten thousand? Fifty thousand?"

"Five or ten thousand. I was there for a different purpose."

"How the hell can an American have a different purpose?"

"Are you trying to tell me you don't have your own people over there? Captain, you frighten me about the way this war is conducted."

"Of course we have our people. I'm merely trying to determine whether or not you're a liar."

"I'll be delighted to give a complete debriefing on everything I saw and heard, so long as it is held from the press until my own stories are published. Why don't you let me go on about my profession, and if you disagree, rebut it?"

"If it is in our best interest to leak, publish or suppress your information we will exercise our prerogative, naturally."

"Now you've compromised the deal."

"There is no deal."

"Then we're boxed. I can't tell you what I know without the guarantee."

"I can hold you incommunicado as long as I like. Nobody knows you're back but me."

"You overlook a squat bastard named Vince Schaefer. The longer you hold me now, the bigger the stink later. You made your goof when you informed him my clearance was pulled. Now he expects to hear from me."

"Fortunately for the country, your Mr. Schaefer does not yet control the military."

"For God's sake, Captain, Vince Schaefer digests people like you for a snack, before lunch. His favorite cussword is military censorship, and he says it through the purple veins in his neck."

"So you decline to cooperate?"

"Not at all. I have voluntarily offered to cooperate to the fullest extent, provided you protect the ownership of my material."

"Empty your pockets, Mr. Wise!"

"Why not? I did it a few days ago for the VC."

I began pulling out the same little baubles. Everything went on and on. I wanted to go to sleep someplace. There was something sweetish in his pipe tobacco. The sound of the air conditioning was like a lullaby.

He came around the desk. He was angry: "You know the Hanoi press has played you as a big hero, I suppose? Picture and all!"

I didn't answer.

"Why didn't you just stay over there with your pals, Danziger, instead of bringing all this bullshit back to us?"

His fatuous face was sort of floating there in front of me and I hit it as hard as I could. It seemed to happen in lovely slow motion. I have never, since, felt sorry for an instant.

Ten days later I was on the way home. Don't fuck around with Vince Schaefer.

He was a life master in the dowdier uses of tactics and strategy, but his shaded area, with which you are supposed to empathize with emotional aberration, had been left on the hospital floor with his umbilical. He was despondent because I had hit Captain Anderson out of anger and frustration and with no deeply rationalized plan in mind.

I said: "It wasn't a blow for anything, Vince. It was an instant emotional response."

"There must have been a better reason. Weren't you persecuted? Weren't they contemptuous of the press? Why do you think I got you out of there?"

"Because you love me, Vince."

The sun was pouring in through the slats of the blinds, and the cigar smoke curling up from his fingers made blue psychedelic designs in the conditioned air. Far below I could hear the muffled sounds of late-afternoon traffic. My mouth was still sensitive where Captain Anderson and the sergeant had successfully belted back.

He said: "I don't give a globule of warm spit for your emotional responses. What can we make out of it?"

"Nothing. Two people doing their individual things. Did you happen to read the stories?"

"The sixth is already enchanting our subscribers around the wire. With certain international political repercussions, I might add. The think piece is ready to go."

"Good."

He looked at me for a while, and I looked back, mainly at the sparse gray mustache which always seemed to me to be a kind of rebellion that stated he didn't have to shave his upper lip if he damn well didn't want to. The little broken blood vessels in his nose were more prominent.

He smiled insincerely: "What exactly are you up to, Danziger? For the last five days there have been more idiots gumshoeing around your past than I can remember since Cohn and Schine."

I was surprised: "I got paddled and sent home. What else can happen?"

"Are you clean?"

"I went across and wrote the stories."

"Forget that. I'm talking about your private contacts."

He pulled out a teletype from a folder: "Ed Dana got this from a Reuter's pal of his in Hong Kong. Read it."

He flicked it across the desk.

It read: "Advised China's Viet rep Li Hsi purged last week due to adverse effect first Danziger story. Formally called Western Deviationism. Leaves Tsen Wu Cheng alone on high which pleases British inasmuch as he considered predictable. Rumored here Cheng arranged all to accomplish said purpose. Wonder Danziger implicated. Details follow."

After a while I said: "Jesus Christ, I kill 'em all."

Vince seemed dangerous suddenly: "Do you feel like a stupid pawn, Danziger?"

There was a long sunlit silence. I felt unreal. I had just got off the plane, and everything seemed to be moving a little faster than I was.

Finally: "I feel like an angry pawn, as usual. The little bastard was just trying to protect himself, but couldn't get around to saying it."

"Are you nervous?"

"Terribly."

"What else did you do? There's more to this than Captain Anderson."

"How do you know they're not trying to manufacture more out of Captain Anderson? Protect your own, and all that—like I wish you were doing."

His eyes were beady: "Who were your contacts in getting across?"

"You wouldn't dream of asking me that if somebody hadn't asked you. I remember the famous old V. Schaefer quote: 'Get your story and keep the dirty details to yourself.' So if I tell you, you'll tell somebody else, and some nice, innocent and confused people will get escalated into the sights of a Saigon firing squad. Bullshit, you know better."

I began to get mad: "Vince, for Christ's sake, what is this? Didn't you like the stories? Since when are you buckling to the military?"

He got up and walked across the room to his fancy refrigerator-cooler and washed his hands under the spout. Then he dried his hands on his handkerchief and put it on the bookcase and came back to me. It should have been a sign.

"I've been asked to suspend you."

"You're as crazy as they are!"

"The accusations go beyond commendable news-gathering enterprise."

"You sound like a bloody Oriental. What are the accusations?"

"Not mine to divulge, unfortunately."

He sat down again. Being short, he felt an advantage sitting behind that expanse of oiled teak. I suddenly realized that I admired him and that he was chopping me off.

Guido always sat in a booth in the back of his restaurant nursing his little black cigar and his big belly and his white pompadour and counting the customers who came in the door as though he were calculating on his mental abacus the number of *paisanos* he had fed in his lifetime.

He waddled forward, as usual, his face pocked with signs of affection and his heart filled with profit.

"Mr. Danziger, the darling, and the lovely signora!" To me, as he led us to a booth: "They have been asking about you."

"Who?"

"A man in a raincoat who ordered veal and peppers."

"What did you tell him, Guido?"

He spread his hands in innocence: "That you are charge customer."

We sat down and he went away.

Esterhazy asked: "What *is* going on, Peter?"

"I have no idea. As I told you, I'm unemployed."

"I'll support you if you'll do the cooking, Peter."

She looked lovely.

"Don't be glib. Something is going on."

"What, darling?"

"I'm being stepped on by something with a big foot."

"For hitting the captain? You really shouldn't have."

"Not for that. Schaefer loves that kind of thing. Something deeper. Something that scared him."

"What else have you been up to, then?"

"Charley Hsi got killed because I went over."

"Oh, Peter!"

"He wanted to tell me something but was afraid of losing face."

"You can't know that!"

"No."

We ordered Francese and salad and a bottle of Valpolicella. I didn't want to talk about my exile any longer. We touched knees and looked into eyes and held hands and thought about other parts and ate and drank and made promises. She thought my letters were mundane, coming from a literary man.

When I couldn't sleep that night I moved away from her quiet breathing and looked up at the dark ceiling and thought about Charley Hsi: the Hong Kong scotch and the smile and the nine children and the six no-trump hand so many years ago.

As a sophomore at Michigan he went by the name of Albie Mart, a skinny apparition from somewhere in the East. He was hooked on terpin hydrate. We never knew whether he bought it or stole it—he was always broke—but you could see the empties in his closet. My first junkie. Once he borrowed a white dinner jacket I had bought on sale at Selinger's in Muskegon, and never gave it back.

He was also hooked on political science and made a few dollars tutoring the less gifted. He was one of the bright ones.

When he was high he used to stand up, wavering slightly, and point his finger at you and whine in a churchy tenor: "Who would you rather be—Jesus Christ or Henry Ford?"

Nobody knew the answer, although I personally opted for Henry Ford, but he received a share of attention and became known as an amiable eccentric.

I didn't even recognize him when he first knocked on my door at the Plaza the next morning; merely smelt that this skinny body in the green loden coat was one of my old ghosts. I had dropped Esterhazy at work and come down to sleep and think and settle in. In jeopardy I always like to live high off the hog, for morale, and I felt jeopardized. The room was already filled with blue funk.

He sidled in: "Peter Danziger, what a joy!"

"You son of a bitch, where's my white dinner jacket?"

"You recognize me! Can we talk? Can we call down for some coffee?"

He sat down. He looked slightly stained. I remembered that sometimes he had affected an English accent. It was a little improved.

I continued pulling off my tie, then unbuttoned my shirt. His presence was like a *déjà vu* flash from an ancient daydream.

I said: "Henry Ford, for your information."

He laughed openly: "You do have a memory, don't you?"

"Also an intelligence. You're working for Uncle."

"How could you deduce that, old boy?"

"I checked in here fifteen minutes ago and no one knew I was coming, so Uncle must have been in tow. Or do you work for some other Uncle?"

He lit a cigarette: "This will be so undemanding and uncomplicated that it will surprise you, Peter."

I went into the john and turned on the shower, then went back to unpack a robe. While I was at it I piled out dirty laundry.

"Just what the hell are you doing here, Albie?"

"Trying to save you some unneeded embarrassment."

I looked at him analytically: "You know, you're at least a year younger than I am, but you look like a dried-up old fart."

He laughed and trembled like a tea leaf: "No

need to go to the attack yet. Really, we thought an old friend might show you a way out."

I put on the robe and stopped on the way back to that magnificent old bathroom: "Out of what?"

He smiled gently at me: "Out of political purgatory. You know. The one that never ends."

"Has this got anything to do with your stupid captain?"

"Not even remotely. In fact, when my superior heard the tape he indicated he might have hit the captain himself."

"Then what the hell?"

He stood up and moved toward the telephone: "Take your shower, Peter. I *do* need coffee. Two?"

He was sipping coffee contentedly when I came out of the shower. I sat down across from him in my robe and dried my hair and wondered whether he'd loaded in a little terpin hydrate. Coffee couldn't be quite that delicious.

He started gingerly: "Peter, we think you're quite possibly an innocent. Some of the people you have known over a long career are not quite that. Not quite innocent. We know that too."

"What did you tell Vince Schaefer?"

"We merely pointed out some strange coincidences. They seemed to deter him."

"They deterred me; not him. What's the rap?"

"Still to be determined. That's why I'm here. To perhaps save you the annoyance of the rap."

I got mad: "I tell you true. I do not understand what the hell is going on. I do not understand the words or the sentences or the nuances. I do not understand why I am fired or why you

are here in my room and why some of the colum-
nists are implying I'm slightly more sinister than
Mao or, for that matter, Albie, why I am sitting
here listening to you."

He poured himself some more coffee and said
wistfully: "I told him you'd get angry."

"Don't tell him that. Tell him I threw you out
—with the proviso that if you stay you get extremely simple about exactly what you're doing
here. Don't keep moaning about the trouble I'm
in. Tell me what the hell it is!"

He finished his coffee and carefully poured another cup: "We might be prepared to make some
beneficial arrangement for you if you would, as
they say, 'spill the beans' on a number of old
friends of yours."

"None of my friends has anything more than
old traffic tickets."

He leaned forward abruptly: "Does that include drug traffic?"

"Jesus, this gets wilder by the minute. Who?
When?"

"There are too many to be a coincidence . . .
on a drug count or some other."

"Show me the list."

"Not until you agree to a hearing."

"I thought this was an internal security thing."

"It is. There are various ways of eroding a government, as you know. Don't you want your coffee?"

"Not without terpin hydrate. Get out of here,
Albie."

"You realize how this will be interpreted?"

"No. I don't seem to know anything."

He stood up: "You must understand why it is impossible to divulge all of our suspicions to you, unless you put something on the record first. It's really so simple, Danziger. All the pigeons might fly. Surely you can understand. For that matter, although I'm sure you're not, you might indeed be implicated."

"What about my job?"

"Perhaps that too can be worked out with your cooperation."

"I'd give my arm to know what you told Vince Schaefer."

He smiled from the doorway: "You already gave your profession."

I closed the door quietly behind him.

Did you ever wake up from a nightmare and find you were still riding a runaway cable car?

I made the rounds: all the people I had known all those years in all those cities. I was received like an impoverished leper walking into 21 on Christmas Eve.

Jack Berkowitz said: "The word is out, Danz. Do not touch. Why don't you try the magazines? Or write a book?"

Elliot Nolan said: "Of course. As soon as the trouble is cleared up. What's going on, anyway?"

Hirsh Bunker said: "No one exactly said so, baby, but it was kind of beautiful the way it was implied. 'Not while investigation is pending . . .' That kind of *shtik*. They got me by my accreditation. You know? The White House and Cape Ken-

nedy and Houston and Saigon and such. The Man
can say yes or no to anyone I sent out. Or he can
just keep saying no. You get my point? I let the
Man say no a couple times and I retire to my apple
orchard which I don't like with my old lady who
I don't talk to."

I wrote an exposé piece about my predicament
for a small Midwestern magazine, and some welcome free-lance speeches and publicity pieces
various friends passed me as sympathy bones.
Esterhazy got me an assignment, a copout really,
comparing miniskirts to Far Eastern fashions. The
pictures made it look good.

The hotel was expensive and I was beginning
to feel a little desperate financially. Esterhazy
tried to buy my lunches. I snapped at her from
time to time. She snapped back. It was a kind of
ugly twilight. We went to the Electric Circus
one night and got a little drugged on sights and
sounds and each other and spent the night at her
apartment. I wanted to leave on a high note, so
next morning I dropped her at work, telling her
in the cab I was going to get away and think a
little, then checked out of the hotel and caught
the next flight to Miami. I was trying to decide
whether to fight these bastards or go into another
line of work.

Jack Walsh opened his cottage door and wasn't
even surprised to see me. His big old party boat,
the *Lady Day,* was groaning against the bulkhead a
few yards away. Wavelets made happy little
sounds against the hull. A seagull was screaming

someplace. Everything smelt beautifully of salt and fish and decay.

He said: "I hear you're a spy."

"Who told you that?"

"My houseman and a guy from a network. C'mon in."

He still looked like a buccaneer.

"How would you like a paying roommate for a while?"

"It's a possibility. As long as you're not copping out."

"I don't think so."

"I don't want you to tell me you have to get away from it all and just think."

"I'm here to not think."

The main room was as clean and bare as ever. The transom planks of all his lovely departed boats decorated the white plaster walls. Nothing else.

"You sound healthy. You got any money?"

"A few dollars. I can always do the buck-and-wing on the afterdeck."

"Okay. We split on groceries. Buy your own booze. We're going fishing at six thirty. Open up the couch. Can you still bait a hook?"

"I'll figure it out, teach."

"I don't want to hear your problems, Danz."

"Who has problems?"

"I do."

And he started to tell me about this broad.

After a couple of months I got healthy and sunburnt and cynical. I kept sending letters to Vince

Schaefer, mainly asking who I could write to, but none of them got answered. I even wrote one to Albie Mart, c/o CIA, but it disappeared into the maw of the void from which he came.

I got a running start on the book. Sometimes it seemed fine to me, sometimes primitive. I felt fibrous enough to write Esterhazy every night without bemoaning the future.

She came down for a lovely sunlit week during which Walsh fell madly in love with her, as he was wont to do with somebody else's woman.

An official document had arrived one day when we chugged up the river after off-loading a party. We had been singing "Charmaine" so soulfully that the Cuban kids on the northern bank kept popping their heads out of their cottage doors to see what marvelous thing was transpiring.

Before I opened the envelope my stomach went far, far back to pre-"Charmaine" days and pre-sun days and pre-fishing days.

Would I voluntarily give testimony in an informal inquiry to clear myself of any possible taint?

"Read this," I told Walsh across rum sours in the yard.

He squinted at it for a while: "I guess you'd better."

I said: "You notice it implies guilt prior to testimony."

"You're not just dabbling with the Dade County cops, either."

"Explain that to me someday."

"Have you got a lawyer?"

"I guess I've also got a girl."

"I noticed. Marshal the forces."

I took a long swallow of the rum sour. Nothing had ever tasted better. The sun dappled the lawn through restless leaves. A breeze was blowing up along the river.

"I guess I will," I said.

The unlikeliest lawyer ever weaned on mother's milk and pure old panther piss is named Gil Ketchum the First. That's how he introduced himself when I first met him at the bar in Lundy's in Sheepshead Bay in the spring of '48. His beard was blond then, but his odd head was already getting bald. I was waiting to have dinner with my mother and her spouse, who were staying in Bay Ridge for some reason. I never did know who the First was waiting for. He'd been married, but I think was in between at the moment. We've been friends and attorney-client ever since.

He's given me some miserably bad advice on several occasions, but always so convincingly that I thought it would be boorish to bring it up later and erode his sublime faith in his rationalizing powers.

I phoned him from Miami and flew up the next night to stay in that monstrous old book-filled apartment on the West Side while we ironed out my legal and ethical status for the inquiry. I wanted Esterhazy exposed to as little guilt by association as possible (the interfraternity of publishing and all that) but wanted her in on the decision-making.

Ketchum's current wife is named Didi. She is fluttery and can't cook, but she is amiable and Gil says she is inventive in bed.

She and Esterhazy were in the kitchen making chili when I got there from the airport.

It was a kind of reunion. After dinner, Didi went back to the kitchen to drop dishes, and we got down to it.

Gil asked: "They mentioned no minor matter such as charges?"

I showed him the letter: "No. Just taint."

"What do you think they're referring to?"

"What could it be but the trip to Cambodia and Laos without authorization?"

"As a matter of fact, why didn't you get authorization?"

"I tried. The press office said I would get it, but after two months nothing had happened. I asked again. They said it was probably bogged down somewhere. They told me how busy they were. I figured my time was running out and I had a chance to arrange it, so I did."

"And I presume that's against war zone regulations?"

"I guess that's what this is all about."

He thought for a while: "Technically, we're not at war. But the offense doesn't seem big enough for scaring off your bureau. For getting you thrown out of the zone, maybe."

"That's what I thought."

"It could have been your contacts in getting across, or the people you saw on the other side, or

some major tactical disaster that happened directly afterward that they could blame on you. Or
even passing security information, I suppose."

"There was no disaster I ever heard of. And I
didn't have any security information. Anyway, I
wasn't in a passing situation, I was in a gathering
situation. By invitation."

We all sat and stared at each other for a while.
Esterhazy poured more coffee. She was wearing a
contoured kelly-green slack suit that allowed her
legs and bottom and et cetera to look superb.

Gil lit a pipe, which I happened to know he detested: "Would you rather be right or employed?"

"I'd rather be right *and* employed."

Esterhazy laughed and said: "That's my boy."

Gil said: "The problem with this thing and how
to handle it is that I don't know what the charges
are. Ergo: how you should defend it."

"Why don't I just find out?"

"I think it's stickier than you think it is," Gil
said. "Else why the security suspicion around
town?"

Esterhazy said: "Perhaps the VC told *you* something important?"

"I wrote about all that."

"But you didn't tell the military."

"I offered to. I wasn't counting troops you
know. Just impressions."

"That's good for a brownie point," Gil said dryly, throwing his pipe at the fireplace.

Esterhazy said: "I think you should be utterly
candid and cooperative with them, on condition

they patch up your reputation at the bureau."

"And elsewhere," Gil said.

"I'm willing to be frank. Like you, I'd also like to know what the taint is. And who these bastards think they are."

Gil got mad suddenly: "You're a lost little fly caught up in the winds of time, you stupid ingrate! All I want to do is get you down with your wings on!"

"At what ethical price?"

"My lost little fly," Esterhazy said enigmatically.

I had bad dreams about Nuy that night. I dreamt he was my son and that people kept killing him.

Monday

DID YOU HAVE A NICE WEEKEND?
  Extremely.
THE WEATHER WAS VERY PLEASANT IN VIRGINIA. A LITTLE HOT.
  Yes.
MR. DANZIGER, PREPARE YOURSELF FOR A SURPRISE. WE ARE TOSSING YOU BACK.
  What does that mean?
AFTER TODAY, YOU ARE FREE TO GO YOUR OWN WAY. THE INQUIRY IS CONCLUDED.
  With a letter of apology and a public statement?
CERTAINLY NOT. APOLOGY FOR WHAT? YOU REQUESTED A HEARING AND YOU GOT ONE. STATEMENT ABOUT WHAT? THAT YOU WERE UNCOOPERATIVE?
  You Machiavellian son of a bitch! What do you tell Vince Schaefer?
I CAN THINK OF NO REASON FOR THIS OFFICE TO COMMUNICATE WITH MR. SCHAEFER.
  (Silence)

What has changed, then, in the last week?

WE HAVE COME TO KNOW EACH OTHER. CAN YOU THINK OF ANYTHING ELSE?

Is it your opinion that my discourse has not cleared me?

OF WHAT?

Of whatever the goddamn charges are!

THERE ARE NO CHARGES, AS I TOLD YOU AT THE OUTSET. THERE ARE JUSTIFI-ABLE SUSPICIONS.

Still?

TELL ME ONE WORD YOU HAVE UT-TERED TO CALM THEM.

What if I went for a jury trial to clear up this nightmare?

WHO WOULD PREFER CHARGES—AND OF WHAT? OR WOULD YOU SUE ME? THERE ARE THINGS IN YOUR RECORD WHICH COULD NOT BE ALLOWED TO APPEAR IN TESTIMONY.

In the interest of security?

QUITE RIGHT. IN THE INTEREST OF SECURITY.

You know, about a thousand times in my professional lifetime I have worried about the frightening disparity between national security and national interest.

IT'S ALL ONE AND THE SAME, I SHOULD THINK.

By whose definition? When you guys think you own the board and the pieces?

WHAT ARE WE TO DO, THEN, WHEN ONE

OF OUR OWN PEOPLE—YOU—REPORTS AN ACTIVE ENEMY SYMPATHETICALLY?

Bullshit! I reported our side a hundred times. Now I've reported the other side too. That's my profession.

ON WHICH SIDE DO YOUR SYMPATHIES LIE?

On the side of the people who are getting shot.

REGARDLESS OF POLITICAL COLORATION?

Regardless of political coloration.

DO YOU INCLUDE VIETNAM SPECIFICALLY?

Yes. Specifically.

SO YOU BELIEVED ALL THAT PAP AFTER ALL.

My stories didn't say I believed it; my stories said I was told it.

BUT YOU DID BELIEVE IT?

About the same as I believe any military figures.

DO YOU INCLUDE YOUR OWN COUNTRY?

I include my own country's military.

IN SHORT, YOU PUBLISHED A CASE HISTORY OF COMMUNIST OBJECTIVES IN AN UNCRITICAL, VIRTUALLY FAVORABLE MANNER.

We're just going 'round and 'round . . . You know, Doc, one of the frightening things about all this is, after all this time we've spent together, I still don't know what you're after.

YOU PLAY THE INNOCENT AS PLAINTIVELY AS I'VE EVER SEEN IT DONE.

Am I accused of going over and reporting Cambodia and Laos and seeing and accepting some of the other point of view? Or of knowing Cybele McCullough and Louis Estimet and Charley Hsi and Mike Chiapa and all the people in my life? Or both? Or are you just wildcatting? Which, Doc? What in God's name is the crime?

YOU NEEDN'T SHOUT. THE FACTS SHOUT FOR YOU.

What facts?

VERY WELL. LISTEN TO THIS. YOUR PO-LITICAL COLORATION IS AN UN-EXPECTED SIDELINE, FOR YOUR INFOR-MATION. BUT VERY INTERESTING TO US. APART FROM THAT: THERE ARE ONLY A FEW LINKS BETWEEN A DANGER-OUS MAN—CHIAPA NÉ CROGER—AND AN-OTHER DANGEROUS MAN, LOUIS ESTI-MET. ONE OF THEM IS THE INCIDENT IN AUSTRIA IN WHICH CYBELE McCUL-LOUGH WAS KILLED, WHICH TIED ESTI-MET AND McCULLOUGH DIRECTLY TO CROGER & LAPHORN.

Okay, what are the others?

THE RECORD OF A MAJOR PURCHASE OF GOVERNMENT CIGARETTES BY ESTIMET FROM A MAN WHO SIGNED HIMSELF AS E. CROGER. ESTIMET GOT AWAY WITH HIS TROUSERS, BUT WITHOUT THE CIGARETTES, SO THERE WAS NO GREAT PRESSURE TO TRACK DOWN CROGER. THAT WAS IN FRANCE IN 1944. YOU

PROBABLY KNOW HOW CROGER GOT HIS
HANDS ON THE TRUCKLOAD OF CIGA-
RETTES, BUT I WON'T BOTHER TO ASK
YOU.

Okay. Keep going.

FROM PASSPORT AND VISA ENTRIES WE
KNOW THAT MORE RECENTLY CROGER
AND ESTIMET WERE IN LONDON SIMUL-
TANEOUSLY, IN FRANCE SIMULTANE-
OUSLY, IN CUBA SIMULTANEOUSLY, IN
HONG KONG SIMULTANEOUSLY, IN TUR-
KEY SIMULTANEOUSLY AND IN SAIGON
SIMULTANEOUSLY. ON MOST OF THOSE
OCCASIONS, SO WERE YOU.

Once I was in the USA at the same time as
Richard Nixon. Simultaneously.

WHICH BRINGS US TO THE FINAL LINK.
YOU, MR. DANZIGER, THE ONLY MAN
ON THIS GREEN EARTH WHO KNEW ALL
THREE INTIMATELY OVER A PERIOD OF
YEARS, AND WHOSE OCCUPATION TOOK
YOU INTO EACH OF THE TERRITORIES
IN WHICH THEY OPERATED.

What am I supposed to have been then? Their
front man?

DON'T FLARE UP SO EASILY. IT DOESN'T
WORK AROUND HERE. I'M NOT SAYING,
INCIDENTALLY, THAT YOU WERE MA-
JOR SECURITY FACTORS. YOU WERE
GRIMY LITTLE THREATS, REALLY, BUT
YOU PRESENTED A DANGER. IT'S NOT
TOO DIFFICULT WHEN YOU'RE ACCUS-

TOMED TO DEALING UNDER THE TABLE WITH AN ENEMY FOR CAVIAR OR DRUGS OR MACHINE TOOLS TO TAKE THAT TINY EXTRA STEP AND EXCHANGE BAZOOKAS OR SECURITY INFORMATION. PROBABLY YOU ALREADY DID, IN SAIGON. WHAT YOU NEEDED WAS ACCESS TO THE PRODUCT . . . WHAT YOU CALL THE MERCHANDISE.

How do you tie in Charley Hsi and the VC, you idiotic bastard?

IT'S NOT TOO BEDAZZLING TO ASSUME WITH YOUR CONTACTS AND CONSTANTLY SHIFTING PRESENCE THAT YOU UTILIZED YOUR INSTINCTS TO POINT OUT PROFITABLE SITUATIONS TO THESE PEOPLE—WHEREVER YOUR ASSIGNMENTS TOOK YOU. YOU COULD EVEN PENETRATE CITADELS OF INFORMATION UNDER THE GUISE OF NEWS GATHERING; THEIRS OR OURS. THEN YOU ARE OUT OF IT AND YOUR PARTNERS MOVE IN TO SEIZE THE OPPORTUNITY AND THE DOLLAR, LEAVING YOU FREE TO SIT HERE AND PROTEST YOUR INNOCENCE AND BLEAT ABOUT FREEDOM OF THE PRESS. IN SHORT, MR. DANZIGER, YOU FURNISHED ACCESS TO THE MARKET.

It sounds like a great business, Doc. You pieced that all together from my conversation?

YOU WERE ONLY VERIFICATION, BUT IT

HELPED. WE KNOW, FOR EXAMPLE,
THAT YOU EXPEDITED A PURCHASE OF
MACHINE TOOLS FOR ESTIMET IN WEST
GERMANY WHICH LATER FOUND THEIR
WAY BEHIND THE BAMBOO CURTAIN AS
PROTOTYPES.

The Ingebritzen deal?

PRECISELY.

What else?

BY YOUR OWN ADMISSION, YOU COULD
EASILY HAVE BEEN PART OF THE AP-
PARATUS THAT BROUGHT ONE OF
MANY SIZABLE HEROIN SHIPMENTS
FROM BEHIND THE CURTAIN VIA TUR-
KEY TO MARSEILLES AND THENCE TO
CROGER & LAPHORN WAREHOUSES IN
BALTIMORE.

What else?

I DON'T KNOW YET WHAT DEAL YOU
AND ESTIMET AND PROBABLY CROGER
HATCHED IN MIAMI AND CARRIED OUT
IN CUBA; BUT I WILL.

What else?

YOU ARE THE ONLY AMERICAN WE
KNOW OF WHO HAS—I SHOULD SAY *HAD*
—AN OPEN AND INFORMAL WORKING
ARRANGEMENT WITH FAIRLY ELE-
VATED PEOPLE IN THE VC, AS WELL AS A
HIGHLY PLACED FRIEND IN THE MAO
GOVERNMENT. THE ONLY AMERICAN
WHO COULD AND DID PENETRATE INTO
THAT AREA WITH REMARKABLE EASE,

AND THEN HAD THE AUDACITY TO COME OUT WITH A BLUSTER AND BANG THAT WE IMMEDIATELY RECOGNIZED AS CAMOUFLAGE. WHAT DID YOU SET UP FOR CHIAPA AND ESTIMET BEHIND THAT JUNGLE, MR. DANZIGER? HEROIN FOR US AND WHAT FOR THEM? INFORMATION THAT YOU COULD EASILY PROCURE IF WE LEFT YOU RUNNING AROUND FREE FLASHING YOUR PRESS CLEARANCE? OR SOME SMALL BUT VITAL ELECTRONIC PART ESTIMET COULD GET HIS HANDS ON? I'LL BET MY LAST DOLLAR YOU HAVE A NUMBERED SWISS BANK ACCOUNT.

I wish to Christ I did, you insane crewcut uptight version of Dr. Strangelove! Why in hell don't you stick me in jail?

I WISH I COULD.

You can't prove it?

I CAN'T. PRIMARILY SINCE THE TWO PEOPLE I NEED TO IMPLICATE YOU FACTUALLY ARE RECENTLY DEAD.

Who?

CROGER AND ESTIMET.

Dead? Mike? Louis?

YES. HOW DID YOU MANAGE THAT?

They're the only two people who might clear me too . . . Tell me about it? What happened?

CERTAINLY. BOTH VIOLENTLY. LIKE YOUR FRIEND McCULLOUGH. YOU APPARENTLY PICKED THE WRONG SIDE IN GUATEMALA. GOVERNMENT TROOPS

OVERRAN THE REBELS THIRTY-FIVE
MILES NORTHWEST OF GUATEMALA
CITY AND KILLED MOST OF THEM, IN-
CLUDING A DANDILY DRESSED GENTLE-
MAN NAMED LOUIS ESTIMET WHO HAD
JUST SOLD THEM SOME QUESTIONABLE
SKODA REJECTS.

What about Mike?

CROGER WAS FOUND FLOATING IN TID-
AL WATER OFF THE BALTIMORE DOCK
FOUR DAYS AGO. HE'D BEEN JABBED RE-
PEATEDLY WITH A SHARP INSTRUMENT.
IT MIGHT HAVE BEEN A JUNKIE OR A
DEALER. HE'S HAD, AS YOU KNOW, THAT
PORT LOCKED UP FOR HEROIN IMPORTS
SINCE WORLD WAR TWO. ON THE OTH-
ER HAND, IT MIGHT HAVE BEEN SOME-
ONE ASSIGNED BY YOU.

Good God!

QUITE. AT LEAST WITH CROGER, ESTI-
MET AND YOUR PRESS CLEARANCE
GONE, YOUR CLAWS HAVE BEEN PULLED.
ANY MINOR ADDITIONAL IRRITATION
AND I'LL PULL YOUR PASSPORT. GOOD-
BYE, MR. DANZIGER.

How long has this bloody investigation been
going on?

MORE YEARS THAN I CARE TO RECALL.

Of me?

OF COURSE, OF YOU.

Then why didn't you drag me in here years
ago?

WE ONLY HAD CIRCUMSTANTIAL EVI-

DENCE OF YOUR INVOLVEMENT, AND NO DIRECT PROVABLE ACT.

Then why now?

YOU GALLANTLY PROVIDED US WITH AN OPPORTUNITY BY CONSORTING FAVORABLY WITH THE VC, BY ASSAILING THE CREDIBILITY OF THE AMERICAN GOVERNMENT, AND BY STRIKING AN AMERICAN OFFICER IN PERFORMANCE OF HIS DUTIES . . . GOOD DAY, MR. DANZIGER. INDULGE YOURSELF. WE SHALL MEET AGAIN.

TO: A. J. Katin
FROM: B. Pike

FORMAL REPORT TO FOLLOW

Case of Danziger temporarily discontinued, as suggested.

B.P.

Love letter from the 5 P.M. Shuttle Flight
My Sweet Esterhazy:

There is no levity in my bones tonight, only a violent and idiotic anger, as much at myself as anyone. For swaying a little with accusation. For wincing a little with guilt.

The horror is: If enough people keep telling you you are guilty, pretty soon you damn well are. And in some hidden little place down inside you begin to feel vaguely guilty. Maybe it's a vestige of original sin.

People who know how to use this syndrome for their own purposes are the dangerous ones. One day you will sit on the wrong side of the judgment bench and you will feel guilty. By then you're lost. That's why it's important to yell too soon, to scream too early, to fight like a maniac before the process takes hold. The sins this lovely language is put to in the name of reason!

Fighting them is like fighting the wind, because their minds are hardened and they occupy space but they have no substance. Bumble onward, you unbroken idiots!

P.

TO: A. J. Katin
FROM: B. Pike

FORMAL REPORT TO FOLLOW

After all these months, it appears Danziger is at it again. There follows a translation of an excerpt from the Baby Lamos entertainment column in Novedades, Mexico, D.F. July 29.

QUOTE:

". . . Jaime 'Pat' Amandarez and his Aztec Productions are doing it again! We had a drink last night on the terrace of Pat's charming apartment overlooking the racetrack with two of our newer celebrities: Mr. Peter Danziger, the celebrated American correspondent and author, and his lovely bride Janice, until recently an editor of a famed

American picture magazine.

"Over delicious margaritas, and while admiring Mrs. Danziger's white silk two-piece cocktail dress, we learned the truth!

"Mr. Danziger is indeed writing a major-budget cinema based on his newly published book *Body Count* for Aztec Productions. It concerns the dramatic and unjust conflict between a newsman and a rigid military government. Sounds exciting!

"The film will be shot in the Pueblo area and on stage in Mexico D.F. A prominent Hollywood actor who has been nominated for two Oscars is enthusiastic about playing the leading role. Pat Amandarez himself will supervise production. With all this talent, personally I can't wait-" END QUOTE

PLEASE ADVISE IF ACTION REQUESTED

TO: B. Pike
FROM: A. J. Katin

ACTION REQUESTED: MAINTAIN SURVEILLANCE

I am referring the Danziger matter to the diplomatic level. Like you, I regard the idea of a motion picture on this subject contrary to our basic interests.

Sr. F. Ramón de Fontana y Menzes will also, I am confident, find it in his country's own best interests to persuade Sr. Amandarez to reconsider the wisdom of the production; particularly since much of his funding comes from our side of the Rio Grande.

When Danziger has descended to a certain emotional and financial level, perhaps with your guidance he will divulge the balance of the intelligence about his own involvement, which you have so assiduously pursued. Then, hopefully, we may close the file on this nasty little gang.

In the meanwhile, fortunately, everyone else concerned is dead.

A.J.K.

Amandarez came down from Mexico City to Cuernavaca in time for lunch. This time he was driving a bright-red Porsche. We sat in the patio of the little place we had rented, drinking beer and eating avocado vinaigrette. He told me he had suffered repeated sledgehammer blows from the Ministry of Culture to abandon production. Amandarez always talks like that. Then, with mustaches bristling and his mouth full of avocado, he said passionately that he, Pat Amandarez, would never capitulate to Yanqui pressure, however elevated the power source. He looked and sounded like Akim Tamiroff in *For Whom the Bell Tolls*, with a little enchilada thrown in, and I wondered whether he would be any more effective under fire. Esterhazy said quietly to the sky: "What do you have to do to live a life?" I reminded Amandarez that I had a contract, and he nodded his head sadly. That blind swelling anger began to grow in my gut again.

Later, a gentle crazy man named Ross Attey

wandered over from next door to give us a house-warming present. He is a retired English civil servant who drinks about two quarts of gin a day but beyond the smell doesn't show it. His hobby is writing poetry, printing it on a handpress and showing it around. He lectured one term at the university. Amandarez says he has tuberculosis. The poem he wrote for us is printed on stiff yellowing paper. It made Esterhazy cry.

> The juice of the juniper screams on high
> Alackaloo, alackalie
> The civilization twist and cry
> Alackadoo, alackadie
> Pursue thy thing
> Alackaling
> And when requited, sing.

If you enjoyed I'M OK—YOU'RE OK,
you will want to read this great book that
sold over a quarter of a million copies in
hardcover.

Love and Will

by ROLLO MAY

* over 4 months on the bestseller lists
* a selection of 6 book clubs
* winner of the Ralph Waldo Emerson
  Award

"An extraordinary book on sex and civilization
. . . An important contribution to contemporary
morality."

—*Newsweek*

". . . a rich and useful book, one that deserves a
thoughtful audience."

—*Saturday Review*

A DELL BOOK $1.75
Also available in a Delta edition $2.95

HOW MANY OF THESE DELL BESTSELLERS HAVE YOU READ?

Fiction

1. **THE TAKING OF PELHAM ONE TWO THREE**
   by John Godey — $1.75
2. **ELLIE** by Herbert Kastle — $1.50
3. **PEOPLE WILL ALWAYS BE KIND** by Wilfrid Sheed — $1.50
4. **SHOOT** by Douglas Fairbairn — $1.50
5. **A DAY NO PIGS WOULD DIE**
   by Robert Newton Peck — $1.25
6. **ELEPHANTS CAN REMEMBER** by Agatha Christie — $1.25
7. **TREVAYNE** by Jonathan Ryder — $1.50
8. **DUST ON THE SEA** by Edward L. Beach — $1.75
9. **THE CAR THIEF** by Theodore Weesner — $1.50
10. **THE MORNING AFTER** by Jack B. Weiner — $1.50

Non-fiction

1. **AN UNTOLD STORY**
   by Elliott Roosevelt and James Brough — $1.75
2. **QUEEN VICTORIA** by Cecil Woodham-Smith — $1.75
3. **GOING DOWN WITH JANIS**
   by Peggy Caserta & Dan Knapp — $1.50
4. **SOLDIER** by Anthony B. Herbert — $1.75
5. **THE WATER IS WIDE** by Pat Conroy — $1.50
6. **THE GREAT EXECUTIVE DREAM** by Robert Heller — $1.75
7. **TARGET BLUE** by Robert Daley — $1.75
8. **MEAT ON THE HOOF** by Gary Shaw — $1.50
9. **MARJOE** by Stephen S. Gaines — $1.50
10. **LUCY** by Joe Morella & Edward Z. Epstein — $1.50

If you cannot obtain copies of these titles from your local bookseller, just send the price (plus 25¢ per copy for handling and postage) to Dell Books, Post Office Box 1000, Pinebrook, N. J. 07058.

Michigan and Father's muttering, "Bumblefoot!" I thought maybe they should have defoliated after all. I thought of Vince Schaefer's round impassive face having lunch at Costello's. I thought of Esterhazy's round impudent breasts. I wondered if I would be shot. I wondered why everything always went haywire. Murphy's law. We walked for a couple of hours.

The camp was a shambles, still smoking. There were eleven small bodies laid out in a line in front of one hut: four uniformed, seven in paddy clothes. I could not tell the sexes. The burp gun was behind my back now, nudging. I kept walking. The smoke was from the remains of a long low shed across the square. Mobs were still running around it. It stank of diesel. The smoke was still pillaring up about a thousand feet to where it shredded and swirled off in the wind. I felt a lot of eyes burning at me as we crossed the square to a Soviet command car that seemed to be temporary HQ. Someone was talking into elaborate radio gear; others clustered around. There was a spiky cluster of mobile antiaircraft dug into the brow of a hill beyond. Beyond that, the woods were smoking. The burp gun was still in my back; I figured we were making a brave entry for the troops. A young man detached himself from the group and moved toward me. He wore dark-rimmed glasses and a muddy denim jacket open over his thin chest. He was tall for a Vietnamese. When he spoke I could see one gold incisor.

He said in Oxford English: "You arrive too late for the picnic, Mr. Danziger."

I couldn't think of a sensible answer.

He smiled vacantly and said: "My name is Nuy. Come with me, please."

I followed him past the command car. The cluster of troops instinctively moved away from me as I passed. I remembered reading that to Oriental nostrils we meat-eating Westerners smell to high heaven. Maybe their deal made me smell even worse. I looked over my shoulder at the lieutenant once, but he pretended he had never seen me before and joined the group by the radio. We stopped by a thatched hut, relatively untouched.

Nuy said: "Come in, please."

We stepped up into a large plain room with a slatted floor, a planked table and two benches. There was an ornate black-and-gold high-backed chair at the end of the table. The table was burdened with transmitting equipment, Japanese. There was a pile of colorful charts alongside which looked as though they had been drawn by a child—but that kind of judgment is a mistake we always make. The floor was covered with unrolled bamboo which crunched when you stepped on it.

A short muscular man had his back to us, talking musically to a pretty young woman in white. When she left through the back I saw that she was astonishingly beautiful and terribly young, like so many Vietnamese women before the sudden moment when everything comes apart. The man turned to us. He wore baggy khaki trousers and a faded-blue tunic, like Nuy's, with insignia. He looked like a small Oriental version of Erich

Von Stroheim, without the menace. When he spoke to us his voice was still musical, a soft resonant tenor. It was short, but apparently it was an order.

Nuy said: "Colonel Nimh would like you to empty your pockets please."

I did so methodically, onto the table. Keychain. Sinus inhalant. Lighter. Cigarettes. Handkerchief. Pen. Address book. Bills in various currencies. Passport. Wallet. Card case. Nail clipper. Coins. Nuy pawed through the pile and looked at me questioningly.

I said: "The rest was abandoned with the car."

He nodded and studied the inhalant, unscrewed the end, sniffed, put it back. He glanced at the card case, studied the picture of Esterhazy, gestured for me to return the gear to my pockets.

The colonel began to speak in Vietnamese, then switched to strongly accented French. I realized he had no English. I said to Nuy: "Tell the colonel I speak no Vietnamese, and I learned my French under bad auspices."

Nuy said: "I will translate. Kindly be seated."

I lowered myself to a bench. The colonel remained standing. It was stifling under the thatch. I had a sudden fear of falling asleep. The colonel began to talk in musical bursts; squinting at me with friendly intensity at the end of each pacing, and quieting Nuy with one hand as he went on and on.

It was certainly not his idea to have an enemy alien in his security area. I had no more right there than he would have in the councils of the

Pentagon. No American belonged in his country—a country of underprivileged people, not of American-backed puppets in Saigon. One day they would welcome us back as benevolent tourists, perhaps . . . Had I noticed the bodies outside? The machinery and the men who created those bodies were products of my country. For all he knew, I too was a puppet of his enemies, trying to ferret out information about the security of his sector. I should know that to the last men the Liberation Front would throw out all renegades of any nationality. The war was going well beyond belief, because Western training was not adaptable to Liberation tactics.

I lit a cigarette. To my surprise, the colonel and Nuy each accepted one too. I lit them all with the Zippo.

If I, perchance, turned out to be beyond confidence, it was unfortunate that I would have to perish in some abrupt manner. If not, as his superiors suggested—men in very high places—if I were indeed searching to report both sides of the question, the hoped-for peace, and the futility of injustice, then we were on the same side, men of goodwill, and the hospitality of the sector was mine.

In the meanwhile, because he was a hardened military man who took no chances, I should acquaint myself intimately with Captain Nuy, who would be my constant companion and escort so long as I remained in Liberation territory. He would also be entrusted to return me safely to Saigon, from which rodent nest I might report my